a life worth
Dreaming about

a life worth
Dreaming about

Nicholas Dettmann

authorHOUSE®

AuthorHouse™
1663 Liberty Drive
Bloomington, IN 47403
www.authorhouse.com
Phone: 1-800-839-8640

First published by AuthorHouse   01/21/2012

ISBN: 978-1-4685-4300-1 (sc)
ISBN: 978-1-4685-4299-8 (hc)
ISBN: 978-1-4685-4298-1 (ebk)

Library of Congress Control Number: 2012900718

Printed in the United States of America

Any people depicted in stock imagery provided by Thinkstock are models, and such images are being used for illustrative purposes only.
Certain stock imagery © *Thinkstock.*

This book is printed on acid-free paper.

Because of the dynamic nature of the Internet, any web addresses or links contained in this book may have changed since publication and may no longer be valid. The views expressed in this work are solely those of the author and do not necessarily reflect the views of the publisher, and the publisher hereby disclaims any responsibility for them.

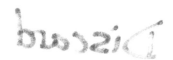

Acknowledgements

A lot of time and effort goes into every project, no matter what the project is. Writing a book is no exception.

This was a project that took longer than I originally anticipated. There were a lot of factors to it, but when it was finally finished, it was a tremendous relief. And there were so many people who helped me achieve my goal of becoming an author.

To me, writing a book was a longtime goal. When my first byline appeared in a newspaper when I was just twenty-one years old, it was such a neat moment for me. Seeing my name here on the cover of this book gives me even more satisfaction. I hope you enjoy the book. If so, I've got more projects in the works and ones I'm very excited about.

To my wife, Elizabeth: Thank you for supporting me in my goals and dreams. Your support means so much to me; words can't express how grateful I am.

To my parents: Thank you for helping me get through this difficult project.

To my sister, Rebecca: Thank you for your help, too. You've got a very proud brother for what you do.

To Aunt Jude: Thank you.

To Bill and Suzanne White: Thank you.

To Alex Gary: You were an inspiration to me to join the writing field. Thank you.

Prologue

*C*ARL ROBERTSON WAKES UP on a Sunday morning wondering why his left arm is sore and why he is feeling out of breath. He brushes off sweat from his forehead.

A two-car garage door hums open. He walks out the back door of his four-bedroom ranch home in a quiet suburban neighborhood an hour from New York City. A neighbor's running lawn mower echoes nearby, and shouts of kids playing football in the backyard next door echo off his house. He walks down the concrete stairs from the back door to the driveway.

With a sore right knee, the fifty-two-year-old limps up the driveway. The sun beams down on a cloudless day, underneath an ocean-blue sky. A gentle breeze passes across the yard. A bird chirps in a nearby tree.

He grabs the lawn mower next to the kids' bicycles. He turns on the radio, which sits on a shelf overhead. The football game is on—the New York Giants against the Chicago Bears. He loves the Giants. It is scoreless midway through the first quarter.

He rolls the lawn mower out of the garage and pulls on the cord to start it. It whirs loudly, and he starts on the backyard. He loves the smell of freshly cut grass.

Jeff, his thirteen-year-old son, comes through the backyard gate with his friend Timmy.

"Hi, Timmy!" Carl shouts over the lawn mower.

"Hello, Mr. Robertson."

Timmy follows Jeff inside the house to play video games. Jeff just got a new football game for his PlayStation 3.

Carl has just started back on the lawn when he feels a pain in his chest. He stops, makes a fist with his right hand, and clenches it over his heart while his left hand holds the lawn mower's handlebar. The mower whirs loudly. The pain quickly subsides.

"Hmm," he says. "That was weird."

Bethany, Carl's seventeen-year-old daughter, pulls up in the family's sedan, returning home from high school volleyball practice.

"Hey, sweetheart!" Carl shouts. "How was practice?"

"It was good."

Bethany shuts the door and notices something's wrong. Dad's skin color looks different. It is slightly pale. She takes off her sunglasses to try to get a better look.

"Dad?"

"Yeah, sweetie?"

"Are you okay?"

"Yeah?"

Bethany notices her father struggling to breathe. He takes a deep breath, trying to get some more air. She watches him closely as he takes a step with the lawn mower.

Suddenly, Carl lets go of the lawn mower. It stops running. He clenches his right hand over his chest. He falls to one knee, struggling to breathe.

"Dad!"

Bethany runs to her father and catches him before he lands flat on the ground. He closes his eyes. His breathing is labored. She reaches into her purse and pulls out her cell phone, holding her dad in one arm.

She fumbles with her phone. Her hands are shaking furiously. With her fingers trembling, she dials 9-1-1.

"Nine-one-one. What's your emergency?" an operator asks.

Bethany is trembling, crying. She's scared.

"It's my dad!" she screams into the phone. "I don't know what's wrong with him. He's all white. His eyes are closed. Not breathing. I think he's dead!"

"Try to remain calm, ma'am. I'll send a unit out right away. What's your address?"

Jeff is in the kitchen getting a chocolate-chip granola bar out of the cupboard over the oven. He catches sight of Bethany holding Dad in her arms, crying, and talking on her cell phone, which sits on her shoulder underneath her right ear. Jeff slams the wooden cupboard door closed and runs outside.

The door swings open violently and slowly closes. Timmy catches Jeff running outside. He follows him.

"*Dad?*" Jeff shouts.

He and Timmy are by Bethany and Dad's side.

"Mr. Robertson? Are you okay?" Timmy nervously asks.

"Call Mom!" Bethany shouts at Jeff.

The boys rush into the house to call Jeff's mother on her cell phone.

"Hello?" asks Sydney, Jeff's and Bethany's mom, picking up the cell phone just outside the grocery store.

"Mom! Something's wrong with Dad. Bethany's crying."

"What's wrong?" she anxiously asks.

"I don't know. Bethany just told me to call you. She's on the phone with nine-one-one."

"Is everything okay?" Worry creeps into her voice. Her hands shake slightly.

"I don't know. She says he's not breathing."

"I'm on my way!"

She shoves her empty shopping cart aside and rushes to her car. She fumbles with her car keys, finally opens the car door, and starts her car.

She pulls up to the house, and there is an ambulance out front. She's scared. She runs up the driveway and finds Carl motionless on the lawn. She drops to her knees next to him.

"Sweetheart!" A tear drips down her right cheek.

The familiar smell of the freshly cut grass is in stark contrast to the paramedics as they are working quickly to stabilize Carl.

"What's wrong? What's going on?" she asks frantically.

"We're not sure, ma'am," a female paramedic says. "Possibly a heart attack. We'll transport him to St. Luke's here in a sec. Once we get him there, the doctors will be able to tell for sure. You can ride along with us to the hospital. You're his wife?"

"Yes!"

Mom looks at Bethany as she follows the paramedics to the ambulance. "Sweetie, I'm going to ride along with your father. Take the car and take your brother to the hospital with you. Meet us there."

Carl is put into the ambulance. Sydney climbs in to sit beside her husband. Her tears drip onto the floor. She takes Carl's right hand with her right hand and holds it tight. The ambulance sirens wail and echo throughout the neighborhood. The neighbors stand on the sidewalk in front of the Robertson house as the ambulance turns the corner and races out of sight.

Ben, a thirty-year-old newlywed from across the street, asks Bethany, "Is there anything we can do?"

"No, thank you. We're okay. We're going to meet them at the hospital."

"I hope everything is okay. Please call us if you need anything."

"Thanks."

*   *   *

As Carl is wheeled through the swinging doors of St. Luke's Memorial Hospital, his wife follows closely. Before the doors swing shut, she sees Bethany and Jeff arrive in the lobby.

"Kids!" she says. "Wait here. I'll come and get you as soon as I can."

"But we want to come with!" Bethany says.

The emergency room doors swing closed. Bethany wipes away a tear from her right eye, turns around, and leads her brother to the nearby waiting area. They sit down on a two-seat blue couch with its back to the window. The sun beams through the window. They are worried about their dad. Loud and overlapping chatter surrounds them. A page is made over the public address system in the hospital calling for a doctor to report to the emergency room. The phone rings behind the front desk. An elderly man sits alone in the waiting area across from where they sit. The TV in the waiting area has a soap opera on. A man on a stretcher is wheeled in through the swinging doors by paramedics. And they lead him through the same set of doors Bethany and Jeff just watched their father go through. Bethany wraps her right arm around her younger brother. A nurse approaches them.

"Is everything going to be okay?" Bethany asks, with tears rolling down each of her cheeks. Her brother sits quietly next to her, worried and afraid.

Doctors frantically attempt to revive Carl. Suddenly, he slowly opens his eyes, and the heart monitor at his bedside starts a high-pitched and sporadic beep.

"What happened?" he asks groggily. "Where am I?"

His wife's eyes are red from crying. He doesn't know why she was crying or why she was leaning over him.

"Sweetheart," she says, sniffling and catching her breath, "are you okay?"

"Yeah. I guess so. I've been better. What happened? What's going on?"

"Well, Mr. Robertson," the doctor says, "you've just had a mild heart attack. We're going to run more tests to see if there is any damage, and we'll also schedule an echocardiogram. Right now, just try to relax and get some rest."

Carl looks at his worried wife confused. He reaches for her hand. She reaches for his hand, and they firmly hold each other's right hands. Faint chatter echoes through the doorway. The heart monitor continues its high-pitched and sporadic beep.

"Is there anything I can get you, sweetie?" his wife asks.

"Water maybe?"

"Okay. I'll be right back."

He watches her leave the room and sighs deeply, trying to relax. He leans his head back into the pillow. Suddenly, the hairs on the back of his neck stand up, and he looks around.

"Hi, Carl," a familiar male voice says from a dark corner in the room.

The voice surprises him.

"Do you remember me?" the voice asks. A faint image begins to appear of a man. Carl rubs his eyes trying to get a better look. He suddenly recognizes him.

"How could I forget?" he replies.

Chapter 1

*H*IS CELL PHONE RINGS.

Thirty-two-year-old Carl Robertson doesn't pick it up. He doesn't dig it out of his suit coat pocket to see who it is. He's too busy. He hustles through the always busy streets of New York City on a late-summer morning with a temperature in the low seventies. A few light clouds hover high in the sky. A soft breeze passes between the tall skyscrapers of the city. A drop of sweat slides down his forehead and continues down his nose. He wipes it away with his moisturized right hand. He's on his way to his $250,000-per-year job as an executive marketing manager for Deluxe Marketing, a highly regarded international company. He's been with the company for five years. He loves it.

His first job out of college was as an assistant marketing manager at a midsized firm back home in Iowa City. He went to the University of Iowa there and received a bachelor's degree in marketing with a minor in business management. He once dreamed of playing in the National Football League but couldn't after an accident in college. He is still a big sports fan, though—a diehard fan most would call him.

He loathed small-town life and loves the big city. The small town in which he grew up was too personal for him. Everybody knew too much, too many rumors, most of which he couldn't care less about. Everybody knew everybody. The big city was his chance to separate himself, concentrate on himself and his career. He loves doing his own thing, being his own boss. He tries to disassociate himself from his roots. He enjoys it. He has no regrets.

To others, though, he is selfish and conceited; he doesn't care about you or the person next to him. The only person who matters to him is himself. He has few friends because of it.

He lives in a twelfth-story condo facing west in Manhattan. The condo is about nine hundred square feet with hardwood floors throughout. It is the ideal setting for him. It is private. He lives by himself and doesn't converse with neighbors much—well, not at all. A wave of hello from a neighbor doesn't trigger much of a response from him, maybe a smile or nod of his head.

A gorgeous kitchen with steel refrigerator, glass-top stove, and light-brown wooden cabinets greets guests once inside. Down the hallway is the bathroom and master bedroom. Opposite the kitchen is a spacious living area with a sixty-inch high-definition television and a light-blue sectional couch. A glass-top coffee table sits in front. The Sunday newspaper is lying on top with only the sports section pulled out of it. A couple of *Sports Illustrated* and *Advertising Age* magazines are strewn about on the table. On the wall are banners of each of his favorite sports teams: the New York Giants of the NFL, the New York Rangers of the National Hockey League, and the New York Yankees.

He has season tickets for each team, too. If work isn't his focus, it is sports. And they're good seats, too. He sits behind the Rangers' bench for the hockey games, fifteenth row back on the thirty-five-yard line behind the Giants' sideline, and in the front row to the right of the Yankees' dugout along the first-base line. He spends a couple thousand dollars each year on the tickets. No worries. He can afford it.

He bought the tickets after his promotion in the company a few years earlier.

Below the window, which has a remarkable view of the city, is an iPod stereo hookup. He has more than five hundred songs on his white iPod. His favorite artists are Johnny Cash, Saliva, Metallica, and Waylon Jennings.

He is high class. His condo costs him three thousand dollars a month. His attire resembles his class, too.

He often wears snappy suits with a matching tie and shirt, and his shoes are often glazed with a new shoe shine. He's wearing another one of his fancy suits on this warm morning in New York.

He's single, never married. Not enough time for dating life, he tells the few friends he has or his colleagues. Pretty girls are aplenty in New York City, or so people tell him. He loathes being set up on blind dates. If he wants a girl, he will make the effort. If she does, she must really spark his interest, which is often hard to do. He has an arrogant approach to women. But to him that's okay. He loves the single life. To him, dating slows him down too much, takes away his focus on work. He doesn't want to share his fortune. He believes women hold him down. The word *commitment* scares him. Past experiences have led him to this belief.

The right girl, he believes, will fall into his lap; he doesn't want to bother looking for her. The right girl must accept his lifestyle—his career, his hobbies, and his way of life—and him for what he is and live with it. If she doesn't? Oh well. Her loss, he says. Women are a low priority to him.

The few friends he has know this, but they still try to set him up on dates. His best friends—his true friends, he says—are single or divorced. But some who are not single are still part of his circle of friends. But most of the other people who've tried to be his friend have tried to set him up on dates and failed miserably. He doesn't speak to them as often.

His job—his career—is far more important than anything else, more important than family even.

Whatever the call is about, he's sure it can wait. It goes to voice mail. His cell beeps to notify him of the new message. He looks at it and puts it back into his suit pocket.

"It can wait," he mumbles to himself, heaves a deep breath, and looks straight ahead. He extends his strides, trying to make up some time.

The bright sun beams down from high above, bouncing off the sidewalks and reflecting off nearby windows from storefronts. The horns sound loudly from passing taxicabs. The streets are shoulder to shoulder, and many people have the same goal: get to work. Some are trying harder to do so than others. They are dreading another Monday. Not Carl. He's excited about what work has to offer today.

There is not a lot of maneuvering room for his big, well-built body. He has blue eyes and dark-brown hair. He has an athletic build from his playing days growing up and maintaining a modest, twice-a-week workout plan at the workout facility at his condominium complex.

Every Tuesday, he spends an hour inside the gym. Most of the time is reserved for upper body work: bench press, chest press, push-ups, and so on. He spends the rest of the time on a treadmill—but not too much. Then on Fridays, he does lower body workouts for about a half hour or so and calls it a week. His knees are often sore because of an injury he suffered while playing football in college.

He does abdominal crunches, about two hundred, every day. He wants to keep his tight, ripped stomach.

The condo also has a twenty-five-yard lap pool on the third floor and an indoor tennis court. There's one outside in the courtyard, too.

Room service with a catering service for residential parties of high class is also available. Everything about him is high class, just the way he likes it.

"Why would I give this lifestyle up?" he says to people when they ask him when he's going to get a girlfriend. "This is the life I always dreamed about."

It sort of is the life he dreamed about. He dreamed of riches, but in a different way. But this is going just fine for him. He still has what he wanted: life in the big city with a pocket full of cash. He's barely thought about how he's treated or continues to treat people from his past. One time, a friend asked him if he wondered what it would've been like if his NFL dream had come true.

Carl thought about it for a moment.

"I don't know," he said.

When he's not at home, he's at his twenty-by-thirty-five-foot corner office on the thirty-second floor of the office building where Deluxe Marketing is located. It overlooks the Brooklyn Bridge.

A good friend of his is Kenny Davis.

Carl and Kenny used to work at Deluxe together. They began at the company just three weeks apart—first Carl, then Kenny. They always had each other's back, in the office and out of the office. It was like they'd known each other for twenty years soon after they began working together.

Two years earlier, Kenny had married Michelle. They have an eighteen-month-old son, Brandon. Kenny left the company a year ago and now works as the ticket office manager at Madison Square Garden. It allows him more time to be at home with his wife and son.

Carl says hello whenever he sees him at games.

Michelle is a professor at New York University, teaching psychology. The two met at a martini bar just three blocks from Carl's place. Kenny couldn't take his eyes off this young, athletically built woman who was wearing a knee-length sparkly dress and had long blond hair and blue eyes. The minute they laid eyes on each other Kenny was in love, he said during his wedding toast. They dated for six months and got married in an elegant spring ceremony in Central Park.

"I'll always remember it being so dark in that room that night, and you walking in and lighting up the room," Kenny said at his wedding.

Michelle's eyes moistened; she was wearing a long, white wedding dress, which hung off her shoulders.

Carl, who was Kenny's best man, was sitting at the head table but didn't pay much attention to the toast. He was ready to hit the open bar. A bridesmaid had her eye on him. He didn't notice. He shook his wrist to look at his watch instead and took a long sip of his mixed alcoholic drink.

Kenny and Michelle's wedding anniversary is in another couple weeks.

Kenny is always happy. He loves being married. He loves his wife. He loves his son. He loves his life. He wants his friend to have the same feeling.

"You know, Carl?" Kenny said one night. "Married life is better than you think it is. It's a lifestyle where you can wake up every day with the woman you love and share your life experiences with her. I always have someone to come home to because of Michelle and Brandon."

"Good for you," Carl replied. "I'm doing just fine."

Kenny said, "Yes, you are. But imagine sharing that with the love of your life."

"I'm fine," Carl bluntly replied.

They are good friends because for the longest time, they did everything together: bowling, parties, and football games. That was until Kenny got married. Now it's not so much, especially after Brandon was born.

Another former colleague, John Watson, echoes the same sentiments about women and married life to Carl constantly.

He's been married for twelve years to his high school sweetheart, Karen.

John grew up in Queens and loves the Mets.

Carl is not a fan of John because of that, but he tolerates it. John began working at Deluxe two months after Carl did. John was a former team member for Carl.

John has two daughters, Callie (ten years old) and Brittany (seven). Callie wants to be an optometrist when she grows up. Brittany wants to be a singer. She loves Carrie Underwood.

"Women are one of God's greatest creations," John told Carl at a Rangers game last winter. "They bring you so much joy and happiness. I can't imagine a day without my wife."

Carl rolled his eyes and said, "Okay, John. Whatever." He stood up and screamed, "That's a penalty, you idiot ref!"

John doesn't go to as many sporting events as he used to when he and Carl first became friends. Callie's into gymnastics and Brittany loves swimming. He goes to both of his kids' events as much as possible. His father didn't do the same for him growing up. He vowed his kids would come first above anything else from the moment they were born.

Carl had hated it when his parents were at his games growing up. He thought they were an embarrassment.

Callie is excellent on the floor exercise. Brittany is a terrific butterfly swimmer. They are each among the best on their club's teams. They also have dreams of being Olympians.

Karen is a nurse. She works the night shift while John works during the day. He makes the kids' lunches every day and takes them to school. He is a waiter at an Italian cuisine restaurant five blocks from Callie and Brittany's school. He left Deluxe a year earlier. They remain somewhat close, but not as close as they used to be.

One single friend Carl does have who still works at Deluxe is Percy Hawkins.

Percy is a twenty-nine-year-old African American, who married Bianca six years ago but has since divorced. They had no kids.

Carl and Percy hang out often.

Percy tells Carl one night, "Don't listen to what Kenny and John keep telling you. You do your thing, man. You've got a good thing going on."

Carl likes Percy. He thinks Percy is the only true friend he has because they share the same opinion on life and women. He's also not setting him up on any blind dates.

"Women are way too controlling," Percy said. "Do this; do that. Uggh! It drives me nuts."

Carl smiles and nods in agreement. Kenny and John vehemently disagree.

Carl's shoes echo off the concrete sidewalk. He walks faster to get to the office. A big meeting is to take place today at Deluxe. Five executives from a company in Paris, France, are in town today to discuss new marketing ideas for their company. The company, Runaway Destination, wants to promote a new, romantic experience for Americans. It's already a smash hit in Paris and all over Europe and even Asia.

They want to expand into the United States. They want to offer a weeklong getaway for American couples where they pay one flat rate, which includes first-class airfare, elegant accommodations, and a memorable experience. They also want to offer opportunities for couples to see the rest of France. They would start in Paris, work their way around into the wine country, and back to Paris where the trip would be capped off with a private dinner at the top of the Eiffel Tower.

How is this company going to be able to lure Americans to this opportunity? It sounds expensive.

The meeting begins in five minutes. He's still seven minutes away from the office. He was up late last night from a night of partying with his friends after the Giants beat their archrivals, the Dallas Cowboys, in overtime.

John and Kenny left Carl's condo when the game ended, shortly after 11:30 p.m., but Carl and Percy celebrated to almost 4:00 a.m. with beers, shots of rum, pizza, and video games.

Carl hates the Cowboys.

He worships the Giants.

He passes a newspaper stand with the headline on the front page reading, "Giants Steal from Cowboys."

Carl smiles and thinks of the six beers and countless shots he and Percy had and the challenge of trying to play a golf video game drunk.

"That was a great time," he whispers to himself. "Man, that was a great time."

He has a small headache. The light is a bit irritating. He got only a couple hours of sleep the night before.

He gets back on his way, almost to the pace of a slow jog, because he has to glance at the newspaper headline. A vendor, dressed in a Giants T-shirt and baseball cap, peers around the side of the stand and notices Carl looking at the headline and skimming over the front-page story. He asks, "Are you a Giants fan?"

"Yes, I am. What a great game last night, hey?"

"Absolutely. I can't complain. I hate the Cowboys."

"Me, too."

Carl turns around and darts across the street to get to the front of the tall, fifty-story complex in which he works. He's nearly hit by a speeding car.

"Slow down, you bastard!" he screams at the car.

"Screw you!" the driver shouts back.

The building has tinted windows on all four sides. The sun glints off its side.

Carl stops just as he reaches out to push the door open to the complex. He catches something out of the corner of his eye.

He blinks.

They're gone.

Two minutes to the office.

Inside, he anxiously waits in the lobby for the elevator. The doors slide open. He rushes inside and pushes "32" on the panel.

"C'mon! Close!" he shouts at the elevator panel and hits "32" again. Two others are on the elevator with him—a man and a woman. He doesn't know either of them. He sees them from time to time at the office. He knows they work somewhere else in the building. He just doesn't know where; he doesn't care to know. He usually smiles and nods to acknowledge them. Rarely are words spoken. The doors close, and the elevator quickly makes its way up the shaft.

He bounces on the tips of his toes and stares at the light panel indicating which floor they are on.

One minute to go and the elevator is passing floor twenty-five.

"This is going to be close," he tells himself. The elevator barely makes a sound going up the shaft.

Suddenly, the door slides open for the thirty-second floor. He turns his shoulders and barges his way through the narrow opening in the elevator doors.

He's off the elevator and notices five people sitting in the office lobby waiting. They are sitting on two long couches facing each other and in front of the main desk.

He looks at his watch.

"Nine o'clock. Phew! I just made it," he says to himself.

"Hopefully you weren't waiting too long," he says to one of them, a thirty-seven-year-old man named Pierre, the leader of the group.

He stands up.

"No," he replies with a French accent. "You are good."

Carl pulls his cell phone out of his right front jacket pocket. Before he turns it off, he notices another missed call.

Hmm. That's strange. I didn't even hear it ring, he thinks to himself. He doesn't check to see who it is.

He turns it off and sticks it in his right front pants pocket. He is unreachable the rest of the day.

He wears a dark, navy-blue suit from Armani. He wears the matching collared shirt with a silk tie. He also has brand-new shoes.

He has a superstition with his suit and shoes. Every time he has a big meeting, he buys a new suit and shoes. Every time he's done this, he's always cashed in on the project. He spends on average $2,500 for a new suit. He has more than a hundred suits in his closest, many of which have been worn only once or twice. Never have any of them been worn three times. They just collect dust and occupy space in his walk-in closet back home.

The ensemble for this meeting cost him three thousand, small change. He bought it on his way home from work Friday.

This is a big deal, a very big deal. If his marketing team, which consists of seven people, plus himself, comes up with the right plan for Runaway Destination, Carl will be a million dollars richer.

Runaway Destination is offering three million to the marketing company that comes up with the best marketing plan for their idea. Carl is second in the chain of command at Deluxe. Only the CEO is above him. He will get one-third of the cut.

It will be the biggest payday of his career and in company history. Deluxe is the third and final marketing company the Runaway representatives have met with in the past two weeks about the project. They know of Deluxe's stout reputation. It is Runaway's last meeting with potential marketers.

He extends his right hand and shakes Pierre's.

"Nice to meet you, sir," Carl says. "Welcome to the United States. Is this your first time here?"

"Thank you," Pierre replies. "No. I came to America when I was ten years old. We visited Washington DC."

Pierre, who is dark-haired and tall and wears blue jeans with dark tennis shoes and a white-collared button-down shirt, goes around the lobby and points out his associates to Carl.

First is Alexandre. He stands up and extends his hand to Carl.

"A pleasure to meet you," he says.

"Likewise."

Alexandre is one of Pierre's closest friends. They are the founders of the company and of the idea. Alexandre stands at about the same height as Carl and is slightly more than two hundred pounds. He's got dark, curly hair and brown eyes. He's twenty-nine.

Next to him is Henri.

"Nice to meet you," Henri says shaking Carl's hand. His accent is like Pierre's and Alexandre's.

"How are you?"

Henri is twenty-six years old and somewhat tall with short, black hair. He has a neatly trimmed goatee and a strong, firm handshake and smooth hands. He's got an alluring facade about him.

Next are the two women of the group. Their backs are to the lobby desk as they sit on the other sofa. A coffee table rests between the two couches with the Monday edition of the *New York Times* and the *Wall Street Journal* on top of it.

The first is Claire.

She stands up, and Carl does a double take. She is gorgeous, stunning—almost model-like.

"Delighted to make your acquaintance, Carl," she says leaning in to give him a peck on his left and then right cheeks and holding his hands gently with hers.

Wow! Carl thinks to himself.

He stammers, "L-Likewise."

Claire is thirty-one and is originally from Paris but currently lives in Boston. A year ago, she moved there to help lay the foundation for the American marketing project that brought them to the Deluxe office today.

Claire has a certain aura about her that Carl just loves. It's a weird feeling. It's somewhat unfamiliar to him, too. He tries to shake it off because today means business. Women are always after work, not necessarily second on the list, either—maybe fourth. But he can't. He's mesmerized by her. She is slender with long black hair and hazel eyes.

He is hypnotized by her beauty.

"Get it together," he whispers to himself.

"What was that?" Claire asks.

"Oh, nothing. I'm sorry. Uhhh. Are you a Red Sox fan at all?"

"No," she says. "I don't know much about baseball."

He cringes.

Next to her is Camille.

Camille is very pretty. She is twenty-five with a light tan, long hair with brown and dark-brown streaks in it, and baby-blue eyes. Camille also works in Boston. She and Claire live in a two-bedroom apartment near Fenway Park.

"Nice to meet you," Camille says.

"Likewise. Geez, if all the girls in France are like this, I think I'll have to move there," Carl jokes and smiles while leaning in to give Camille a pair of kisses on the cheek like Claire did to him.

They all laugh.

"Well, it's a pleasure to meet you all," he says. "Follow me to the conference room."

They walk past the main desk and down the hallway. Soon after, they pass the break room, where Carl's assistants are talking, having coffee and doughnuts, and waiting for the meeting to begin. All of the conversation is centered around Caitlin, an assistant, and her date last night.

"Let's go," Carl says to them.

Before he leans back out of the break room, he turns around to Pierre, Alexandre, Henri, Claire, and Camille and asks, "Would you like any coffee? Can I get you anything to eat?"

They all say, "No, thank you."

"We ate at the hotel," Pierre adds.

Carl, the five executives, and his six assistants make their way down the brightly lit hallway from the break room to the conference room for the meeting.

It is a large-sized room with glass surrounding it. The room is at the center of the office. All the hustle and bustle revolves around this room. At any given time, people can see what is happening inside.

Carl calls it, "The Center of the Universe."

The room, which also has white blinds, which could be drawn up or down to help give the room some privacy if needed, can hold twenty people at a large, light-brown table in the middle of the room. On another side of the room is an entertainment center with a fifty-inch television screen hooked up to a laptop.

Nine softly padded chairs line up along each of the long sides of the table. At each end are two more chairs. Carl usually sits on the end furthest from the television. The chair by the entertainment center is used for the presenter.

He asks one of his assistants, Tammy Layman, to pull the blinds shut.

She says, "Sure thing."

She closes the blinds and flips on the light switch, brightly illuminating the spacious room.

Tammy is twenty-three years old and in her first year out of college. She attended the University of Arizona in Tucson where she majored in marketing and business management. She graduated with a 3.8 GPA and honors.

She is short and thin with brown hair and blue eyes. She always has a smile on her face, and she lights up the room whenever those pearly whites shine.

She is one of Carl's top assistants. She is already one of the best in the field at attracting the twenty—and thirty-something women for companies. Tammy is not married but has been dating her boyfriend, Drake, for six months.

Then there is thirty-nine-year-old Tucker Beahm.

Like Tammy, Tucker is new to the business. Tucker went to the University of Maryland to be a marketing designer. He got a degree in multimedia design and development. He graduated fifteen years earlier from Maryland and worked in a newspaper in Annapolis, the *Capital*, as an advertising designer. He joined Deluxe a year ago. But already, he's proven to be quite an asset for the team because of his razor-sharp design skills.

Tucker is tall and burly. He's got brown hair and hazel eyes. He works out five days a week for about two hours at a time. He is single and has never been married. He's the ladies' man in the office, and he's got a smile that paralyzes women. But he has a rule, "I don't date coworkers."

"I want to keep business and pleasure separate," he tells the ladies in the office. They groan every time, especially after he flashes that infectious smile with dimples.

He certainly captures the attention of Claire and Camille.

"Hi, Tucker," they say simultaneously, batting their eyelashes and smiling.

"Hello, Claire and Camille," he replies. "Very nice to meet you."

Carl is slightly agitated.

Tucker is not much of a sports fan, but he is good to talk business to and is one heck of a billiards player. However, Tucker will go to the occasional game if Carl asks.

But unlike Carl, Tucker likes to go to places and meet people, especially women. He has no problems walking up to a pretty girl at the bar and asking if she would like a drink. Carl would rather go about his own thing. "That way, I know they're interested."

"Chasing the ladies is half the fun of the game," Tucker said.

"Eh."

Tucker also has an assistant. His name is Nick Johnson.

Nick is twenty-six years old. He is a three-year veteran in the field. He went to school at the University of Southern California and worked in Los Angeles for two years as an intern. He came to Deluxe in April. It's his first full-time job. He worked retail back home in San Diego while in high school. He and Tucker usually toss ideas back and forth with one another, trying to develop sharp, eye-catching marketing and advertising plans. They are a good team—one of the best.

Nick is engaged. Her name is Ashlee. They met in college. She's in her final semester of school at USC. She's on the cheerleading squad and is a dance major. She dreams of being a Broadway musical dancer. They are to wed in December. When she finishes school, she will move to New York City with Nick, which will help her pursue her dream. She's had a couple of auditions for plays and musicals already but has come up empty each time. She's not a quitter, though, which is one reason why Nick fell in love with her.

"Your time is coming, sweetheart. I just know it," he told her over the phone after her latest rejection.

Nick's place is a couple blocks from Central Park. It's a long hike for Nick to get to work, but he loves the park where he plays football with the friends he's made in a relatively short time in New York on Saturdays.

Nick is a San Diego Chargers fan.

He and Carl don't hang out much oddly enough. He often tied up with wedding planning. He and Ashlee fly back and forth to Los Angeles monthly to see each other.

He is thin with a light tan, spiked blond hair, and brown eyes. He played soccer and tennis in high school. He was all-state in both sports and was the prom king. Ashlee was the prom queen of her high school. She grew up in Phoenix. Nick wants to be a family man.

He wants three kids, all boys, and hopes they are each athletes.

The fourth member of Carl's marketing team is Caitlin Reese.

She is a young intern, twenty-two, from Georgetown University in Washington DC. She joined the team in August to begin her twelve-month internship credit. Upon completion, she will receive her bachelor's degree in marketing. Whether she wants to stay at Deluxe is unknown at this point. But so far, everything is going okay. She wouldn't mind moving closer to home, say Boston.

Caitlin was a standout athlete in high school, playing on the soccer team, the basketball team, and the tennis team in her hometown in New Hampshire. She was a four-year varsity starter in all three sports. She had full-ride scholarship offers to play soccer at Indiana, Notre Dame, and North Carolina; basketball at Duke; and tennis at Butler University in Indianapolis.

She was also the valedictorian of her high school graduating class with a 4.0 GPA. She decided to bypass athletics to pursue her career and attend Georgetown on a full academic scholarship.

She's been an athlete for as long as she can remember. She was four years old when she participated in her first soccer camp. She had loads of fun and stuck with it. She found basketball while playing with her two older brothers, and she found tennis when she met her best friend, Karen, freshman year of high school.

Karen asked her friend to give tennis a try.

"Sure, why not?"

Caitlin is a tightly toned brunette with hazel eyes. She has the best sense of humor on the staff. She is an office favorite because of it. It's also an on-the-edge sense of humor. She's very ambitious to learn the ropes of her future career. Her main responsibilities are to make sure guests are properly accommodated with snacks and drinks and assist Carl with his day-to-day tasks. It's tedious work, but it gets her foot in the door in her profession.

"Whatever you need me to do, I'll be glad to take care of it," she told Carl at her internship interview in June. She is also very good with computers and is helpful when it comes to web page design. She'll sometimes help Tucker and Nick if they have trouble.

Carl, who doesn't often compliment people, believes she has a bright future because of her smarts and witty personality.

The fifth member of the team is thirty-year-old Steve Hammond.

Steve is a newlywed. He got married in July to his longtime girlfriend, Susan. She is older than Steve at thirty-six. They met online, "Datemaster.com," and it was love at first sight. They were smitten with each other. They couldn't believe how much they had in common.

On an unseasonably warm December evening in New York City, they went out to a nice steakhouse restaurant for dinner, but they barely ate. They just talked the whole time.

Steve, who's somewhat tall with a trace of gray hair on the sides of his head mixed with dark-brown hair and green eyes, proposed to her two years ago, and she excitedly accepted.

They went back to the steakhouse where their first date was for the big proposal. Steve was nervous, clumsy. Susan was scared. She thought something was wrong with him. She couldn't figure it out. She carefully watched his every move. She thought he was having some kind of anxiety attack or something. Sweat was dripping off his forehead.

About an hour into the meal, three members of the wait staff brought out a cake but held it high so Susan couldn't see it.

Steve said, "Susan . . ."

The three staff members—two girls and one guy—lowered the cake into Susan's view.

"Will You Marry Me?" was written on top of it in icing.

Susan bawled in excitement. She didn't answer the question immediately.

"So?" Steve nervously asked. "Will you?"

"Huh?"

"You haven't given an answer yet."

"I didn't, did I?"

Steve, Susan, and three staff members laugh.

"Of course I will, Steve."

The wait staff clapped, and the rest of the restaurant, which was full this evening, followed suit. Susan got up out of her chair, walked around the circular table, and kissed Steve. He pulled out the ring from his pocket and slid it onto her left ring finger.

"Oh, it's beautiful," she said, tears dripping down her cheeks. The ring was glistening under the restaurant lights. Her hands were shaking.

"Now who's shaking?" Steve joked.

"Oh shut up." She leaned over and gave him another kiss.

After months of planning and delays, they finally married after overcoming a near family tragedy. Susan's mother, Anne, was diagnosed with breast cancer three months after the proposal. They decided to be as supportive as they could be and postponed the wedding until everything was okay. The focus needed to be on Anne. She went through months and months of chemotherapy. Thankfully, the cancer was caught at an early stage, so they were able to detect and remove it after a lengthy surgery. About a year after the diagnosis, Susan's mother was as healthy as she had been before, and the wedding was back on. There have been no signs of recurrence.

Since then, Steve, Susan, and the whole family have participated in any charity event related to breast cancer research. They took part in a five-kilometer, or 3.1-mile, walk through Central Park just last week.

Anne cried throughout the wedding. Susan is her only daughter. Just to be able to be at the wedding was a relief because of how far she'd come and how close she had been to dying.

Today, Steve and Susan are as happy as ever together. They plan to have kids in the near future. He is another one of the people who constantly gets on Carl's case about finding a soul mate.

"Your career will only be there for a short period of time," Steve once told Carl. "But the love of your life will always be there, and she'll always support you."

Carl did his usual and reluctant, "Okay," and proceeded to return his attention elsewhere.

The last of Carl's assistants is Amber White, a thirty-four-year-old, with curly blond hair down to her shoulders and blue eyes. She has a half-inch red mark on her upper lip. She's had it since she was born. It was hard for people to look at her without looking at the mark when she first started at the company in January. But she has a strong attitude about it.

"It's what makes me unique," she says. She quickly became a likeable person around the office.

Like Caitlin, Amber also has an outrageous sense of humor. She loves playing practical jokes around the office.

Carl takes his usual spot at the head of the table, furthest from the laptop computer. Tammy, Tucker, Nick, Caitlin, Steve, and Amber are on one side of the table. On the other side are Pierre, Alexandre, Henri, Claire, and Camille. Carl keeps one eye on Claire. The other is focused on Pierre.

Camille keeps a close eye on Tucker. So does Claire.

Carl begins the meeting by again welcoming the guests from Runaway.

"It's a pleasure to have you all here today at Deluxe Marketing. We're excited you've selected us as a potential partner for your idea. Pierre, please begin."

Pierre stands up. He walks over to the laptop and plugs his flash drive stick where all the information about their idea is saved into the side of the computer.

He sits down at the chair in front of the computer.

"Okay," he begins. "We have an exciting product that we think you will be able to help us with promoting here in the United States."

As he goes through his presentation, Sharon Davison's phone rings at her desk. She is Carl's secretary.

"Good morning, Deluxe Marketing. This is Sharon, how may I help you?" she says into the receiver. She wears a portable headset which helps her with filing and typing when she's on the phone.

She's been Carl's secretary for three years. She was hired three weeks after his promotion. Sharon is fifty-one years old and has been married for twenty-seven years to her husband, Larry. They met at Boston College. They're both big Red Sox fans.

Sharon and Larry have two grown sons—Tom is twenty-four, and Drew is twenty-two.

Carl and Sharon tease each other constantly when the Red Sox and Yankees play against each other in baseball's most-heated rivalry. Carl's arrogant about it, while Sharon is playful.

She pauses to hear who's calling the office. It is Carl's twenty-four-year-old sister, Elizabeth.

Elizabeth is a very pretty woman; she's tall with long brown hair down to the middle of her back, green eyes, and an athletic build. She is a former volleyball player. She lives in Tampa, Florida. She is in her first year out of law school as a public defender. She moved to Miami to go to school six years ago and moved to Tampa two years earlier. She had a six-month internship at the law office—Turner and Steele—before landing a full-time job at the firm she currently works at, Schroeder and Dunham.

Sharon met Elizabeth when she came to New York to help Carl move into his current place a few years ago. She also came up for a visit a couple months later. Since Carl moved to New York City, he'd not been to his hometown in Iowa much—well, ever. Elizabeth is the only family he's seen in the past three years. He's barely talked to anyone else.

Mom and Dad—Mary and George—hate that he never wants to come home for the holidays.

"I've got too much going on," he says.

"There's always time for family," Mom replies.

"Sorry, Mom, but I can't make it this year. Maybe next."

The year after? "Maybe next year." His parents still wait for his visit. They miss him. He doesn't miss them.

Sharon says, "Hi, Elizabeth. How are you?"

She doesn't respond immediately. "I'm okay. How are you?"

"I'm good. Thank you. How's the job treating you?"

"It's nice so far."

Curious as to why Elizabeth's answers are softly spoken and short, she asks if she needs to speak to her brother.

"Yeah."

"I'm sorry, sweetie. He's in a meeting right now. Can I leave him a message?"

"Not really."

"Is everything okay?"

"Ummm . . . Not really."

"Is there anything I can do to help?"

"Can you get him? It's really important."

"Okay, I'll see if I can pull him out of the meeting. Can you hold on for a second?"

"Sure."

"Okay. Just a sec."

She puts Elizabeth on hold, takes off her headset, and walks around her desk and down the hall toward the conference room. She knocks softly on the door.

"I'm sorry, Mr. Robertson? Sorry to interrupt," she says.

"What is it, Sharon?" Carl asks angrily.

"You've got an urgent phone call from your sister."

"Tell her I'll call her back later. Right now, I'm busy."

"But, sir, it doesn't sound good. You should really—"

"Please, Sharon."

Upset he won't take the call, she turns around, slams the door, and rushes back toward her desk. Carl rolls his eyes and turns his attention back to the meeting.

"I'm sorry, Elizabeth; he just won't come to the phone right now," she says into the microphone on her headset. "But I'll be sure to have him call you immediately. Take care, sweetie."

"Okay," Elizabeth softly replies.

Sharon hangs up the phone.

She swiftly seeks out a pad of paper and a pen on her desk, rifling through piles of paperwork. Finally, she finds a blank piece of paper and writes down in big letters, "Urgent. Call Liz." She stands up, goes inside Carl's office, which is just past the conference room, and places the message on his desk. She sticks the note on top of his desk where she knows he will see it and returns to her desk. She gets back to calculating last month's expenses.

The meeting continues.

"I apologize for that interruption," Carl says.

"No problem," Pierre replies.

"Please continue."

About two hours later, the meeting wraps up.

"Well, Pierre," Carl says. "I think your product is magnificent. Tell you what I'm going to do. My team and I will get to work right away to come up with a marketing plan, and we will have it ready for you, say, tomorrow morning."

Pierre and his associates are stunned. Impressed.

So are Carl's. Well, they are stunned but not impressed, a bit agitated actually. They know their plans for tonight are shot.

Steve and Susan had a dinner date planned. Caitlin had a date with a good-looking guy she has been seeing for a little bit, Dean. Tammy had tickets to a Broadway show with her boyfriend Drake.

"We'll meet here again at nine in the morning to discuss what you've come up with," Pierre says.

"See you then," Carl replies.

Everybody stands up and shakes hands. Carl asks his team to stay put in the conference room while he escorts Pierre and his associates out of the office.

Just after they leave the room, Tammy, Tucker, Nick, Caitlin, Steve, and Amber all look at each and loudly scoff in frustration.

"There goes my date," Caitlin says. "I better call him."

Caitlin picks up her cell phone, which is in her purse beneath the table, and calls her date.

"Dean?" she says. "Hi, it's Caitlin. Listen, I'm really sorry, but I'll have to postpone our date tonight. I'm really sorry. I really wanted to see you tonight. My boss is making me work late tonight. Can we go out tomorrow night?"

"Okay, great. I'll see you then." She closes her cell phone.

While she's doing that, Steve and Tammy cancel their plans. The others didn't have plans that night, but they still hate working late.

Nick's fiancée is in California. She's not due to come back to New York until next week. Nick misses her terribly.

Everybody's bummed and complaining as Carl says good-bye to Pierre and his associates. "We'll see you in the morning," Carl says as Pierre and his associates reach the elevator.

On his way back to the conference room, he and Sharon cross paths at the copying machine.

"Did you see the message I left you about your sister?" Sharon asks.

"No, I'm busy right now. I'll check it later. I'm sure whatever it is, it can wait."

"No, it can't," Sharon tells Carl.

"Yes, it can," he angrily replies.

He gets back into the conference room and tells everybody to take a fifteen-minute break and return promptly. Everybody leaves the room, except Carl.

He stands up slowly and goes to his office, which is just a few feet down the hall from the conference room. He closes his door, sits behind his desk in a comfortable reclining leather chair, and pulls his cell phone out of his pocket.

He turns it on and dials "1" for voicemail. He waits.

The automated voice message tells him, "You have six new voice messages. To hear your messages, press one."

He presses "1."

The first message is from his brother Bill.

Bill is Carl's oldest brother at thirty-five years old. Carl also has a thirty-year-old brother named Steven. And there is Elizabeth.

Bill lives with his wife, Mary, and three sons. Tanner is the oldest at thirteen; Tyler is eleven; and Trey is eight. They are still in Wisconsin. Steven still lives in the Robertsons' hometown in Iowa. He helps Mom and Dad and works at the high school as a math teacher and an assistant football coach.

Bill is notorious for calling for no reason whatsoever. One time, he called just to tell Carl that he got a new lawn mower.

"Big deal, Bill," Carl had said.

"Just thought you'd like to know," Bill said. "This thing is awesome. It's got five speeds!"

"I don't care. Call me when you have something really interesting to tell me."

In the voice mail message, Bill says, "Hey, Carl. It's Bill. Listen . . ."

Carl deletes the message without even hearing the rest of it.

All the messages are from Bill. When Bill says on his message, "Hey, Carl. It's Bill . . ." Carl just hits delete and moves on, not even bothering to see what is so important that Bill would call six times in two hours.

On the sixth message, Bill is screaming into the phone, "Call me now!"

"It's probably about some stupid thing he did today," Carl says.

He opens up the desk drawer to his right, puts the phone on silent, and places it in the drawer.

He picks up the television remote control, turns on his fifty-inch plasma television, and flips on an old episode of *Home Improvement*—it's one of his favorite shows.

He puts the control down on top of the message from his sister. He pushes the control aside, looks at the message, and reads it.

"Hmm," he wonders, "what could it be about?" He suddenly feels a chill go down his spine. He shakes it off.

He is reaching over to get his cell phone out of his desk drawer to call and find out when his office phone rings. It's his colleague, Percy. He's off work today after closing a deal last week with a client.

"Hey, man, how are you?" Carl says.

"Man, that was a lot of fun last night. What are you up to?"

"Listen, I've got a meeting and a business matter to take care of today. I can't go to the lounge tonight. Would tomorrow be okay?"

"All right, man. Take care, and I'll catch you later."

Carl hangs up the phone and realizes he's got two minutes until the meeting with his assistants is to begin. He looks at the note from Sharon about his sister and puts it back on his desk.

"I'll call her later," he says.

Chapter 11

*C*ARL WALKS DOWN THE hallway from his office and turns into the conference room where his assistants are sitting, waiting. Each has an irritated look on his or her face. They each wonder how long this is going to take.

"Oops," Carl says. "I forgot something. Be right back."

He goes back down the hallway toward his office. He grabs a large, white dry-erase board. He picks it and the stand up and heads back to the conference room.

Just as he walks out of his office, he bumps into Sharon.

"I'm sorry, Sharon. Are you all right?"

"Yes, thank you."

Carl continues on his way.

Sharon shouts at him, "Hey, did you call your sister?"

He hears her but ignores her.

Sharon scoffs and heads back to her desk. She's angry and irritated.

He's always so caught up in his work, Sharon thinks to herself. *He really needs something or someone to straighten him up.*

Carl closes the conference room door and begins the meeting with his assistants.

"Well," he says. "What are we thinking, folks?"

Just as he says that to his team, Sharon, genuinely concerned, calls Elizabeth.

"Hi, sweetheart. How are you doing?"

One of the other lines on Sharon's phone begins to ring. She ignores it. Whatever it is, it can wait. This is more important. She never understood why her boss lost touch with his family members.

On the other end of the line, Elizabeth is crying.

"Calm down, sweetheart. Everything is going to be okay," Sharon tells Elizabeth.

Trevor Marks, a forty-three-year-old web page designer, walks past Sharon's desk to head out for an appointment. He sees a serious look of concern on her face.

"What's wrong?" he asks.

She holds up her right index finger to say, "Hold on."

"Listen, sweetie, you keep strong, and I'll stay on Carl to call you immediately. I promise I'll have him call you before he leaves the office tonight." She disconnects the call, takes off her headset, and looks at Trevor.

"Okay, what's wrong, Sharon?" Trevor asks.

"That was Carl's sister, Elizabeth. Something is wrong and he won't call her to find out what it is. He's too wrapped up in that Runaway deal. He's in the conference room with his team right now."

"What's wrong?"

"I don't know. We didn't get that far. She was pretty upset, though."

"Let me talk to him."

Trevor takes a quick moment to head over to the conference room. He knocks on the door.

"Who is it?" Carl angrily asks.

"Hey, Carl, it's Trevor. Can I come in?"

"Yeah, sure."

Trevor opens the door and pokes his head inside.

"Hey, man, you busy?"

"Yeah, why?"

"I really think you should call your sister back. Sharon just spoke to her, and she looks a little shaken up."

"I can't. We have to get this marketing proposal done tonight. Runaway will be here again first thing tomorrow morning."

"But it's really important."

"I'm sure it isn't. This needs to get done first. Whatever it is, I'm sure it can wait. My sister tends to blow things out of proportion a lot. I'm sure it's nothing."

"Sharon has a very concerned look on her face. And you know, she's usually pretty calm. Whatever it is doesn't appear to be a good thing, man. I really think you should check it out."

"Thanks for your concern, but we've got work to do. Now shut the door."

"But, Carl—"

"Shut the door!"

Carl turns his attention back to the meeting with his associates. Trevor rolls his eyes and goes back into the hallway, slamming the door behind him, upset with Carl. Carl screams back, "What the hell?"

Trevor briskly walks past Sharon's desk and says, "I'm sorry, Sharon. I tried."

"Thanks for trying. Have a good day, sir."

"You too, Sharon."

Just as Trevor leaves Sharon's desk, he pulls out his cell phone to call his appointment.

"Hey, it's Trevor with Deluxe Marketing. I apologize, but I'm running a few . . ." His voice fades as he moves away from Sharon's big but cluttered desk.

Sharon is struggling to focus. She gets up to get a cup of water from the water cooler across the hall. There, she comes across Peggy Larson, another secretary in the office.

"Hi, Peggy. How are you?" Sharon asks excitedly.

"I'm good. You?"

"Not so good. See, Carl has this very important message from his sister, but he refuses to take it. The Runaway deal has got him tied up."

"What's wrong?" Peggy asks.

"It doesn't look good. Someone is in trouble. I don't know what it is. His sister has called here a couple times crying. She sounds pretty rattled. I'm really worried and scared. But Carl doesn't know what's going on, and I can't get him to stop for two seconds to call his sister. He won't put the Runaway deal down."

"Do you want me to try?" Peggy asks.

"No, Trevor already tried, and Carl nearly bit his head off. He did the same to me. But thank you though for the offer."

"I'm sure everything's going to be okay."

"I hope you're right."

The meeting has gone on for two hours since the Runaway representatives left. Tammy looks at the clock over the doorway and asks, "Hey, Carl, is it okay if we take a short break? We've been at this for two hours. I don't know about everybody else, but I'm getting pretty hungry."

"Yeah. Me too," Nick says. Everybody else nods in unison.

Carl's hesitant at first. But he eventually agrees. "Okay, take a half-hour break. Be back here at two thirty."

Tammy, Tucker, Nick, Caitlin, Steve, and Amber shoot out of their seats and rush toward the elevator to get something to eat from the cafeteria on the fifth floor.

Carl hangs in the conference room. He picks up a couple sheets of paper, documents handed to him by Pierre. He leans back, picks up a legal notepad covered with notes he's written. He evaluates what he's gone over with his team. Then he realizes he's hungry himself, so he heads toward the elevator. But he doesn't go to the cafeteria. He heads outside to a hot dog vendor who is usually in front of the building about this time of day.

"Hello, sir. What can I get for you today?" the man asks.

"I'll take two dogs with mustard, ketchup, and relish."

"Okay. That'll be seven dollars."

"Here's ten. Keep the change."

"Thank you, sir. Enjoy your hot dogs, and have a splendid afternoon."

Carl walks toward the building and leans up against it, watching the buzz of the city pass in front of him. A burly man, wearing a cutoff grey shirt and blue jeans, holds a construction jackhammer. He looks up at Carl and restarts the jackhammer. It echoes off the buildings. They are repairing the pothole in front of the building.

"It's about time they fixed that," Carl says.

That pothole has been there for months. He's nearly tripped in it a number of times.

He finishes his first hot dog, crumbles up the paper wrap it was served with, stuffs it into his right pants pocket, and begins on the second one. Trevor pulls up in a cab. He's returned from his appointment for another project. He'd met with some representatives from a company in California in Times Square.

"How'd your meeting go?" Carl asks.

"Fantastic. Couldn't have gone better. We should be able to close on the deal no later than the end of next week."

"That's awesome, man."

Trevor hesitates and gives Carl a dark stare.

"Is there something else?" Carl asks.

"Yes. I'm sorry for earlier," Trevor says. "You know I wouldn't bother you in a meeting like that unless it was real important. Don't you trust me?"

"Yeah, I do. But like I said, my sister gets worked up about a lot of things. I'm sure this is no different."

"I think you're making a big mistake."

"How do you know that?"

"It's just a hunch I have."

"Well, that's your opinion. I know my sister better than you do."

Trevor walks through the revolving door of the office building and heads back to the office.

Irritated, Carl looks at his watch, which reads 2:25. He rushes to finish his last hot dog, tosses the wrapper onto the pavement, and heads back to the office. Following him onto the elevator is Karen, a twenty-seven-year-old red-haired woman, whom Carl went out to dinner with one time last year. It was only the third date he had ever gone on since moving to New York City almost six years earlier.

Karen is a former client of Deluxe. Today, she works in the same building as an attorney. Her office is way up on the forty-seventh floor. It's got an exquisite view of the Statue of Liberty and Ellis Island.

"I love looking out my office window every day," she said on their date.

They met when she was working with a tourism group out of Buffalo and for Niagara Falls. The two were immediately attracted to one another. After the first meeting, Carl did something he didn't normally do: he asked a woman out on a date.

"Karen, would you like to go out for dinner sometime?" he asked.

"Is that okay? Would we get in trouble?" she replied.

"No. It's perfectly fine. It'll be fun."

Sharon remembers the interaction well. It happened right in front of her desk, shortly after a meeting in the conference room.

They went to a restaurant in Chinatown, which wasn't far from Karen's five-story apartment building. She has a spacious apartment, almost a thousand square feet. She pays about a thousand per month on rent, but it has full amenities. It's not as elegant as Carl's place, though.

Dinner went well. They talked throughout the meal. Everything clicked between them. At least that was what Karen thought.

Carl walked her home afterward. It was about 9:00 in the evening. He left work at 4:00 that day to meet her at the restaurant at 6:00. When they got to the doorstep of her building, she hoped for a hug or some kind of kiss.

Neither happened.

Instead, he extended his right arm, shook her hand, and said, "Thank you for the evening. I'll see you and your associates Friday, correct?"

She sighed in disappointment. "Yes."

He walked down the stairs and whistled for a cab. Karen stood and watched as he got into the cab and headed back to his place. She slowly rifled through her keys and opened the door, disappointed but curious as to whether he actually liked her not.

The next day, Carl came into the office with the same expression as usual: no smile and a heavy stare straightforward. He passed Sharon's desk before going to his.

No matter how bad of a mood he may be in, he always asks how Sharon's morning is thus far. It makes her feel good that he at least acknowledges her.

"How was your date last night, Carl?" she asked.

"It wasn't a date. It was a business dinner," he replied.

"No, it wasn't Carl. It was a date. Admit it. I saw the sparkle you had in your eye when you asked her out yesterday. You were smiling like I've never seen you smile for as long as I've known you. You liked her. You were standing right here in front of my desk. Remember?"

"Yeah, well, she wasn't what I thought she was. She was pretty and all but not very intellectual at all."

Sharon had a stunned look on her face.

"That's mean, Carl," she snapped at him.

"Well, it's true."

Sharon mumbled to herself, "That's what you think."

"What was that, Sharon?"

"Nothing, sir."

Carl gets on to the elevator, anxious to return to the meeting. He's followed by Karen. There's a moment of awkwardness between the two.

"Hello, Karen," Carl says softly and reluctantly.

"Carl," she replies slightly more emphatically. "Nice to see you."

He leans over and hits "32" for his floor.

"What floor are you on?" he asks.

"Forty-seven," she responds.

"Oh yeah. That's right."

The elevator doors close, and they head up the shaft. No words are spoken. Soft orchestral music plays on the speaker over their heads. The elevator is dimly lit. He's trying to avoid eye contact. Karen is staring at him. She wants to talk. He doesn't. The engine and cables pulling the elevator up whir softly. She keeps looking at Carl, waiting for some kind of conversation. Carl stares at the floor between quick peeks at the floor screen above the door.

10 . . . 11 . . . 12.

"You know, you can talk to me, Carl. I won't bite."

"I'd rather not."

"I saw the Giants won last night."

Carl nods and softly says, "Yes, they did. Great game. Great win."

"Did you go to the game?"

Before he can answer, the elevator reaches Carl's floor. The doors slide open. They aren't even all the way open before Carl nudges his way through them. The elevator doors close slowly.

"Bye, Carl!" Karen shouts just before the doors close.

Just before the doors close, he takes a quick glance back at Karen. The elevator motor hums, taking her up to her floor. She sighs. She still remembers and thinks about their date. She still has a thing for him.

He looks back from the elevator and speeds past Peggy's desk in the lobby. She is not there. Then he goes past Sharon's desk, and she is not there, either. He is too busy to wonder where they went. He's too busy to care.

Peggy and Sharon are in the fifth-floor cafeteria grabbing a snack. Peggy gets an apple, a salad with French dressing, and a Diet Coke. Sharon gets a ham-and-cheese sandwich and an orange juice. They take their snacks, which Peggy paid for—$9.50—and head back to their office.

Waiting for the elevator to come, they talk about Carl.

"I don't know how you stand to work for him sometimes, Sharon. He can be awfully rude."

"Yeah, I know, but he means well. He just cares about his job so much and wants to do a good job. You really can't fault him for that, can you?"

"But at the expense of having a normal life?"

"Yeah, I know. I don't know how else he'll learn."

"Let's just hope everything's okay."

"But you know, Peggy, there's a part of me that hopes everything's not all right, because if something is truly wrong with them and he doesn't pay attention to it, maybe he'll regret it and that'll change his ways. Does that sound terrible?"

"You know, not really. But I've heard great things about his sister. Let's hope they're okay, and that it's nothing."

"Yeah, you're right."

The elevator reaches the cafeteria floor, and they walk on together. While going back up to their office, they talk about Sharon's two older sons.

Tom had just been hired to be the program director for a country music station in Knoxville, Tennessee. Tom's been working in radio for a couple years already. He interned at a station in Grand Rapids, Michigan. Most recently, he was the assistant program director for a country station in Indianapolis. He was there for one year. He starts his new job next month. He is engaged. His fiancée's name is Lisa.

Tom loves working in radio. He's met many celebrities already, including his favorite singer, Garth Brooks. It was his dream come true to meet Garth Brooks.

Drew is in his last year of college at the University of Buffalo. He wants to be a psychologist. He plans to enroll at the University of Michigan to get his master's degree and soon his doctorate.

Drew is single; he just broke up with his girlfriend of almost two years, Amy. He and Sharon have been talking on the phone almost every day for the past two weeks since the breakup.

"Keep strong, sweetheart," Sharon said during a recent phone conversation. "Another great girl isn't too far away. I promise."

"I hope you're right. I really cared about her. She was special."

The elevator doors slide open on the thirty-second floor.

Peggy leads the way off the elevator, gets behind her desk, and says, "Catch you later."

"Don't work too hard."

"Oh, I won't." Peggy giggles.

Sharon walks down the hall from Peggy's cluttered desk and around the conference room to her desk, pulls up the chair, sits down, and eats her sandwich. Ten minutes later, Carl comes out of the conference room to get a drink of water from the cooler.

"Hi, Carl," she says.

"Oh! Hi, Sharon. I didn't know you were there. Where'd you go?" he asks.

"To the cafeteria with Peggy. We just got a snack."

"Okay."

He tosses a pile of papers onto Sharon's desk.

"File these." He storms back to the conference room.

"Okay," Sharon says.

At five o'clock, everybody is getting ready to leave for the day. However, the meeting is still going on for Carl and his assistants.

"Grr! This is going to take forever," Caitlin whispers into Steve's ear while Carl stands at the dry-erase board from his office, his back turned.

"Is there something you'd like to add, Caitlin?" he asks.

"No, sir. I'm sorry."

"C'mon, guys, let's focus here. The sooner we get this done, the sooner you can go home."

Already irritated with having to stay late, the team continues working on the Runaway plan as best they can. Nick yawns.

Sharon knocks on the door, opens it, and asks, "Is there anything else you need from me today, sir?"

"No, Sharon. You can go home. Have a good night. See you tomorrow."

Before she closes the door, she says, "Carl, don't forget about that message from your sister."

"Okay, Sharon."

She gently closes the door and walks toward the elevator. She knows he is irritated she brought that stupid note up again, but she doesn't care. She just wants to remind him of it even if he gets upset again. Peggy is already waiting at the elevator.

"Hi, Peggy."

"Hi, Sharon. Long day?"

"Yeah, you could say that."

"Did Carl ever get to that message from his sister?"

"No, they're still working on the Runaway project."

"Still?"

"Yeah. They're supposed to be back here again tomorrow morning at nine."

"Why?"

"Because that's when Carl told them they'll have the plan ready."

"Is he insane?"

"I think so. But I don't argue with him anymore. I never get anywhere with him."

"I'm sorry, Sharon."

"It's okay."

The elevator doors open. Karen is already on after leaving her forty-seventh-floor office just moments earlier. She is also heading home for the night. No date planned. She hasn't gone on one since her dinner with Carl.

"Oh hi, Karen. It's nice to see you," Sharon says.

"You are?" she says inquisitively.

"Sharon. Carl's secretary. We met last year at his office."

"Oh yeah! How are you? So nice to see you. How was your day?"

"Rough. Carl got a phone call from his sister Elizabeth, did you ever meet her?"

"No, I didn't. Is everything okay?"

"Not really. Elizabeth called pretty upset. Apparently something happened to their mom and dad, and he needs to get home immediately to be with the family. But he's so caught up in his work and this project he's working on he hasn't stopped to check on it. I left a message on his desk this morning about it. Trevor and I reminded him a couple times later in the day. Each time we brought it up, he just got more and more irritated. I'm afraid something is really wrong."

"What happened?"

"I don't know. That's all she could tell me. She was crying pretty heavily."

"Do you want me to talk to him?"

"I don't know what good it'll do, but you can try. I'll just warn you, like I said, he's bitten the heads off of everybody who's brought the note I left him from his sister up to him. I'm just forewarning you."

"Thanks. I'll give it a shot."

The elevator reaches the main floor. Sharon, Peggy, and Karen all get out. Sharon and Peggy continue out the building to the parking garage across the street where their cars are parked.

"Good night, Karen!" Sharon shouts as she heads out the door.

"Good night, Sharon."

Karen waves bye to them. She hangs in the main floor lobby, digging in her purse for her cell phone. She still has Carl's number in her phone. She doesn't clean out her address book too often. She hopes that someday she can have another shot at him. She calls the number, hoping it's still the same.

It is, but it goes straight to his voice mail.

"Hey, this is Carl from Deluxe Marketing," it says. "I can't take your call right now. Please leave a name, number, and a message, and I'll get back to you. Thanks and have a great day."

Beep.

"Hi, Carl. It's Karen. Sorry for earlier today if I said anything that bothered you. But I wanted to see if you wanted to grab a bite to eat tonight. I've got some business things I'd like to discuss with you. Can you call me later? Thanks. Bye."

Karen closes her cell phone and heads out of the building, hoping—praying—he calls her back. After an hour of waiting outside on a still pleasantly warm late afternoon, Karen waves for a cab and heads home to her apartment. She has a firm hold of her cell phone and glances at it every three seconds, wanting to be available immediately when he calls her back. If he calls her back.

It's going on eight o'clock at night, and Carl and his team are still in the conference room discussing the Runaway project. A couple of them are dozing off, struggling to stay focused and interested.

"Hey, Mr. Robertson?" Tammy asks, yawning.

"Yes, Tammy. What is it?" he replies.

"It's eight o'clock; can we take a break? My butt feels numb."

The others vehemently agree in unison.

"Can I call my wife to give her an update and let her know when I might get home?" Steve asks.

Reluctant at first, Carl gives in.

"Okay, ten minutes. Then it's back to work."

"What time should I tell her?" Steve asks.

"Not sure," Carl replies. "Probably at least another one to two hours."

"One to two hours!" they shout in unison.

Everybody is now frustrated, because it'll likely be close to ten before they can go home, or at least be able to think about it. As they scoot out of the room, they all stomp past Carl.

"Knock off the attitudes!"

He follows them out and goes to his office. He sits behind his desk and turns on the television to see how the Yankees are doing. They're winning 6 to 1 in the bottom of the fifth against the Chicago White Sox in Chicago.

The note from Sharon about Elizabeth is still on the desk. He picks it up, looks at it, and tosses it back on the desk.

"Yes!" he screams.

The Yankees just turned an inning-ending double play with the bases loaded. The Yankees lead the division by just two games with three weeks left in the season.

He opens his desk drawer and pulls out his cell phone just as the game goes to commercial. He turns it on to see if he has new messages.

There is one message.

He dials up his voice mail inbox to see who it's from.

"Hi, Carl. It's Karen. Sorry for earlier today if I said anything that bothered you. But I wanted to see if you wanted to grab a bite to eat tonight. I've got some business . . ."

Beep.

He deletes the message.

"I'm not into you. Leave me alone," he says. He silences his cell phone, puts it in his desk, and goes back to the conference room. The phone loudly beeps from his desk drawer. It's almost out of battery power.

He's the only one back in the conference room. The rest of the office has just a few scattered overhead lights on. All the lights inside the conference room are still on. They glare off the conference room table. His eyes start to wander around the room as he thinks. An elderly male janitor starts the vacuum cleaner inside an office just outside the conference room.

"What could be so important that everybody just has it out to interrupt me today?" he softly asks himself.

First to walk back in from break is Nick. Still another six minutes before break is over.

"Wow, that was fast, son," Carl says.

"I just needed to stretch out my legs."

He and Carl talk about the day's events and the Runaway deal.

"I think it's a great opportunity for the company," Nick says. "I'm glad to be a part of this. I think it's going to be a special thing for us."

"I agree," Carl says.

Caitlin is next to walk in. Five minutes left until the break is over.

"You okay, Caitlin?" Nick asks.

"Yes, I'm fine," she reluctantly says and with a pout on her face. She plops back into her chair next to Nick.

Carl just looks at her and says nothing.

"You're still going out with Dean tomorrow right?" Nick asks her.

"Yes, thank goodness. I really like him. He's cute and has a sweet personality."

"Gosh, I remember when I first met Ashlee. It was like there was nothing else in the room and there was a spotlight on her. I'll never forget the eye contact we made. I still quiver when I think about it."

"Dean is so sweet. He's also got nice, well-built arms, which is always a plus with me."

"Yeah, Ashlee has got a petite body that I love wrapping my arms around."

Carl listens to this conversation in disgust. He doesn't like the mushy details.

"Why get married, Nick? Women are so controlling," he interrupts.

Both Caitlin and Nick are offended, especially Caitlin.

"Well, Mr. Robertson, that's your opinion. But I love Ashlee very much," Nick says. "Do you date much yourself? You're a good-lookin' guy."

Uncomfortable with the compliment, he says, "Thanks. But I love my life just the way it is."

Caitlin jumps in. "I agree with Nick, Mr. Robertson. You are very good-looking. I bet you get a lot of dates." Carl doesn't reply.

The rest of the team walks in together, sharing a laugh as they do.

Caitlin, Nick, and Carl stop and look at Tammy, Tucker, Steve, and Amber, and Carl asks, "What's so funny?"

The break room, which is located just down the hall from the conference room, is spacious with a black-and-white linoleum tile floor, a kitchen counter, a refrigerator, a stove, a microwave, and a few tables with chairs. It's a bright room because of the lighting and white-painted walls, and it looks out to the skyline. At this time of the day, you can't see too much but the lights of the city.

"Gosh, he needs a girlfriend bad!" Amber said to the group during the break, referring to their supervisor. "He'd be so much easier to deal with. We'd probably go home at a decent hour more often. I bet we wouldn't still be here if he had a girl."

"Couldn't agree with you more," Tucker said, while Tammy and Steve nodded in agreement.

"Does anybody have any female friends he can meet?"

"No," Tucker said.

"No," said Steve.

Tammy took a minute or so to think of one. She couldn't think of anybody, either. While she knew she'd being doing something good and all, she also knew about his past and lack of desire to meet anybody. She wanted to see her supervisor happy, but at the same time, she knew he would probably not be interested in her friend right from the start. Then she'd have to hear about it from her. She didn't want to jeopardize any friendships she had because of his arrogance and how mean he was.

"Nope, I can't think of anyone," she said.

Oh wait! she thought.

"Did you guys happen to notice how Carl kept looking at Claire at the meeting today?" she asked them.

"Claire?" Tucker asked.

"One of the cute girls with Runaway."

"Oh yeah! Why?"

"Boy was he smitten. I saw a sparkle in his eye I don't think I've ever seen, including that one girl he dated last year very briefly. Oh, what was her name?"

"Karen!" Steve said.

"Yes! Karen," Amber said. "I'd only been here about a month or so when they met. I thought Carl was so sweet. Then I heard what happened and obviously have gotten to know him a little bit since."

"I thought he really liked her. I think he had a, 'Man that girl is hot,' look on his face during that meeting today."

"You know," Steve started, "I do think I remember that. But I didn't get the feeling she was that into him, though."

"Yeah, she and Camille were in to me," Tucker said.

"How are you so sure?" Amber asked.

"Because every time I looked at them, they were looking back at me, and I thought I felt one of them graze my foot under the table."

"That was just your imagination, dude," Steve joked. Amber and Tammy laughed.

"Shut up!" Tucker said.

"Sorry, Tucker, that was my foot," Steve joked again.

Boisterous laughter echoed down the hall but couldn't be heard in the conference room because the door was shut.

"But what do you think?" Tammy asked. "Do you think it's worth a shot?"

They all looked at each other kind of confused and worried, because they knew their supervisor's history and his opinion of women.

"Let's see what happens tomorrow," Steve said.

"I think she's interested in him, too," Amber said.

Tucker looked at his gold watch and said, "Hey, we better get back to the conference room. If we want to get out of here at a decent hour, we better not be late."

"That's if we get out of here," Amber said. "I wouldn't be surprised if he made us sleep here tonight."

They made the short walk back to the conference room. Before they opened the conference room door, Steve said, "Okay, here we go, into the temple of doom."

Everybody laughed at the doorway. Steve opened the door and was first in sight. He peered into the room.

"What's so funny?" Carl asks.

"Oh, nothing, sir. Steve just told us a funny story about him and his wife," Tammy says.

"Oh, what is it?" Carl asks, pretending to be interested.

Tammy stammers and looks at Tucker, Amber, and Steve. "It's not that important, sir. Let's get back to work so we can get out of here."

"Okay."

The team works for another hour, and the entire time, Tucker, Tammy, Amber, and Steve constantly glance at each other, thinking about what they had talked about in the break room a short time ago. Carl is discussing a course of action for the plan, hopeful he's putting the final touches on the presentation for tomorrow morning's meeting. He's focused, not attentive to the lack of concentration being demonstrated by his assistants. Tammy yawns. Steve yawns. Nobody is paying attention. All of them are fighting fatigue and drowsiness. Nick's eyelids dip closed. Caitlin nudges him to wake him up. Tammy mouths some words at Tucker. He nods in agreement.

". . . if we can figure out these two scenarios—" Carl says.

"Mr. Robertson?" Tammy asks with a soft quiver in her voice, interrupting her boss.

Carl angrily stops, throws his notepad onto the floor, and asks her, "What?"

"Well, sir," Tammy starts, "Tucker, Amber, Steve, and I were talking in the break room earlier, and we were wondering what you thought of Claire today? Did you think she was pretty?"

Carl is angry—furious.

"What brings this up?" he asks sternly. "You bring this up in the middle of my meeting? What the hell is wrong with you?"

Steve jumps in, "We thought she was giving you a look today."

Suddenly, Carl's voice has a hint of curiosity.

"What kind of look?" he asks.

"The one where she's almost undressing you with her eyes," Steve replies with confidence.

They all hold their breath nervously.

"Well," he starts, "yeah. I thought she was pretty. But she is a client. I don't think it's such a good idea. You know how it worked out with Karen, remember?"

"Yeah, true. But every girl is different, and I thought she seemed pretty into you at the meeting today. At least every time I looked at her, she had an eye on you. I think you should ask her out at the meeting tomorrow. It'd be fun. It'd be good for you."

Carl is upset.

"Oh, so that's what this is about!" he shouts. "Good for me, huh? You stopped this meeting because of some girl you thought would be good for me? What the hell is the matter with you?"

Everybody gasps.

With an even more elevated and angrier voice, he continues, "I don't need you guys to tell me what's best for me. I've done pretty well on my own. I don't need your input. If any of you bring up dating ever again to me, you will be fired. I'm not kidding this time!"

He slams his hands onto the table. Drinks shake. All drowsiness has fled. Everybody is awake now. They're all focused, wondering what's going to happen next. Who's getting fired?

Nick and Caitlin look at Tammy and mumble, "Way to go."

"What was that, you two?" Carl hollers.

"Nothing, sir. I'm sorry," Nick says.

"Me, too, Mr. Robertson," Caitlin adds.

"You know what?" Carl says, still fuming. "I'm tired of everybody trying to hook me up with women. If I like them, I'll go after them. I don't need you people to do that for me."

"But don't you like her?" Tucker asks.

"I'm tired of dealing with this. Everybody go home; I'll see you all here at six tomorrow morning. Since we can't get the work done tonight, we have to do it first thing in the morning.

"You better come here ready to work, not concerned with which girl I should be dating or hooking up with. Is that understood?"

They all softly say, "Yes."

"If it comes up again, the person who is responsible is gone."

The assistants all think, *Hey, he can't fire us over that.* But at this point, they don't dare say anything. They don't want to find out what could happen.

They each stand up avoiding eye contact with Carl and dart out of the room and straight for the elevator. Carl hangs out in the conference room a bit longer before heading to his office. He angrily leans back in his chair and exhales deeply. He's upset. He runs his hands through his hair.

He gets up out of the chair in the conference room and grabs his notepad and pieces of paper with the information from Runaway. He places them into a light-brown file folder and closes it. He puts the notepad underneath the folder, picks them up off the table, and turns to head out of the conference room. He turns out the lights and gently closes the door.

He takes the short walk down from the conference room and opens the door to his office. He flicks on the light switch. His spacious office is brightly lit.

He grabs his keys off the top of his desk, turns out the lights, and heads out the office to the elevator to go home.

He forgets his cell phone in his desk.

*   *   *

It's the next morning. The sun peeks from behind the horizon. It's 5:00 a.m. on another beautiful day in New York City. A few clouds hang high in the sky. It's a tad cool this morning. The sun's glare creeps into Carl's bedroom.

His meeting with his assistants is in just one hour. The meeting with Runaway begins in four hours. Carl whips off the covers of his king-sized bed and places his feet on the chilly hardwood floor. He yawns. He stretches.

"Phew!"

He goes to the kitchen and grabs a bowl out of the cupboard and a box of Cheerios off the top of the refrigerator. He grabs a half-gallon—almost full—of milk out of the refrigerator and pours it into his cereal for his breakfast. He fills the bowl just past halfway. He opens his front door to pick up today's newspaper, which sits on the floor in front of his condo. He picks up the paper, gently closes the door, yawns, and sits on his coach. He rifles through the paper until he gets to the sports section. The main story is about the Cowboys' coach and his comment regarding Sunday's game.

"What an idiot."

He reads a couple of paragraphs of the story, closes the paper, and tosses it onto his coffee table. He stands up, retrieves his cereal bowl, and stands in the kitchen, leaning against the counter next to the stove. He takes a big scoop of cereal and milk and places it into his mouth.

At 5:15, he's getting dressed. He lays out a gray suit and pants; black shoes; a long-sleeve, white-collared button-down shirt; and a gray tie.

At 5:35, he's out of the house and riding down the elevator to the first floor. He is alone. He realizes he forgot his cell phone. He hits a button on the elevator floor panel, "6," and waits for the elevator, which is now on floor "9" to stop.

He gets to the sixth floor and gets off the elevator. The doors slide closed, and the elevator heads down. Too impatient to wait for the elevator to come back up, he darts to his left down a long hallway to the stairwell. He violently pushes the door open and goes up the stairs to his condo on the twelfth floor, two steps at a time.

Nearly winded, he reaches the twelfth floor and quickly pulls open the door. He runs down the long hallway to his condo. He searches through his keys, heaving deep breaths, trying to regain his breath. He opens the condo door and frantically looks around his place for the cell phone. Kitchen counter? No. Coffee table? No. Bathroom? No. The pants he wore yesterday hang on a hanger. He reaches into both pockets. Nothing turns up. He looks on the nightstand next to his king-sized bed, sheets still all scattered. He didn't make his bed. No sign of his cell phone.

"Oh crap. I left it at the office," he realizes. "There wasn't much battery power left on that sucker."

He then looks for his cell phone charger. It's sitting on top of a dresser in the corner of his room. He grabs it and puts it into his suit coat pocket.

He rushes out of the condo, slams the door, and locks it. He speed-walks down the hall, still catching his breath from running up six floors of stairs. He reaches the elevator and presses the button for the lobby. The elevator is already there.

He stops and hears soft top-forty music playing over his head from the speaker. It's Vertical Horizon's "Everything You Want."

Carl bobs his head up and down in approval. "Great song." It's on his iPod.

Soon, the elevator reaches the first floor. The doors slide open, and he steps out of the elevator. The night guard, Jack, is on duty at the front desk. He will be until 7:00 a.m.

"Good morning, Mr. Robertson."

"Good morning."

"It's awfully early for you to be up, isn't it?"

"Yeah, it is. But I've got a meeting early this morning."

"Is there anything I can assist you with?"

"Yeah, can you call me a cab? I need to get to work ASAP."

"Sure thing."

Carl waits outside while Jack calls for a cab.

At 5:47, the cab shows up.

"Deluxe. On the double."

The cabdriver, Shane, according to the nameplate on the rear of the front seat, speeds away from Carl's condo complex. He has National Public Radio on. The disc jockey is discussing something about a new tax proposal for the city. Carl doesn't pay much attention. He's focused on the meeting with his assistants, which starts in less than ten minutes, and the Runaway one shortly afterward.

The roads are fairly clear at the early hour in New York City. It's a bit warmer than it was earlier, but still on the cool side. They drive past a sign that reads, "Expected high temperature today: 68. Current temperature: 49."

They pull up to the office building. It's 5:58.

"Fourteen thirty-five is your total sir," Shane says, turning over his right shoulder toward Carl.

"Here's fifteen; keep the change."

"Thank you. Have a good day . . . Carl."

Carl stops just after he gets out of the car. He hears his dad's voice.

"What did you say?"

"I said, 'Have a good day.'"

"Did you say my name?"

"No. I'm sorry . . . Carl."

Carl is upset. "Knock it off!"

"What is the problem sir?"

"You keep saying my name. I don't know you. I never told you my name. How do you know my name?"

"You're hearing things."

"No, I'm not."

"Well, it's on your briefcase, sir."

"My briefcase?" Carl looks at the briefcase on the seat next to him. A small nameplate reads, "Carl Robertson, Deluxe."

"Oh."

Shane gives a half smile. Carl's embarrassed.

"I'm sorry about that. I'm just a little skittish today."

"Something big going to happen today?"

"I sure the heck hope so . . . Here is five for me giving you a hard time."

"Thanks, Carl."

They share a laugh, and Shane drives away. Carl walks away and smiles, still slightly embarrassed. He walks through the revolving door and past a group of people talking and laughing. He's avoiding any eye contact with anybody. He looks at his watch: 5:59.

He pushes the thirty-second floor button on the elevator panel. The elevator is already on the lobby level. He steps inside, by himself, and pushes "32" on the panel, and the elevator doors close.

John Denver's "Thank God I'm A Country Boy" plays softly on the speaker.

Soon, the elevator doors slide open for the thirty-second floor. Peggy is not at her desk yet. She won't be in for another two hours. The office is half lit. Only he and his team are in the office, which has a clean smell to it. The janitor had used an orange-scented carpet cleaner last night. Everybody, except Carl, is waiting in the conference room.

All are about half awake and have tall cups of coffee in front of them. The room reeks of the freshly brewed coffee smell.

Carl walks in. It's 6:02. Amber and Caitlin both yawn. Steve and Nick look at their watches to see what time it is. Tammy sips on her coffee. Steve stirs his coffee and adds a small packet of sugar.

Carl has no explanation for his lateness. He demands that his employees be on time, which they were, and he isn't. Each of them is thinking that, but they don't dare say anything. Not a good idea to upset the boss two minutes after he walks in the door and especially after last night.

"All right. Let's get started," Carl says.

The staff goes over the details they couldn't finish last night. Tammy goes first.

*   *   *

Sharon walks in to the office at 8:47. She's a few minutes early. She walks past Peggy's desk.

"Good morning, Peggy."

"Good morning, Sharon."

"Why are all the lights on?" Sharon asks.

"Carl and his team are in the conference room. I guess they've been here since six this morning."

"Why?"

"Apparently, they never got the work finished last night. I think they left here at around ten last night."

"Wow. Really? How do you know?"

"I overheard Steve talking about it in the break room when I was getting a cup of water."

"That's terrible." Sharon walks away toward the conference room to put a small brown paper bag with her lunch inside in the refrigerator in the break room.

"Hey!" Peggy says loudly. "Did Carl ever call his sister back?"

"I don't know. I'll ask him later."

Five minutes later, Pierre and his associates from Runaway step off the elevator.

"Good morning, Pierre," Peggy says.

"A good morning to you, too."

"What brings you here this morning?" Peggy asks.

"We are meeting with Carl and his assistants again."

"Are they expecting you?"

"Yes, indeed."

"Oh, okay. They're in the conference room. I'll let them know you're here." Peggy picks up her phone and calls Sharon's extension. Sharon has just sat down at her desk after dropping her lunch off in the break room.

"Hello?" Sharon asks.

"Pierre and his associates from Runaway are here."

"Okay. Thank you. I'll let Carl know." They hang up the phone.

Peggy looks at Pierre and says, "They'll be right with you. Please have a seat."

Sharon opens the conference room door and pokes her head in. "Pierre and his associates are here."

"Okay," Carl replies. "Thanks." He gets up out of his chair in the conference room and greets Pierre in the lobby.

"Good morning," Carl says, extending his hand to shake Pierre's and then each associate's, including Claire's. Carl flashes a smile at her. She does the same to him.

"Good to see you this morning," Carl tells Claire.

"Thank you. It's nice to see you, too."

"Let's head back to the conference room and wrap this up today, shall we?" Carl says. While walking, Carl thinks about the argument—the disagreement—he had with his staff last night. He then looks over his right shoulder and takes a quick peek at Claire. She has a small smile on her face. She's wearing a knee-length black skirt with high heels and a low-cut white blouse, showing off a little cleavage. He smiles at her. She smiles back. He looks back ahead of him.

His mind runs wild about her. He's had good times with women in the past. It remained a mystery as to why he didn't try it more. At least that's what his friends thought. Carl's admitted a couple times there have been women he's liked and considered hooking up with them. But date them? That's a different story.

But, for some reason, Claire is different. A lot different.

He escorts them back to the conference room. Each of his assistants is there, except Amber.

"Where's Amber?" Carl asks.

"Bathroom," Tammy replies.

"Well, ask her to hurry up please."

Tammy gets up and quickly heads down the hall toward the bathroom. Halfway to the restroom, they bump into each other.

"Oh. I'm sorry. Carl just wanted me to check on you," Tammy says.

"I hope if we close this deal this morning, he'll let us go home for the day. I'm exhausted," Amber says.

"I doubt it."

The meeting finally begins.

*　　*　　*

Sharon works on her computer, typing at a high rate of speed. The keys click and echo off the walls around her desk. She glances at the clock on her desk: 11:32. She hears muffled voices inside the conference room.

"Wow. They've been in there a long time," she says to herself.

Moments later, the door opens. Applause echoes out of the room. She can't see what's happening because the blinds are drawn again. Everybody is all smiles walking out. Carl and his team escort Pierre and his associates out of the office. He says thank you to them as the Runaway group walks onto the elevator.

Carl has the biggest smile on his face he's had in years. Sharon's never seen a smile like that; it's even bigger than the one he had when he met Karen.

"I'll be in touch," Carl tells Pierre as the elevator door closes.

In front of Peggy's desk, Carl tells his assistants to take a break and return at 2:00 p.m. He's giving his assistants more than two hours off. He must be in a good mood.

The team is excited and stunned. They go to the conference room, collect their things, and head out. Amber's place is the closest, and she offers her colleagues a chance to crash at her place to take a much-needed nap. All graciously accept.

Carl stays at the office. There is a hop in his step. He's excited. He thinks about the luxury items he's going to buy with his new payday. A new laptop computer is on his list. A vintage rug for the center of the condo is also on his shopping list.

"I'm guessing things went well?" Sharon asks Carl before he goes into his office.

"Yep. We closed the deal. But can you book me a flight to Paris first thing in the morning. I'm flying there with the contract to finalize the deal. We would've done it here, but they have a two o'clock flight."

"Right away," Sharon says.

He goes into his office and closes the door. He lets out a huge sigh of relief and pumps his fist, too.

He pulls up to his computer and begins looking up information about Paris. He's never been to Paris. What is there to do? Where is it? He looks for a hotel.

"Book me a hotel, too, Sharon!" he screams out to her through the open doorway.

"Yes, sir."

"Something near the Eiffel Tower."

Sharon wants to ask him about the message from his sister. But she's scared to. She doesn't want to ruin the good mood. It's a rare thing to have him in a mood like this, and she doesn't want to be the one to spoil it. He's much easier to deal with.

"Ah, he'll see it," she mumbles to herself. "Maybe since he's in a good mood, he'll check it, too."

He does neither.

*   *   *

Shortly before 2:00, all of Carl's assistants arrive from their extended break. They are awake and refreshed. They're also relieved to have the deal done.

Coffee is still their beverage of choice. They have a late night of celebrating planned.

They each go to their desks, which are scattered throughout the office.

Just before they split to their desks, Steve says, "We're going to drink it up tonight!"

Carl goes to each of their desks, pats them on the back, and tells them they did a good job. He calls them over to his office. They all stand inside his spacious office. The sun beams inside.

"Before we leave tonight, let's get everything in order so I can take it to Pierre tomorrow in Paris," Carl tells them.

"Yes, sir," Tammy says. They leave his office and get back to work with urgency. Everybody's in a good mood. It's been a while since there has been this kind of buzz in the office.

After Tammy shuts the door to the office, Carl notices the note from Sharon about Elizabeth. He realizes his cell phone is still in his desk drawer. He opens it and reaches in to get it. The phone is out of battery power.

"Crap!" Carl screams. He can't call her because the number is on the cell phone. He reaches for his cell phone charger in his pocket and it's not there.

"Where the hell is it?" he nervously asks. He goes back to the conference room to see if it dropped out of his pocket there. He looks under the table and on the chair he was sitting in; he retraces his steps as best he can throughout the office. Nothing.

He quickly walks back to his office. Then his office phone rings.

"Yes?" Carl asks.

"It's Sharon. Your sister is on line one."

"Great. I was just about to call her. Transfer her to me."

"Yes, sir. Hang on just one second." Sharon transfers the call, and Carl hears crying as he places the phone to his ear.

"Elizabeth? What's up?" Carl asks.

Elizabeth struggles with words.

"What are you crying about?" he asks.

It's hard for Carl to make out what she's saying. Elizabeth gasps, trying to catch her breath.

"I can't understand you."

Elizabeth tries to collect herself on the other end of the line, deep breaths, one after another. But she continues to struggle.

Carl's other office line starts.

"Listen. I don't have time for this. I've got another call coming in. I've got to go to Paris in the morning, and my cell phone is out of commission. I'll call you after I get back. I should be back Monday. We can talk then. Okay? I promise."

"Wait, Carl!"

He hangs up the phone.

Chapter III

*C*ARL RETURNS FROM HIS visit to Paris late Monday afternoon. It's much later than he expected. He stops by the office on his way to his condo from the airport. Some of the office staff has left for the day or is getting ready to leave.

Orchestral music plays softly on the speaker in the elevator going up to the thirty-second floor. The elevator stops on the fifth floor. The doors slide open. Tucker and Amber get on. Tucker holds a turkey breast sandwich on white bread and a Diet Coke. Amber holds a BLT sandwich with an iced tea.

"Mr. Robertson," Tucker says, surprised. "I see you're back from Paris. How was it?"

The elevator doors close, and the elevator goes up. The music continues softly.

"It was good," Carl says. "The contract is all finalized, and we're ready to go."

"Fantastic," Amber replies. "What's next?"

"Well, we got to get going on the plan we discussed and settled on. I'd like that up and running by the end of the week. They'd like to get this out to consumers by next Monday."

"Shouldn't be a problem," Tucker replies.

The elevator doors open on the thirty-second floor of the office.

"Hello, Mr. Robertson. Welcome back. How was your trip?" Peggy asks.

"Good."

He walks past Peggy's desk and toward his office. Sharon is not at her desk just outside of his office. She's left for the day. Her husband had a doctor's appointment. He checks the mailbox hanging outside his office. There's a note from Sharon about the doctor appointment hanging on the outside.

"*Mr. Robertson. I left at 3:30 today to take my husband to a doctor's appointment. I'll be in an hour earlier tomorrow.—Sharon.*"

He continues to sift through the papers in his mailbox, about twenty sheets of paper. There is additional paperwork on the Runaway deal. Pierre had faxed it over earlier in the day.

Then there is a bright pink piece of paper. It's another message from Sharon. It says:

"*Please call Claire from Runaway as soon as you can. She has a few additional questions she couldn't ask at the meeting. She's still in town. Call her at the hotel. The number is 212-555-3600—Sharon.*"

"I wonder what this could be about."

He puts it on top of his pile of papers, opens the door to his office, and walks in. He places the stack of papers on his desk. He sits down behind his large cedar desk with glazed shine. Everything is neat and tidy. He calls the number from his office phone.

"Hello and thank you for calling the Ritz-Carlton. This is Jane. How may I help you?"

"Yes. My name is Carl Robertson from Deluxe Marketing. I'm returning a message left for me by Claire from Runaway Destination. I don't know what her last name is."

"Yes, sir. I have a message from her to have us transfer you when you call. I'll connect you to her room. Please hold."

Dave Matthews Band's "Ants Marching" plays softly in the phone while the hotel connects Carl to Claire's room.

"Ms. Claire Morel?"

"Yes."

"This is the front desk. You have a call from a Mr. Robertson. Do you accept?"

Claire's nervous. "Yes."

"Claire?" Carl asks.

"Yes? Who's this?" she asks, pretending to be surprised.

"Carl. I got a message asking for me to call you."

"Oh yes. Hi, Carl. Are you back in town?"

"Yes, I got in about two hours ago. What's wrong?"

"Nothing. I wanted to know if you were available for dinner tonight. There's a nice restaurant here at my hotel."

"Like a date?" He's excited and reluctant—more reluctant.

Tammy comes up to the door of Carl's office, wanting to ask a question about the Runaway project. She hears the conversation Carl's having on the phone. She hopes it's Claire. She pauses and listens. Carl has his back to her. He's sitting in his chair facing the window, overlooking the cloudy day in New York City. Raindrops splash onto the window.

"Yes and no. I wanted to ask you about some additional things with your marketing plan. But I wanted to do it in private and away from your office."

Tammy spots Amber walking toward the break room. She waves at her to get her attention and to get her to come over by the office. Amber obliges, her curiosity aroused.

"Shhh," Tammy whispers to Amber. "I think somebody's trying to ask Carl out on a date."

"Do you think it's Claire?" Amber asks.

"It has to be."

She and Tammy both listen intently and as quietly as possible. Both are grinning ear to ear. They're doing all they can not to make a sound.

"What are you still doing in town?" Carl asks Claire.

"I've never been to New York City before, so I wanted to stay for a couple days. Then when I found out you were going to Paris. I just waited until you got back so you can show me around a little bit and we can discuss the marketing plan."

"Oh, okay. I suppose we can do that."

"There is something else."

"What's that?"

"I'll tell you at dinner."

"No, what is it?"

Claire lets out a deep sigh, trying to compose herself. She's nervous.

"I don't know how to tell you this, but you are really attractive and I'd like to get to know you better, on a more personal level. What do you say?"

Carl hesitates. Then he lets out a sigh.

"What's wrong, Carl?" she asks, scared.

"That's really nice, Claire. I'm honored. But I don't think it'd be great to mix business with pleasure. If you want to meet in regards to the plan, I'd be happy to do so. But if it's for a date, I don't think it's a good idea. I don't want any conflicts. You're pretty and all, but I just don't think it'd be a good idea."

Claire is disappointed. So are a watchful Amber and Tammy. They sigh simultaneously in disappointment, but just soft enough to where their supervisor can't hear them. They now know it is Claire on the other end of the phone conversation.

"Okay. I guess I can understand that. I probably shouldn't be out too late anyways. My flight leaves at seven in the morning. But if you're ever in Boston, let me know."

"Okay. Bye."

He hangs up the phone.

Claire hangs up the phone, looks at it, and sighs heavily, very disappointed. Carl spins his chair around and spots Tammy and Amber standing in the doorway.

"What do you want?" he asks angrily.

Both pause with blank stares, not knowing what to say for an excuse.

"We had a question for you," Tammy says, stammering over her words. "But we figured it out. Never mind." They walk away, but not before Carl stops them.

"Wait, you two. Were you listening to my phone conversation?"

Tammy and Amber look at each other not knowing what to say.

"Okay. Yes. We were," Tammy says.

"How much?"

"Just a little," Amber replies.

"Don't tell anybody about it. Understood?"

"Yes, sir," Tammy and Amber reply simultaneously.

"It's just it's been so long since you've been out with a girl," Tammy says. "We got a little curious. Was that Claire?"

"No . . . Yes. Why?"

"Well, we couldn't help but notice how she was looking at you last week. She totally looked like she was into you. She has the hots for you."

"Whatever."

"No, she does," Amber says.

"We all saw it," Tammy says.

"Who?"

"We did," Amber says, pointing at herself and Tammy. "Tucker, Nick, everybody did, sir. What did you think of her?"

He hesitates. "Well," he starts. "She is pretty. I'll at least agree with you there. But I don't like to mix business with pleasure. It's unethical. You know that by now."

Tammy and Amber scoff.

"No, it isn't," they say in unison.

"You're just looking for an excuse," Amber says.

"Now I've told you guys before, don't set me up with dates. I'll date when I feel like it. Stop trying to set me up. It's getting really irritating. You understand me?"

Disappointed, they nod their heads.

"Yes, sir," Tammy says reluctantly.

"Yes, Mr. Robertson," Amber replies in a disappointed tone.

"Good. Now get out of here. You've got work to do."

Amber and Tammy walk away. He gets out of his chair and slams his office door shut. It echoes down the hall. Amber and Tammy walk back to their desks.

He goes behind his desk and switches on his computer. He picks up his television remote to turn on the Yankees game. They're playing the Twins. The game started ten minutes ago. It's in the bottom of the first inning—no score. The Yankees are now on the outside looking in, hoping to make the playoffs with only a few weeks left in the season. They had a rough road swing while he was in Paris.

*   *   *

An hour later, Carl stops working on the computer. He analyzes data research given to him by the reps from Runaway during the meeting at the office—market population, demographics, and so on.

There's a soft knock on the door of his office.

Carl looks at the clock on his computer: 7:23 p.m.

"Who the hell is still here?" he asks himself.

"Who is it?"

The door opens. It's Percy.

"Hey, man. How was Paris?"

"Good."

"Do anything cool?"

"Not really. Just worked."

"Did you go up the Eiffel Tower?"

"No. No time."

"Ah. That sucks. Hey, listen, I heard about the Runaway deal. Congratulations."

"Thanks, man."

"Everybody's going out to celebrate at Famous Dan's. Want to come?"

"Not right now. Let me get this work done, and maybe I'll meet you over there."

"Okay. It'll be fun. C'mon out. See you over there."

Percy closes the door behind him and meets up with Carl's assistants to go to the bar and grill for drinks and dinner. It's the usual choice of destination for the Deluxe employees after landing a big deal. The Runaway deal more than qualifies as a big deal. Some are still recovering from a heavy night of partying from a couple days before, but that doesn't slow this group down. They're excited.

Plenty of beers, wine coolers, and shots are consumed. They don't care that they have to be at work in nine hours or so.

Carl wants to finish off his work before going over. He never makes it to Dan's. It's just before ten at night. The place closes at ten.

"Ah, I'll never make it."

He shuts down his computer and watches the final outs of the Twins-Yankees game. He lets out a long, loud yawn, stretching his arms above his head, and then shivers.

It's five after. The Yankees win, 5 to 3. They take over the division lead from the hated Red Sox. They'd be in the playoffs if they were to start now. But there's still too many games left in the season before he can feel comfortable.

"Yes," Carl says, gently pumping his clenched right hand.

He hates the Red Sox as much as he does the Cowboys—probably more. The television broadcasters go over the upcoming schedule for the Yankees during their postgame show. The Red Sox are in town next weekend, followed by the season-finale weekend against them in Boston.

"Hmmm. Claire's in Boston."

He picks up the message left for him about Claire. He holds it gently on the tip of his fingers. He smiles, partly confused. He thinks about their conversation earlier in the evening.

"Oh, I really do like her. But it'd never work. Never."

Denial.

He picks up his things, including his cell phone. "Suppose I should charge this thing."

He's the only one left in the office, except for the janitor. The vacuum cleaner sounds throughout the office. Only two or three lights remain on for them.

Carl bumps into him.

"Oh, I'm sorry. Have a good night," Carl says.

The janitor smiles and continues vacuuming. He has a walkman hanging off his right hip on his belt loop. He has earphones plugged into the radio, and the volume is turned up on high. Carl's cell phone slips out of his coat pocket, which he had draped over his arm and falls onto the floor, but he doesn't realize it.

He is already on the elevator when the janitor notices it on the floor. He picks it up and places it on Carl's desk. He finds a small, white piece of paper and writes, *"You dropped this last night."*

Chapter IV

THE STEEL ELEVATOR DOORS slide open on the lobby floor. The entire time on the quiet elevator, he thinks to himself about the conversation with Amber and Tammy. *Gee, why does everybody insist on setting me up with someone?*

Then Claire crosses his mind again. "She is pretty."

He has arguments with himself out loud, trying to talk himself out of going out with Claire. "No, I shouldn't date her or ask her."

"Yes, I should."

"No, I shouldn't. Grrr."

It reads 10:17 p.m. on his watch.

"Phew! What a long week this has been."

His mind is all over the place. It's been a long time since he's had these emotions. That pretty gal he dated not long after he moved to New York, Ginger, certainly had her bright spots—red hair with a petite body and green eyes. But like all the others, it didn't work out—at least it wasn't working for him.

A few weeks later, there was a brunette named Cindy. It lasted only a matter of days. Another brunette named Amber followed. That lasted a week.

Karen? She had the best potential. It lasted one night. And now there is Claire. Something makes this girl unique. He hasn't figured out what. He's half curious to find out. The other half doesn't care to know. It won't work out anyway. They never do.

"She's a client."

The lights are dim throughout the large lobby. Only Bill, the night security guard, is in the area. A guard of twenty-three years, Bill sits behind a desk in his black slacks, black shoes, and light-blue collared shirt. A name tag hangs off his left front shirt pocket.

"Evening, Mr. Robertson," Bill says. "A late night for you, huh?"

"Yes, it is," Carl replies. "She wanted to finish up some important paperwork."

"Any good news lately?"

"Listen," Carl says, ignoring Bill's question.

"Yes?" Bill asks curiously.

"Did my assistants come through here already?"

"Yes, they did, sir. Hours ago. Why?" the guard asks confused.

"What were they doing? Were they talking about anything?"

"I couldn't tell. I was on the phone with my wife, Caroline."

"Oh, how is she? Still doing well, I hope?" Carl asks pretending to care.

"Yes, thank you. Sorry I can't be more helpful though."

Carl had met Bill's wife four years earlier at the company Christmas party. He remembers her being a sweet lady with a sweet personality. She kept calling Carl "sweetie" all night long. Two years earlier, she made some of the most delicious eggnog he's ever had. He comes across her every once in a while when he's leaving the office and Bill's just coming in for the night. She usually takes him to work, gives him a kiss on the right cheek, and goes back to the car.

"I love you, sweetheart," Bill says after he shuts the car door.

"I love you, too," she replies.

Carl often ignores the pleasantries between the two. It's not a pleasant or desirable thought or sight to him. But he always raises his arm and halfheartedly waves at her.

Carl gives a half-smile, "Good night, Bill."

"Good night."

Just before he approaches the revolving door, Bill stops him and says, "Sir, it's locked."

"Oh. Well, can you do me a favor then?"

"Sure, what is it?"

"Can you call me a cab? I don't feel like walking tonight."

"Sure thing, Mr. Robertson. Just a moment."

Bill picks up the phone behind the desk a short distance from the front door. Carl finds a wooden bench to sit on by the door. He reaches into his pocket for his cell phone.

"Maybe I'll finally see what Bill and Elizabeth needed so bad," he says.

He can't find it and checks every coat pocket and every pants pocket.

"Where the hell is my phone? Eh, I probably forgot it in my desk again. I don't feel like getting it. I'll call them tomorrow."

Bill hangs up the phone with the cab company.

"Sir, the cab will be here in ten minutes."

"Okay, thanks."

"You're welcome. I've got to make some rounds. Are you going to be okay for a few minutes down here by yourself?"

"Yeah, but don't you have to unlock the door."

"Oh, sure. I apologize. I'll wait till your cab gets here."

Bill stands up from his chair and walks toward Carl on the wooden bench across from the lobby desk near the door. He sits down next to him.

"Is everything okay, Mr. Robertson? You look upset," Bill says.

The argument with Amber and Tammy has hit him hard this time. He thinks about how Claire asked him out and he didn't accept. He doesn't know why. Both the argument and Claire are hard on his mind; it's more than a girl usually does—more than a girl ever has done.

He's bothered by it. Why? He doesn't know. He is frustrated, curious.

"Well," Carl starts, "everybody is so determined to set me up on a date. They think it'd be good for me. But I've never had good luck with women. I don't know why. I'm rich, successful, and good-looking. What more could they want?"

"Well, when was your last date?" Bill asks.

"Do you remember Karen at all?"

"Yes, I do actually. Very beautiful young woman. I see her quite a bit now that she works here in the building. How'd that go?"

"We went out for dinner once. That was it. I didn't like her too much. She's not a sports fan. Plus, I didn't think she was that pretty after all."

"Are you kidding? She's stunning."

"She wasn't bad."

"Mr. Robertson, I think your standards are too high," Bill continues. "Maybe even you think too highly of yourself. I've known you since you got here, so I think my opinion matters to you. Right?"

"I guess so," Carl says softly, slightly agitated.

"I think you should be more receptive to the idea of women and dating. I bet you'd be surprised if you gave it a shot. Women don't like men who are cocky about themselves. There's a dramatic difference between confidence and cockiness. I think you're getting the two mixed up."

Carl is irritated and offended but tries to be reasonable and comprehend what Bill is trying to tell him. Still, he tries to convince himself to ignore it. He can't. Claire is something special.

"Almost every time I see Karen, she looks disappointed."

"Why?"

"Sir, I really believe she likes you."

"Look, I appreciate you and everybody's concern. I really do. I'm just tired of hearing the same thing from everybody. The right woman will come around when I'm ready."

"Yes, that's true, but are you even allowing it to happen?"

Carl stops to wonder.

"What do you mean?"

"Because you're so wrapped up in your work. I've heard and seen what you've been doing for the company up there. You're doing great work. I know because I hear others talk about it. But are you even giving a woman a chance to open your eyes and heart?"

Carl sighs.

"My job is very important to me, and I've worked very hard to get where I am. I don't want to lose it or have my work be influenced because I put my job behind dating. I let that happen to me once before in college, and it was disastrous. Like, Claire, one of the associates with Runaway, asked me out to dinner tonight. She's pretty, but she's a client, and if something goes wrong, it could mean problems for everybody involved. I don't want to take that chance. Don't need to take that chance."

"Well, I can understand that. Relationships are tough no matter what. But you just need practice with it. It's not something you just jump into. It takes work."

"But I don't want to do the work. I've got more important things on my plate."

"See, that's part of the problem, sir. Women like a man who can give them attention and make them feel loved. The attention doesn't always have to be 100 percent of your day. They just like to know they are appreciated. You want them to worship you. And I think you believe you have to constantly give them attention. You don't have to. Once you learn the balance, I guarantee you will feel better about yourself and the prospect of dating. Your stress won't be as high, and you won't be this uptight about work all the time. You'll actually be more fun to deal with, more fun to work with. Give it a chance. I bet you'll find happiness. I've heard from colleagues you can be pretty mean on most days. A woman who really cares about you can change that. But it only happens if you allow it. Can I ask you what brought this up?"

"Like I said, one of the clients from Runaway thinks I'm cute."

"What do you think of her?"

"She's pretty and all. But I already told you. I just don't like the idea of mixing business with pleasure. It never ends well. It hasn't before."

"How often have you tried? Once?"

"A couple times."

Bill lets out a deep breath.

"Have you ever given thought to why people want to help you?"

Before he could answer, Carl's cab pulls up and honks the horn. He quickly gets up from the bench. Bill isn't as quick. He's in his sixties. Carl waits for Bill to unlock the revolving door and then quickly goes through it.

"Thanks for the chat, Bill. I'll think about what you said and all. Good night."

"Good night, sir," Bill says. He locks the door behind Carl.

He opens the car door and says, "Luxury Living, please."

"Okay," the cabdriver says.

On his way home, in the backseat of the taxi cab—a yellow Chevy Lumina—Carl thinks about what he and Bill talked about in the lobby.

Is he right? he wonders. *Do I allow it to happen? No. Probably not. But whatever, this is the life I wanted, and I'm pretty happy with it. I'm doing pretty well for myself. Why can't people just accept that and leave me alone? I shouldn't have to be everybody's concern. I don't want college to happen to me again. That was a pain. But Claire is certainly someone different. Why can't I stop thinking about her?*

His admiration for Claire is increasing.

The cab pulls up to the front of his condo complex. He looks at his watch: 10:46 p.m.

"Wow. We got here pretty quick," he says. He was so caught up in his thoughts about Claire. "It's good to be home. I need a drink."

"That's seventeen seventy-five," the cabdriver says.

Carl hands him a twenty-dollar bill and waits for his change.

Suddenly, Carl has a quick blackout moment, and his mom and dad flash before his eyes. It lasts just a split second, but long enough to make him jump and let out a soft, quick scream.

"*What?* What's wrong, sir?" the cabdriver frantically asks.

"I don't know. I just saw a vision of my mom and dad. Weird."

He wipes his eyes and shakes his head. Everything's back to normal.

"Ooooookaaaay," the cab driver says. "Two twenty-five is your change. Have a good evening."

Still stunned about what just happened, Carl just waves at the cabdriver and rushes inside his condo complex.

The guard at the door of the complex says, "Good evening, Mr. Robertson. Late night I see." The guard, Tim, wearing a long black coat with black pants, black shoes, and white gloves, pulls the door open for Carl.

"Yes!" he shouts quickly and avoids eye contact. "Work."

"Is everything okay, sir?" Tim asks.

"Yes, I'm fine!" he shouts back, and runs to the elevator. He slams his right hand onto the floor panel to the right of the elevator doors. Nothing lights up on the panel.

"Damn it!"

He extends his right hand at the panel and presses "12." Tim stares at him, making sure Carl is indeed all right.

He nervously bounces on the tips of his toes, waiting for the elevator to come.

"C'mon! Open up, you damn thing!"

The doors slide open. He rushes in and hits "12" for his floor. Repeatedly. Then he hits the "close door" button. Repeatedly. The doors slide closed, and the elevator makes its way up the shaft. A soft, upbeat, jazzy tune plays on the elevator speaker. Mirrors surround the inside of the elevator, which is big enough for about ten grown men. He's the only one on the elevator.

Carl looks at his watch on his left wrist: 10:59. His arm is shaking. He feels a bit chilled. He glimpses himself in the mirror. "Hmm." His face is red. He holds up each of his hands. They are shaking.

The elevator reaches the twelfth floor. He reaches into his pocket and rifles through his keys nervously, sweating and shaking.

He finds his keys and drops them onto the floor. He reaches down, picks them up, and frantically searches through them. He unlocks the door, violently pushes it open, and then quickly slams it shut behind him, the sound echoing down the vacant hallway. He locks the door and the deadbolt. He flips on the lights to his apartment. He searches in his pocket for his cell phone and realizes again he forgot it.

"Damn it!" he says. He has a phone in his condo, but it doesn't have an answering machine. He always tells people to call his cell. It's usually the best way to reach him, unless it's his family—his parents or siblings—then he seems to be unreachable. He rushes to the phone in the kitchen, which is hanging on a wall next to the refrigerator, and calls Percy.

"C'mon. Answer the phone, dude!" he shouts still shaken up.

"Hello?" Percy asks.

"Dude, you busy?" Carl asks.

"Not really, but I was about to head out to the bar. You want to come?"

"Yes! Yes! Yes!"

"Okay," Percy replies nervously. "Settle down, man. I'll be at your place in ten minutes."

Carl hangs up the phone.

A concerned Percy, dressed in blue jeans, a light-green polo shirt, and brown shoes, grabs his wallet, keys, and jacket, and heads for Carl's place, which is a ten—to twenty-minute walk from his.

Carl opens his refrigerator and pulls out a bottle of Miller Lite. He opens it and pounds it. He doesn't stop until the bottle is finished.

"Phew!" he says. He slams the bottle on the countertop.

He reaches into the refrigerator, grabs another, and takes another big swig. He doesn't finish it. He finishes a third of the bottle. He takes a deep breath and finishes it. He reaches into the refrigerator and grabs a third bottle. He takes a shorter swig. He sweeps his right arm across his mouth to clean up his face.

"Oh, man, I needed that," he says and then tips his head back and takes a long swig of his third Miller Lite. He swallows, clears his throat, leans his head back, and finishes the rest. "Phew!" He tosses the bottle into the garbage. It clangs against another bottle from last night. The other two sit on top of the counter in front of him. He grabs both and tosses them into the garbage. The bottles loudly clang against the others.

He suddenly hears a voice.

"Carl! Carl! Carl!" it says in a faint, high-pitched voice.

"What? Who is it? Who's here?" he shouts out. He heads to the door and looks out the peephole. Nobody's there. He unlocks the door, swings it open, and looks left down the hall. Nothing.

Then he looks to the right. Nothing.

He slams the door and then shuts and locks it. The deadbolt remains unlocked.

"Carl, Carl," the voice continues.

He starts to make it out. It suddenly sounds familiar.

"Mom?" he asks uncertainly. He looks out the window. Next he searches around his condo. Nothing. He looks under the couch and the coffee table, behind the TV, under the bed, behind the shower curtain. His search frantically continues.

He reaches into his pants pocket, looking for his cell phone. No phone, he realizes again. Flustered, he looks for his phone inside the unit. It has a speaker system. He picks up the phone, a constant dial tone sounds in his right ear. He picks up the receiver and yanks it off of the wall just past the kitchen and throws it onto the couch in the living room.

The voice continues, "Carl, Carl, Carl."

"Stop it! Stop it! Leave me alone!"

Carl grabs a fourth Miller Lite, takes one long swig of it, getting through half of it, and throws it into the sink. The bottle breaks. He grabs his keys and heads downstairs. He presses the button for the elevator, but it's up on the twenty-third floor.

Instead of waiting, he turns to his right and sprints down the vacant hallway to the emergency stairwell. He slams the door open, pushing it open with his right shoulder. It closes behind him after he's gone down one flight of stairs, echoing off the walls throughout the stairwell.

He's running down the stairs, almost two and three steps at a time. His deep breaths echo inside the stairwell. He feels his heart racing, like it's about to hop out of his chest. He gets down to the main level and opens the door to go into the lobby, pushing it open with his right shoulder. He's out of breath. He collides with another security guard, Joe, and the two fall hard to the ground.

"Oh, I'm sorry, Mr. Robertson," Joe says. "Are you okay?"

"Yes, yes. I'm fine. Sorry. Are you hurt?"

Carl quickly pushes himself off the floor and heads for the door. He passes Tim, still standing at the front door.

"Going out, Mr.—" he asks before Carl interrupts him.

"Yes!"

Once outside, in the cool evening air, which has the scent of rain, he runs toward Percy's place. He hears the voice again.

"Carl, Carl, Carl."

He's scared to death. He is covering his ears, singing, "La, la, la, la, la, la, la," trying to drown out the voice. But it grows louder.

"Carl, Carl, Carl."

"Leave me alone!"

He turns the corner and runs into a man, knocking them both over onto the cold pavement. It's Percy.

"Geez, Carl, what the hell is the matter with you?" he asks.

"Nothing, let's just go."

"Okay." Percy is puzzled by how his friend is acting.

The two flag down a cab. One pulls up—a yellow Chevy Lumina. Carl recognizes the cab for some reason.

He blinks his eyes a couple times.

"Is everything okay, Carl?" Percy asks.

"Yes, I'm sorry. Let's just go."

They get into the cab, and the driver asks, "Where to, guys?"

Carl recognizes the voice. He looks at the driver's ID plaque on the seat behind him. It's the same driver who drove him home.

"Get out!" Carl screams to Percy.

"Why?" Percy asks confused.

"Just do it!"

The two slide out of the car, and Percy tells the driver, "We'll get the next one. I apologize for my friend here. Here's a couple bucks for your troubles."

Percy tosses in a ten-dollar bill, not attentive to how much money he just threw at the driver.

The cabdriver says, "I come across weirdoes all the time."

Percy slams the door, and the cab drives off.

"All right, Carl, what the hell is going on?" Percy angrily asks him.

"Nothing."

"Bullshit. Something is bothering you. Your face is all red. Your hair is all over the place. What is it?"

"You wouldn't believe me if I told you."

"Carl, I'm your friend. I'll believe anything you tell me."

Carl thinks quickly and tells Percy what the problem is.

"Well, that cabdriver drove me home tonight from work. It was a late night because of the Runaway deal. When I was waiting for my change, I saw my mom and dad. It was like they were right there in the cab, driving!"

"What?"

"Yes, it's true. Then I get to my condo, and I hear voices, 'Carl, Carl, Carl.' I tried to drown it out, but I just couldn't do it. It sounded like my mom."

"Your mom?"

"Yes! I was running toward you, and I kept hearing the voice. I tried to sing to drown it out, but the voice just kept getting louder. That's when I ran into you. Sorry about that, by the way."

"Then what happened?"

"Well, that's pretty much it."

"Have you had anything to drink tonight?"

"Yes, I slammed a couple Millers when I got home."

"How many is a couple?"

"Uh, four?"

"How quickly did you have them?"

"Oh, I don't know, two or three minutes."

"That's probably it."

"No, I saw my parents before the drinks. I started hearing the voice afterward."

"Okay, so it looks like we need to get your mind off of it. How about doing something a little different tonight?"

"What do you have in mind?"

"How about a club or something? Some shots will make you better. Promise."

"Perfect! Let's go!"

Carl whistles for a cab. One pulls up. It's another Chevy Lumina. It's green.

He immediately jumps into the backseat and looks at the driver's ID tag on the back of the seat. "Phew! A different driver," he says.

"Is this all right, Carl?" Percy asks.

"Yes. Let's go."

Percy tells the driver to head to the club district. The driver, confused by Carl's curiosity about who's driving the cab, pulls away. Percy gives his good friend a pat on the back in the backseat of the cab, "It'll be okay, buddy. I'm here for ya, man."

"Good. Thanks, dude."

Chapter V

PERCY DOES ALL HE can to help his friend take his mind off what's been going on by talking Giants football with him on their way to the club.

"Did you by chance happen to hear what the Cowboys' coach said about the game against the Giants?" Percy asks.

"No, I was in meetings all day. What happened?"

"Apparently, their coach said the win was lucky because the Giants got all the refs' calls and they didn't."

"*What?* That's insane. What's he smokin'?"

"I don't know. That was my reaction, too. They've been talking about it on the radio and sports channels all day. Everybody I've listened to said it was idiotic to blame the loss on the refs."

"He's just miffed they lost. I hate the Cowboys. That's why I hate the Cowboys."

Carl's mind drifts away from the voices he had been hearing earlier and the image of his parents in the cab when he got to the complex. He's calmed down. His face isn't as red.

"They're always blaming the loss on something or someone other than themselves," he says. "Why don't they just man up and accept it like a man?"

"Amen, brother!" Percy says and high-fives his friend.

The cabdriver shakes his head in the driver's seat. Percy and Carl both notice it.

"What's up?" Percy asks. "Why are you shaking your head?"

"Nothing," the cabdriver says.

"Oh yes, it is," Carl says. "What's up?"

"Nothing," the driver says more adamantly this time.

"Okay, man. You don't have to snap on us," Percy says.

The driver slams on the brakes, Percy and Carl nearly slide off their seats, and the driver whips around at them, looking over his right shoulder. When he turns around, Carl has the illusion of his father's face on the man's. "Come home, Son."

"Aaaaaah!" Carl screams at the top of his voice. "Get me out of here!" He opens the car door, rolls out of the car, and runs away.

"Carl!" Percy says.

Percy throws the cabdriver a twenty and chases after Carl.

"The fare is twenty-one thirty-five, sir!" the driver yells with his normal face and voice. Percy stops and reaches for whatever he can find—a ten—runs back to the cab, and throws the money at the driver through the front passenger side window.

"Thank you. Have a good evening," the driver says and speeds away.

Carl is running full steam ahead; his destination is anyone's guess.

"Get me away from him!" he shouts, his voice echoing off the buildings. "Leave me alone."

"Carl! What's wrong? Wait up!"

Carl stops, allowing Percy to catch up to him.

"That driver is possessed," Carl says shaking, his heart racing. He put his arms over his head.

"What? What are you talking about?"

"I saw my dad!"

"Your dad?"

"Yeah."

"How so?"

"When he turned around, my dad's face was on his, and he talked just like my dad."

Percy wants to believe Carl, but he's finding it harder and harder to do so. He's worried.

"Did he say anything?" Percy asks.

"Yeah, he said, 'Come home, Son.'"

"'Come home, Son'?"

"Yes. 'Come home, Son.'"

"What does that mean?"

"I don't know."

"Listen, let's walk back to my place. You can crash at my place tonight. I can assure you nothing weird is going on there."

"How can you be so sure?"

"Because it's my apartment. I live there. I think I'd have a pretty good idea if anything weird is going on in my own apartment."

Carl is hesitant. Scared. But he reluctantly agrees, knowing his place is not any safer. "Okay."

Percy glances at his watch: 11:51 p.m. They're about fifteen minutes away from his place. Percy wraps his right arm around Carl to comfort him and calm him down. Their walk is slow. Percy can feel his friend shaking. He tries to think of a subject the two of them can talk about to help calm him down.

"What do you think about next week's game for the Giants? They play the Bills, right?"

"Yeah, I think so. They're not that good."

"Easy win, you think?"

Carl is silent.

At 12:20 a.m., they arrive at Percy's apartment. It's in a six-story, redbrick building. It's got a four-step concrete staircase leading up to the front door. Each of the windows are dark with the lights inside turned off, except for a dim light on the second floor—Percy's apartment.

The street lamps illuminate the street in front of his apartment.

"Hang on, Carl, let me get my keys," Percy says.

Carl quivers.

Searching through his keys, Percy finally finds the front door key. He unlocks it and leads his friend inside. They go up one flight of stairs to Percy's second-floor apartment. It's at the top of the stairs—twenty-six of them. Carl counted, hoping to use it as a way to calm down.

Carl is shaking—scared, mortified, confused.

Percy rifles through his keys again to find the ones for the doorknob and deadbolt locks on his apartment. Carl is searching all around the area for any kind of sign something might be up again.

Nothing.

"There we are," Percy says excitedly as he pulls out his keys. A dog with a medium-pitch bark starts up next door.

He unlocks the door and takes Carl inside. Percy gently closes the door behind him and sits Carl on his black-velvet, three-cushion couch facing the television. "Want me to turn on the TV?" Percy asks.

Carl nods his head.

Percy turns on his forty-inch plasma television. ESPN's *SportsCenter* is on. They're talking about the comments made by Dallas's coach, which Percy had mentioned earlier in the cab.

"Is there anything I can get you?" Percy asks.

"No," Carl replies softly, still shaking. He wraps himself in a red wool blanket and lies down. He stuffs a pillow under his head and lies on his left side to face the television. He still has his shoes on. He slides them off onto the floor.

Percy's apartment is small, but it's not as expensive as Carl's. It's in an older building. His place is dimly lit, but it's cozy. There are wooden floors throughout with a small kitchen, big enough for one or two people, a refrigerator, a sink, a stove, and a counter. But the counter has two sides: one inside the kitchen, one on the outside, like a breakfast bar table. White, wood cabinets line the kitchen. The countertop is tile. It's a one-bedroom apartment with one bathroom. It's not much, but Percy likes it. It is home.

The floor creaks loudly with every step. The neighbor's dog is still barking, but faintly. Percy spends nine hundred dollars per month on rent. He heads into the kitchen to grab a glass of water for Carl, while he grabs a beer for himself.

"Here you go," Percy says.

Carl gives half a smile and takes the glass of water. He slowly sips it and puts it on the end table.

"I'll be right back," Percy says, and he heads for his bedroom. He shuts the door softly behind him and grabs his cell phone out of his right-front jeans pants pocket. He dials his good friend, Joe Young, a doctor at St. Luke's Hospital.

"Hello?"

"Joe?"

"Yeah?"

"Hey. It's Percy."

"Hey, Percy, how are you?"

"I'm fine. Listen, I've got a friend of mine here who's having these visions of his parents popping up everywhere, and he's hearing voices. What should I do?"

"Voices?"

"Yeah, and seeing his parents when they're not there. Like about a half hour or so ago, we were riding in a cab, and the driver turns over his shoulder at us, and my friend, Carl, jumps out of the car. He screams and runs away. Carl says he saw a vision of his dad screaming at us."

"What's he doing now?"

"He's here at my place, relaxing on the couch. What should I do?"

"Give him some warm tea. That should knock him out for the night. Then call me in the morning, and we'll see if he can meet with me and our psychologist, Dr. Roberts."

"Okay. Thanks. Have a good night."

Percy places his phone on the dresser opposite his bed, opens the door slowly and softly, and heads back out to the living room. Carl is still watching TV, clutching a pillow. His eyelids drop.

"You still okay, chief?" Percy asks.

"I'm doing better."

"That's good."

Percy sits down on his blue-velvet recliner to the left of the couch and kicks up the leg rest.

"How'd the Runaway meeting go today?" Percy asks.

The faint but high-pitched voice resumes, "Carl, please come home."

"Aaaah!" Carl jumps up and screams.

"What?" Percy asks, alarmed.

"I've got to get out of here. Now!"

Carl hops up, throws the pillow on the couch, and slides his shoes onto his feet. Percy kicks down the leg rest, jumps out of his seat, and grabs Carl at the door.

"No. You've got to stay here tonight. Too many weird things are happening to you man. You'd be safer here."

"No, I've got to go home."

"Why?"

Carl struggles to put an excuse together. "I've just got to go."

"Fine," Percy says adamantly. "If you don't want to stay here, then I'm crashing at your place."

"No!"

"No? Forget it. I'm coming with you. Let me grab my keys."

Percy grabs his keys off the kitchen counter next to the stove and turns off the lights to his apartment, and they head to Carl's place. Carl's at the bottom of the stairs. Percy locks up his apartment.

"Carl, is everything okay?" Percy shouts as he heads down the stairs with the neighbor's dog barking loudly and rapidly.

"Yes. Absolutely," Carl replies. "You stay here. I'll be just fine by myself."

They're twenty to thirty minutes away from Carl's place or about five miles. Percy wants to hail him a cab.

"No way!" Carl screams. "I'm going to run."

"Run?" Percy asks with his voice getting higher at the end. "Are you nuts?"

"Yes! Run!"

"It's pretty late to be out running around crazy. Carl!"

Carl takes off.

"Wait! Carl!"

Carl ignores him while in a dead sprint for his apartment. Percy says to himself, "Forget this."

Carl's shoes echo off the pavement.

"Good night, Carl!" Percy's voice echoes off the buildings. Carl darts around a corner and disappears. Percy gets his keys out and heads back up to his place.

There's minimal pedestrian traffic in the wee hours of the morning. Carl glances at his watch: 12:59 a.m.

"What is going on?" Carl asks himself, heaving breaths. "Man, I need to work out more."

"Carl!" a loud whisper says.

"Carl!" it says again.

Carl hears it. "No! Stop it!" He covers his ears while running and starts singing gibberish notes as loud as he can. He passes a homeless man sleeping on a bench.

"Hey, what is your problem?" the man asks startled and angry. "I'm trying to sleep here!"

Carl ignores him and keeps going. The man lies back down and falls back asleep. Carl continues screaming in gibberish.

"Blah! Blah! Blah! Blah!"

He ignores every traffic stop. He nearly gets hit by a car; it blares its horn just a couple feet from him.

"Blah! Blah! Blah! Blah!" he continues to scream with his hands covering his ears and still running as fast as he can.

"Blah! Blah!" he screams, heaving deep breaths.

He comes up to his condo complex, and the night guard is sitting inside.

"Hello, Mr. Robertson," he says. "Is everything—"

Carl interrupts him. "Yes, yes. I'm fine. I just need to get to my place."

He runs past the elevators and bolts up the emergency stairwell, striding two steps at a time. He gets to the twelfth floor, swings the door open, and jogs down the hallway. He's almost out of breath, heaving deep breaths.

He grabs his keys out of his pocket, opens the door to his condo, and heads inside, slamming the door behind him and locking it. He turns on the light. He kicks off his shoes, whips off his suit coat, and tosses it on the couch. He throws his keys at the coffee table but misses. He goes into the master bedroom, turning those lights on too. Quickly, he changes into shorts and a grungy T-shirt and hops into bed. He whips the covers over his head, leaving the lights on.

Having forgotten to take his watch off, he looks at it: 1:12 a.m.

He can't sleep. All he thinks about is the flashbacks of his parents and the voice which seems to follow him wherever he goes.

Ten minutes later, there is silence. He slowly slides the covers from over his head to see if there is anything going on around him.

Nothing. He gives a small sigh of relief.

He tries to settle down to get some sleep. He closes his right eye but keeps the left one open.

Nothing.

He can't sleep.

"This is going to be a long night."

He gets up and looks for sleeping pills in the bathroom medicine cabinet. The box is empty.

"Damn it!" he says, slamming the empty box onto the floor.

He wanders down the hall into the kitchen, looking for something—anything—that could put him to sleep for just a few hours. He digs through his refrigerator to see if anything's in there.

Nothing.

He looks around the room.

Nothing.

"Aha!" he says.

He opens up a cabinet above the refrigerator. Inside is half a bottle of Jim Beam. "This should do the trick," he says.

Instead of getting a glass out of the cupboard, he takes one big swig straight out of the bottle.

He cringes.

"Phew! That's good stuff."

He takes another swig. He cringes again.

"Eww! That's tough."

He takes another gulp. The bottle is almost three-quarters empty now. He's polished off almost a fourth of the sixty-four-ounce bottle in less than two minutes. He feels a tingling in his stomach. He suddenly feels nauseous.

"Uh-oh," he says.

He slams the bottle onto the counter, breaking it, and darts for the bathroom. He slams open the toilet seat and vomits. While sitting there on his hands and knees with his face buried in the toilet bowl, he remembers he hasn't eaten anything in hours. He becomes very nauseous.

Dizzy.

He sits at his toilet for almost twenty minutes. He finally builds up enough energy to dampen a washcloth, which hangs on a bar over the toilet. He grabs the cloth, gets off his knees, and moistens the small towel in the sink under cold, running water. He heaves a deep sigh, holds the wet towel in his right hand, and calls Percy at his place from the telephone in the kitchen.

He feels cold. The temperature is 68 degrees. He is shivering.

"Damn it! No answer," he shouts, wiping off his face and lips with the moist towel.

Percy's answering machine starts.

"Hey, what's up? It's Percy. I can't take your call right now. Leave your name and number at the beep and I'll get back to ya."

Beep.

"Percy!" Carl shouts into the phone. "Percy! Percy! Pick up the phone, man! It's an emergency."

Percy picks up.

"Carl?" he says groggily. "What's wrong?"

"Man, I think I got alcohol poisoning," Carl says. "I just pounded a fourth of a bottle of Jim Beam. Now I don't feel very good at all."

"You did what?"

"Just get over here."

"Dude, I can't. Call an ambulance."

"No. Get your butt over here!"

Silence.

"Okay, fine. I'll be right over." Percy hangs up the phone.

Carl heads back to the toilet with the moist cloth still in his right hand.

Percy slowly puts blue jeans and a sweater on over his pajamas. He grabs his keys off the counter, his cell phone, and heads downstairs.

He looks at his cell phone: 1:42 a.m.

He whistles for a cab coming down the street as he gets outside. The cab stops. New driver. He gets in and tells the driver, "Luxury Living, please. Step on it."

The cab speeds away. Percy with his cell phone still in hand calls Carl's cell.

"Shoot! Straight to voice mail."

Carl's head is buried in the toilet bowl at his condo; he's holding the towel on his forehead.

The cab pulls up to Carl's complex.

"That'll be sixteen seventy-five," the driver says.

Percy gives him seventeen and says, "Keep the change."

The driver pulls away, and Percy quickly knocks on the glass doors of Carl's complex. One of the many night guards, Joe, is at the front desk. He gets up and heads for the door. Through the glass, Joe asks, "May I help you?"

"Yes," Percy starts. "I'm Carl Robertson's friend. He called me. He sounds very sick. Can I come in?"

"Oh. You're Percy, right?" the guard remembers. Percy's at the complex often. "Certainly. I'll go with you. Is everything okay?"

The guard opens the door, and Percy comes in. "I don't know," Percy says to the guard. "He called me a bit ago and sounded really sick. He said he thinks he got alcohol poisoning. He may need to go to the hospital."

The two go to the elevator and up to Carl's floor—the twelfth floor. They get off the elevator and go to Carl's apartment.

Percy quietly knocks on Carl's door, trying not to wake any of the neighbors.

"Carl? Hey. It's Percy. You in there?"

Percy and Joe look at each other. No answer. Joe reaches for the door to see if it's unlocked. Locked.

"Carl! Open up," he says. The door lock rattles, and Carl opens the door. He's got the cloth over his lips. Some of the vomit is on his T-shirt. He looks a bit blue.

"You don't look good," Percy says. "You need to get to the hospital."

Carl can barely speak. He's so nauseated. He gulps in his mouth and bolts for the bathroom again. Joe and Percy follow Carl inside, and Percy softly closes the door behind him.

He glances at a clock on the wall: 2:01 a.m. He opens up his cell phone and dials 9-1-1.

"Nine-one-one operator, what's your emergency?" a woman asks.

"My name is Percy Hawkins, and I'm with Carl Robertson at the Luxury Living Complex. I think my friend may have alcohol poisoning or something worse. He's vomiting and doesn't look good."

"Okay," the operator says.

While the operator takes the information from Percy, Joe is with Carl in the bathroom.

"What the hell happened to you tonight?" he asks.

Hovering over the toilet, "I don't know," Carl says. "Everything was fine up until I got home tonight. While I was waiting for my change from the cabdriver, I had a vision of my mom and dad. They were in the front of the cab. My dad was driving, and my mom was in the passenger seat. It freaked me out. So I came up here to try to drink myself to sleep. Then I started to hear voices, calling my name back."

"Voices?"

"Yes. It's like they've been following me all night, and I keep seeing my mom and dad somewhere. It's messed up."

"You look and sound awful, Mr. Robertson."

Carl spews more into the toilet. The guard turns away. Percy, in the living room, says, "Okay. Thank you." He hangs up his cell phone, puts it in his pocket, and comes into the bathroom.

"The ambulance is on its way," he shouts to Carl from the living room.

"*Ambulance?*" Carl says. "No way. I'm not going. I'm staying right here."

"Carl," Percy says, "do you realize what time it is?"

"I don't care! I'm fine. Leave me alone so I can get some sleep."

"It's quarter after two in the morning."

Carl and Percy are still arguing back and forth with one another when there's a buzz on the intercom inside Carl's place.

"If that's the medic, I'm not going anywhere."

Joe goes to the speaker and answers it. It's the paramedics.

"I'll be right there," Joe says into the intercom.

*   *   *

Joe gets downstairs to the lobby, and the paramedics are already inside. Jack is standing at the door, locking it. "Where is he?" a male paramedic asks.

"In the bathroom in his apartment," Joe says. "Right this way."

He leads the two paramedics—a man and a woman—to Carl in his twelfth-floor unit.

They ride the elevator with no music playing. The doors slide open on the twelfth floor, and Joe leads the two paramedics down the hall to Carl's unit. He opens the door and leads them inside to Carl who still sits on his knees with his left arm draped around the toilet seat. Percy stands just outside of the bathroom in the hallway.

"Here they are," Joe says, pointing to Carl on the floor with his head resting on the toilet seat.

"Get the hell away from me," Carl says angrily at the paramedics.

"It's all right, sir," the woman says. "My name is Bridget. You'll be just fine."

"Stay away from me. I'm warning you."

"Sir, you need to listen to us," the man, named Roger, says.

Carl is forceful. He's swatting Roger's and Bridget's hands as they try to hook him up to their equipment to get some readings and evaluate him.

"I'm fine. Look, no vomit!"

He continues to reject everything the medics are doing. He then turns his head into the toilet and gags.

"What's his name?" Bridget asks Percy.

"Don't you dare tell them!" Carl screams at Percy.

"Carl. Carl Robertson," he says.

"Damn it! I told you not to tell them."

"Sorry, man. But I have to. You look like crap."

Carl tries to get up off the floor but falls right back down, barely missing hitting his head on the toilet. He's light-headed.

"See, Carl, you're not fine," Percy says.

Bridget and Roger agree.

"You look like you're in bad shape. We better run you over to the hospital as a precaution," Bridget says.

"No. I'm not going," Carl says.

"Yes, you are," Percy says.

"It's in your best interest that you go, Mr. Robertson," Joe says.

Carl lets out an enormous scoff—he's not shy about revealing his frustration and disagreement with the idea of going to the hospital.

"Fine," he finally says. "But I'm not staying overnight."

Bridget, Roger, Joe, and Percy all pick Carl up off the floor and walk him down to the ambulance on the first floor. Percy takes the once-moist washcloth and rinses it underneath the faucet with cold water. He wrings it out and moistens it once more. He hands it to his friend.

Percy takes the stairs while everybody else takes the elevator. He begins calling a couple of Carl's other friends—Kenny and John—to let them know what's going on. First, he calls Kenny.

No answer. The answering machine picks up.

"Hello. You've reached the Davises. Leave a message. Thanks. Bye!"

Beep.

"Hey, Kenny. Sorry to bother you so early in the morning, but I wanted to let you know we are taking Carl to the hospital. It looks bad for him. We're going to St. Luke's. I'll call later with an update."

Next he calls John.

John is up. He's getting a drink of water in his kitchen at his three-bedroom ranch just outside the city.

"Hello?" a surprised and confused John answers.

"John? It's Percy. I didn't expect you to be up."

"Do you know what time it is?"

"Yes, I do, and I apologize for that. But listen, Carl's on his way to St. Luke's. He's in bad shape. C'mon on over when you get a chance."

"Is he going to be okay? What happened?"

"I'll explain it to you later. I've already called Kenny, but he wasn't up, so I left a message."

"All right. I'll be right over."

"Later."

They each hang up the phone, and John heads to his bedroom to throw on a pair of pants, socks, and a sweater so he can meet up with them at the hospital. It's about a twenty-five-minute drive with minimal traffic.

Percy meets everybody downstairs. He waits outside the elevator until it comes down. The elevator doors slide open. Carl's arms are draped over Roger and the guard. Bridget is leading the way. Carl is in rough shape. He reeks of vomit. His face is a light shade of blue. He's weak.

Percy heads to the door to lead everybody outside. He glances at his watch: 2:59 a.m.

They get Carl outside. Bridget opens the back door to the ambulance, and they all walk Carl up into the back and lay him down on the stretcher inside. Bridget and Roger hook Carl up to some equipment to monitor his vitals—blood pressure, heart rate. Percy hops into the back with them, while Roger gets out and goes to drive the ambulance to St. Luke's. It's a short drive. Roger closes the ambulance door, gets in the driver's side, turns on the siren, and pulls away.

Joe watches them pull away. He looks at his watch: 3:03 a.m. He goes back inside the complex and returns to his spot behind the desk in the lobby. He logs the events in the security diary. Jack sits in a chair close by.

"Is he going to be okay?" he asks.

"I hope so."

*   *   *

The ambulance siren wails in the background, echoing off the buildings on a cool night just a few hours before sunrise. Carl, Bridget, and Percy are inside. Percy is sitting on a small ledge while Bridget is on her radio with dispatch, updating Carl's status, relaying it to the hospital.

Percy watches his friend closely. He's worried, concerned, even scared. He takes a peek at Bridget, a good-looking girl in her mid-twenties.

"Is everything going to be okay, ma'am?" Percy asks.

"He'll be fine."

Carl's eyes begin to close. He's exhausted. He hears a very faint female voice just as he drifts off to a deep sleep.

"Carl . . . Carl . . . Carl."

It's the same voice he heard inside his apartment and while running home from Percy's.

"Carl . . . Carl . . . Carl."

He's so tired, he can't open his eyes. He falls asleep and begins to dream.

*   *   *

He finds himself standing in front of his boyhood home in eastern Iowa. He grew up in Cedar Lake, population 2,800, on the edge of Cedar and Pitt Counties. It's a small town where everybody knows everybody.

The house looks brand new—no way near, not even close to the way he ever remembered it. It was in great shape—trimmed yard, trimmed hedges. The roof shingles are in place. None of the windows are broken or cracked. The paint is not chipping off. A red 1959 Chevy sits in the driveway; it also looks brand new.

He hears a deeper voice this time. An excited voice.

"Carl! Carl!"

He opens his eyes and wakes up.

"Carl, wake up!" Percy says.

"Ah!" Carl screams, startled.

"What?" Bridget asks. "What's the matter?"

"Nothing," Carl replies. "He just scared me. I was sleeping. He woke me up from my dream."

"You were dreaming?" Percy asks. "We've only been in the ambulance for a couple minutes."

"Yes. I was standing in front of my parents' house. But I wasn't. It was like a completely different house."

Bridget and Percy look at each other confused. Both are concerned.

The ambulance pulls up to the hospital.

The loud, wailing siren shuts off. Roger hops out and opens the back door. Bridget stands inside the ambulance and grabs one end of the stretcher Carl's lying on, and Roger gets the other end. They roll it out. The legs extend, and they roll Carl into the emergency room.

Percy follows close behind.

The doors to the ER slide open.

Percy looks at his watch: 3:17 a.m.

Roger and Bridget wheel Carl past the counter at the ER, and a nurse comes in. "What happened?" the nurse asks.

"Possible alcohol poisoning," Bridget responds.

"What are the symptoms?"

Bridget and the nurse trade information. Percy is looking at his good friend half awake. He looks terrible. Percy looks up and sees John sitting in a chair in the waiting room.

"Percy!" John shouts out to Percy.

"Oh hey! Glad you made it."

"Is everything okay?"

"What happened?"

"I don't know," Percy says hurriedly and John follows closely. "He says he's had visions of his past, seeing his parents at different places, like illusions, and he's hearing voices. He couldn't sleep, so he tried to drink himself to sleep. He called me. I went over to his place, and he was draped over the toilet. He's been vomiting for about the past thirty minutes or so."

"When did this happen?"

"About an hour or so ago. Then on the way over here, he fell asleep, and when I woke him, he said he was standing in front of his parents' house."

Silence.

They wheel Carl into a room for evaluation. A nurse and a doctor show up. The nurse asks Percy and John to wait in the waiting room. "We'll come and get you when he's ready for visitors."

"Hang tough, Carl!" Percy says to a half-conscious Carl. He doesn't acknowledge him.

Carl hears noises around him. The heart monitor continues its beep . . . beep . . . beep . . . beep. Excited voices give one another instructions.

"What are his vitals?" the doctor asks.

"Blood pressure: one forty-nine over ninety-six," one nurse says.

"Heart rate one forty," another nurse says.

"Symptoms?"

Carl's eyelids are getting heavy and weak. It's been a wild night. The lack of sleep is kicking in. The room gets blurry and bright. He stares at a bright light above his head in the hospital operating room. Carl dozes off to sleep.

The sounds of the room disappear.

Chapter VI

GROWING UP FOR CARL Robertson was tough. His family didn't make much money. They lived in a small house way outside of town—ten to fifteen miles away. He had to share his bedroom with his brother Steven. Bill and Elizabeth shared another room. Mom and Dad had the other bedroom.

The living room had a three-cushioned couch, a love seat, and a nineteen-inch television—black-and-white and no cable. The lighting was weak throughout. They had hardwood floors, but they were not in great shape and creaked with every step. They had wooden walls, too. Living quarters were tight. It got awfully cold during the winter and very muggy in the summer. During the winter, the floors felt like ice, and there was no air-conditioning for those muggy nights of June, July, and August. A wood-burning furnace was all that kept the Robertsons warm during the cold months of winter. The family used water out of a well in the backyard. It didn't rain much.

The house sat on a field surrounded by unused farmland. The closest neighbor was more than a mile away.

Mom worked a minimum-wage job as a waitress at the truck stop near the interstate. Dad brought in more cash but not much. He was an assistant manager of the grocery store in town. He and his wife shared the only family vehicle, a red pickup truck.

Both Mom and Dad grew up there. They didn't leave too much. They met there. They went to school there. They got married there. Not much life existed for them outside this town.

As he got older, young Carl wanted nothing to do with it.

"I hate it here!" Carl yelled at his parents during an argument when he was eight.

"Well, when you grow up," Dad said, "you can go wherever you want. Live wherever you want. But as long as you live under my house and my rules, you will abide by what I say and live where we live. Is that clear?"

"Uggh!"

Carl never gave any thought to enjoying life in Cedar Lake. He wanted out as soon as possible. He would do whatever he had to do so he could get the hell out as fast as he could. The less time spent in Cedar Lake, the better.

But he liked to study. He loved it. It was a way to keep his mind off of the awful life he was living with his two brothers, one sister, and parents. He didn't respect his parents. He hated them. He barely tolerated his siblings.

He was jealous of the lifestyles he saw among his classmates growing up. They always looked so much happier than he did. They also dressed well and had neat haircuts. That was not the way it was for little Carl.

His clothes were always raggedy, torn, and dirty. He didn't smell too good, either. His hair always had snarls and was out of place most of the time. No brush or comb was available for him.

Growing up, everybody liked to make fun of him.

"He looks like he's homeless," one girl, Katie Johnson, snickered to her friends one day in fourth grade.

"You mean he isn't?" another girl, Nicole Jennings, said, eliciting a loud laugh from his classmates in the hallway as he walked past, holding a couple textbooks on top of his right arm and a couple yellow pencils in his left hand.

One thing he did enjoy was geography. At the library, he often read travel magazines and books.

"When I get older, I can't wait to live in New York City," he told the librarian when he was six years old. "It looks like there are so many neat things there. I want to go up the Statue of Liberty. That's the first thing I'm going to do when I get to New York is go up the Statue of Liberty. She's so pretty."

"Yes, she is," the librarian said.

"I also want to be rich! That way I can build a big house as far away from here as possible."

Silence.

Nobody ever wanted to sit by Carl in class or in the lunchroom, except for one person: Chuck.

Chuck was Carl's best friend, his only friend.

Chuck lived three miles from Carl's house on the outskirts of town. He had one brother, Charlie. His dad had died a long time ago. His mom still hadn't gotten over his death, so she drank constantly. They lived with their grandma instead of their mom. She was at home, usually passed out drunk on the couch, barely making ends meet.

Chuck, Carl, and Charlie did everything together; they fished, hunted, and played baseball.

They were close friends. Girls entered the picture in sixth grade—at least for Chuck they did. Carl and Chuck hung out together less after that. Girls were the priority for Chuck. He was curious. Not Carl. He wanted to hang out with Chuck. If he didn't hang out with Chuck, he would study to be really smart so he could get the big job in the big city.

"Girls are gross!" Carl said.

"No, they ain't," Chuck replied.

In sixth grade, Carl started to play football. He was puny, barely eighty pounds. There was no growth spurt in sight yet. Everybody else was bigger than he was. Even the girl who filled up the water bottles was bigger than he was.

"How can you play football? You're so tiny," the girl, Stephanie, once told him.

The cheerleaders overheard her say that to him, and they pointed and snickered.

"I can't believe the coach lets him on the team," one cheerleader, Mary Jennings, whispered to her friend, but loud enough for Carl to hear. "He stinks!"

"In football?"

"And he smells."

Laughter.

Carl dumped water on the water girl. She cried. Her daddy was the coach of the team.

"Robertson!" the coach yelled. "What'd you do to my daughter?"

"She called me tiny."

"You are! Now give me ten push-ups. Now!"

Carl got on the ground and began the push-ups.

"One. Two. Three. Four." He thought to himself, *This is so stupid.*

He stuck with the push-ups, because when he was on the field, he loved to play. He thought he was the best. Just getting onto the field was the problem. Not even five feet tall, it was hard for him to make an impact.

Not even a thud.

He usually played when his team, the Chargers, was leading by a big margin. Even then, he'd be the last guy in.

Uggh! I can't wait to get away from here, he kept thinking on the sidelines every game and during practice every day.

The following year, the growth spurt he had longed for finally came. In a matter of months, Carl grew to almost five foot ten but was still scrawny. He began lifting weights that summer before seventh grade.

By September, Carl was much bigger at five foot ten, 165 pounds —quite the size for a seventh-grader.

The laughing, the criticism, and the insults dwindled. Everybody was so small compared to him now. He loved it. He always had a cocky smirk on his face from then on.

"Look at me now!"

He was on the field that fall, and he was on the field all the time—offense, defense. He was a lineman. He loved it. He got to take out some of the anger and frustration he'd built up for years.

"Robertson," his seventh-grade coach said, "you're one of the meanest seventh-graders I've ever seen out here. You're going to be in the NFL someday, son, if you keep that up."

"Yes, sir!"

He liked his coach, Coach Hall. He was a big man at six foot six, 290 pounds. He had played in the NFL for three years for the Chicago Bears. He played in college at Iowa, just down the road from Cedar Lake. Like Carl, he was also a lineman.

Carl wanted so much to be like Coach Hall. He was a better dad than his own father. He got out of Cedar Lake and made something himself. But Coach came back home.

"Why did you come back here, Coach?" Carl asked him one day.

"I love it here. This is where the real people of America live. Not in the big cities like Chicago. Too many distractions. Good family values here, son."

"That sounds like fun to me. I want to live in the big city someday. I can't stand it here."

"Ah, you say that now, but trust me, that'll change when you get older and after you move away from here. I thought much like you did when I was your age."

"No, it won't."

No man was as good as Coach Hall in Carl's young eyes. Carl's dad, George, wanted to provide for his family, something his father never did for him. Grandpa died three weeks before Carl was born.

When Carl started to play more, his dad made it a priority to be at every game. But every time he came, Carl, in his mind, played terribly. Beyond terribly. It was embarrassing. Finally, after his eighth-grade season, Carl told his dad to never come to his games again.

"You just make me play bad," he told him. "You're bad luck."

Dad was stunned and sad.

"Okay, son. If that's what you want."

He was reluctant to tell his son that, but he wanted what was best for him and he wanted to be there for him. If that meant giving up going to his games, so be it. He wanted to be the best father he could. He just had to figure out another way to be there for his son.

Carl's siblings were all athletes, too. Bill played baseball; Steven played soccer and wrestled; and Elizabeth was in tennis and track.

Dad had been a pretty fair athlete himself. He'd played football and baseball and wrestled in high school. He was all-state in football and wrestling. He won a state championship in his senior year in wrestling at 171 pounds.

Carl hated wrestling.

"It's stupid. A bunch of sweaty guys grabbing each other. Sick!"

Still, Dad watched games out of sight, usually from beyond the edge of the tall steel bleachers at the football stadium, Crisman Field. Carl never knew he did this, but everybody else in town did. They thought it was so tragic Carl didn't want his dad at his games.

After his last game in high school, George peered from behind the bleachers as the team jogged back to the locker room.

"I'm proud of you, Son."

Carl was angry.

"Why didn't you listen to me?" He stormed off, running back to the locker room.

Mom and Dad watched disappointed; a tear dropped out of Mom's right eye. The coach looked at them and said, "I'll talk to him."

Assistant Coach Dan Reed called Carl into his office. Coach Reed was the team's offensive line coach, Carl's position coach.

"Robertson! Get your butt in my office."

Carl sat down with his football pants and cleats still on and a grungy, torn white shirt, which he wore underneath his shoulder pads and jersey. Sweat rolled down his face. Grass stains covered his arms. His face paint was smeared.

The office was small with a wooden desk in the middle. Four steel folding chairs lay folded up against the wall next to the door. A tall, steel bookcase stood behind the coach's chair. It held hundreds of videotapes of game film. There was only one window—on the door. A twenty-two-inch television sat on top of the desk. The floor had a thin red carpet with concrete underneath it. On the wall hung a sign with an inspirational message from Coach's favorite college coach, Ohio State legend Woody Hayes: "You win with people."

Also on Coach's desk was an autographed picture of him with Hayes. Reed had played for Hayes in the 1970s.

"What is it, Coach?" Carl asked.

"I saw what you did to your dad. How disrespectful can you be?"

"He lied to me, and he didn't listen to me."

"About what?"

"I told him not to come to my games. I play bad when he's there."

"No, you don't. He's been doing that all through high school."

"What? That asshole!"

"Robertson! Watch your mouth!"

Carl was silent.

"You should be grateful that you have parents who support you the way they do. Not everybody has that."

"Yeah, well, have you seen my house?"

"Who cares? You have a house. When I was your age, I was living in a car with my mom, dad, and sister."

Carl was surprised but pretended not to care.

"Apologize to your dad."

"Okay, I will. Sorry, Coach."

He never did.

When Carl began high school, he was six foot two, two hundred pounds, and still growing. He was fit. He was lean. He was angry. Area newspapers called him meaner than Mean Joe Greene from the famed Pittsburgh Steelers' defense in the 1970s; he was meaner than Coach Hall at that age.

One newspaper reporter called Carl "the best athlete ever to come through Cedar Lake." He was even better than his idol, Coach Hall.

Carl started on the varsity football team as a freshman. He played right tackle. Then he moved to linebacker as a sophomore and was all-state there for two years. Football became as much a part of his life as studying was. Whatever kept him away from home as long as possible was fine by him.

He would go to school at 7:00 a.m., sit through classes all day, practice until six, workout until ten at night, and then study in the library until midnight. He loved the routine. He was extremely dedicated to his athletics and his studies. He graduated from high school with a 3.755 GPA. He got a full scholarship offer to play football at Iowa. He grew to 235 pounds, and he was fast. He also ran on the school's track team. He signed the National Letter of Intent in February after his last high school football game in November.

"Finally, I'm going to get out of this town and make a living for myself," he said.

The ceremony took place in front of the office at the high school as a celebration for his accomplishments. Despite his arrogance, he was still a popular guy in the halls at school. The girls wanted to wear his jersey at games. They liked his bad-boy persona and hard-to-get attitude. He didn't pay attention to it. He didn't care.

Thirty students huddled around a tiny table in the hallway just outside the main office. Among those in attendance were his best friend, Chuck, and a couple of the girls who always tried to wear his jersey on game day. They were also the same ones who used to make fun of him for his body odor and size. Now they were itching to go on a date with him. Carl never forgot that. He didn't date anybody in high school. He held a grudge against them.

One day, a couple weeks before, one of those girls at the ceremony—Stephanie—had passed Carl in the hallway after school. She was a volleyball player. Carl was finishing up his workout, which he usually did after practice. He was heading back to the locker room when he came across Stephanie sitting in a small wooden chair outside the locker room, waiting for him.

"Hi, Stephanie," he said.

"Hey," she replied. She stared at him.

"What is it?" he asked just as he approached the door to the locker room, sweat glistening off his face from the hallway lights and dripping down. He was wearing mesh workout shorts and a cutoff T-shirt. His muscles bulged from beneath it.

She stood up and planted a long kiss on Carl's lips. He pushed her off.

"What the hell was that?" he asked angrily.

"I want you," she replied. "You're so hot."

"Yeah, well forget about it. I remember sixth grade and all those times you made fun of me. It's not going to work. Now beat it."

He placed his hand on the door to push it open. She grabbed his arm and glared into his eyes.

"Whatever. You want me. I know it. It's only a matter of time until you realize it."

"Keep dreaming. Now let me go."

She let go and walked down the hall toward the girls' locker room, swaying her hips back and forth with each step. Carl stood there and watched. At the locker room door, she glanced back at him, smiled, blew a kiss with her lips, and walked into the locker room.

Carl, still surprised and upset, went back to the gym to get his mind off what had just happened. He took it out on the punching bag for the next thirty minutes.

At the ceremony, a newspaper reporter asked him, "Why Iowa?"

"Because it's a great school which could lead me to my lifelong goals."

"What would those be?"

"Live in a big city, making a lot of cash."

"Playing in the NFL?"

"That'd be great because this town is a joke. I can't stand it here. Everybody here is a disgrace to humanity. All this lovey-dovey crap is sickening. Have you ever stood on the end of Main Street and just looked down it? This town is a dump, an embarrassment. Everybody here is trash. It's disgraceful. You are all idiots for wanting to live here and calling this a good place to live. You're kidding yourself if you believe that."

He pulled out a picture of New York City and showed it to everybody. They all stood there in disbelief.

"Now this is a way of life."

His parents were sitting next to him. They were stunned. All of the thirty people in the hallway around the table were stunned.

"Carl! How could you say that?" his mother asked, still stunned. Everybody's mouths were open. Some girls' eyes were tearing up.

"What? I've been saying it since I was six. It's nothing new. I've never been one to hold anything I'm thinking back. The man asked a question, and I answered it."

He looked at the reporter. "Any other questions?"

The reporter shook his head no—still shocked and clueless about what to write.

"Okay, thanks for coming. Go Hawkeyes!"

The reporter grabbed his bag, put his notepad away, and left. He thanked the principal on the way out.

"Please ignore what he said," the principal requested.

Silence.

Everybody stormed off back to class angrily. The principal, ashamed of what had just happened, yanked Carl into the office.

"What in the world was that?" Mrs. Warner asked.

"Look, I've been grateful for what everybody has done. Really. I am. But this town is not the place for me. It never has been and never will be. Telling the reporter my feelings was my way of saying what needed to be said."

"Regardless, you are a bad representation of this school, the football program, the athletic program, and this town given your actions here today. You're the real disgrace of this town."

Carl slid the chair back rapidly and headed back to class. For the rest of the year, his classmates gave him a cold stare anytime he walked past them in the hallway. He didn't care. In a few months, he would be on his way out of there, and nobody was going to stop him. So he continued to focus on his studies and made sure he got in shape for fall football camp in August.

The next day, the local newspaper headline from Carl's signing read, "Cedar Lake's Robertson Bashes Town in Signing."

He read this and was angry. "Why did they focus on that? I hate reporters."

His parents looked at him and said, "You made a mockery of this town. You should be embarrassed."

He wasn't.

When graduation came in June, Carl didn't even show up. He was drinking with the one person who supported him: Chuck.

Carl's relationship with his parents deteriorated more as he got older. He listened to them less. He respected them less. He never appreciated what they did for him or tried to do for him. He was home a lot less. He only came home to sleep.

"All you did was deprive me of a decent childhood with this awful house and this awful lifestyle," he said during a heated argument shortly after graduation. When Carl turned eighteen a few weeks after graduation, his parents told him if he wanted to leave, he could, but regardless of the past, they still welcomed him with open arms.

"Yeah, whatever. I'm gone." He packed up his things, got into his orange Chevy pickup truck, and headed to Iowa City. He and Chuck got an apartment together close to campus.

While doing workouts one day a month later, working on running drills with Chuck's help, Carl planted his right leg and felt a snap in his right knee.

"Aaaahhh!" he screamed.

He collapsed to the grass of the Iowa football practice field. Chuck dropped the football he was holding and fell to his knees next to his best friend.

"Carl! Carl! Are you all right?"

"No! I think I tore my ACL. Get somebody! Hurry!"

Carl sat on the ground in pain, while Chuck ran to the trainer's office. It was a short run to the office.

"Hurry! I think Carl hurt his knee!" Chuck screamed at the trainer.

They ran back to Carl and then carried him back to the training room. The trainer called for an ambulance to take him to the hospital. The paramedics wheeled him through the doors of the hospital and straight into the emergency room. Three nurses and a doctor were at his side. Chuck was in the waiting room just down the hall. They diagnosed him as having torn almost every ligament in his knee.

"Will I be able to play?" Carl asked, screaming in pain.

"Play? That's the least of my concerns," the doctor said.

Soon, a nurse walked down the hall to get Chuck waiting in the waiting room. He was standing back against the wall, crying. He hoped to come along for the ride with Carl, because he also dreamed of living in a big city. Chuck wanted to be his agent if—when Carl got to the NFL.

They had it all planned out, too. Chuck saw all those dreams going away.

"Chuck, is it?" the nurse asked.

"Yes."

"You can go see him now."

Silence.

"Don't you want to see him?" the nurse asked.

Chuck turned away and sprinted down the hall toward the exit of the hospital. Tears were rushing down his cheeks. Carl never saw him again.

A month later, after the surgery, Carl was taken home by a member of the coaching staff, Coach Williams, his position coach, and was dropped off at his apartment near campus. Coach Williams took the crutches out of the backseat, opened the front passenger-side door to his four-door sedan, and handed the crutches to Carl.

"Thanks, Coach."

"Do you want help up to your place?"

"No, that's okay. I got it."

"All right. Get some rest, Robertson."

Carl walked with the aid of his crutches to the front door to his complex. The coach slammed the car door shut, walked around the front of his car, and got in. He started the engine and watched Carl limp inside.

Carl struggled up the stairwell to his apartment building, which was two stories with white siding and red window frames on the outside. Inside, it was well lit and carpeted. There were eight units in the building. His unit was at the top of the stairs. He dug in his right front jeans pocket to get his keys. He opened his door and saw an emptier place than he remembered.

Chuck's things were gone. Carl saw a note sitting on the dining room table to the right of the doorway. He limped over with his crutches underneath his arms and picked up the note: *"Gone back home. Sorry 'bout the leg. Chuck."*

Carl crumpled up the note and threw it into the nearby garbage can. There was a soft knock on the door frame. His parents were standing in the doorway.

"What are you doing here?" he asked them.

They had been notified by Coach Williams, who told them what had happened. He had called them when the injury took place, but Carl was adamant about not seeing any visitors. He just wanted to sulk in self-pity and disappointment.

On his way to pick up Carl from the hospital, Coach Williams called Carl's parents to tell them he was taking him home.

"Thanks, Coach," George said. They hopped in the car and drove to Iowa City to be with their son.

"I thought you guys hated me," Carl said after they arrived. Strangely, he was kind of glad to see them.

"We still love you, Carl," Mom said. "Always have and always will. No matter how much of a jerk you may be to people. We'll always be your parents."

Silence.

"How's the leg, Son?" Dad asked.

Carl shrugged his shoulders. "It's okay. Could be better."

Dad handed Carl a note from Bill. "Hang in there. You'll be back up on your feet in no time, clobbering those pansies from Minnesota."

Carl laughed.

Elizabeth had sent a card with Mom and Dad as well: "Get Well Soon! I love you!"

Carl closed the card and tossed it on the chair next to his bed.

"What did it say?" Mom asked.

"Nothing. Just get well soon."

Silence.

"Why don't you guys just get out of here? Don't you work tomorrow?" Carl said.

"Yeah, but—" Mom started before being interrupted.

"No! Go home. I'll be fine."

Silence.

"Well, call us if you need anything," Dad said.

Silence.

Mom and Dad walked out of his apartment and gently closed the door behind them. They walked down the stairs. Mom glanced over her right shoulder to see if her son was poking his head out. He wasn't.

Mom and Dad got back in the car and headed back home.

"What did we do to deserve that?" Mom asked Dad. A tear moistened her eye.

"Nothing. He's just upset," Dad replied.

Carl limped without his crutches over to his couch and lay down, staring at the plain white ceiling.

Two months had passed since the surgery. Carl had struggled getting to and from class with the crutches and big knee brace. Some teammates tried to help by carrying books. A couple others came over to the apartment to hang out, play video games, study, watch game film, and talk football.

On a cold late November morning, John, a fellow freshman linebacker at Iowa, gave him a lift to the doctor's office. Bad news awaited him.

Carl wouldn't play football ever again. He was devastated.

"Are you sure?" Carl frantically asked.

"I'm sorry to say so, but you tore every ligament in your knee," Dr. Andrews said. "It'll be a long recovery. You're going to be lucky to have mobility in the knee after it's all said and done."

*   *   *

After the appointment, John took Carl back to his apartment.

"You going to be okay?" John asked.

Silence.

"Well, if there's anything you need, let the team know."

Carl limped with a large black knee brace around his leg back to his couch and lay down. He turned to his right side and looked into the back rest of the couch.

The next morning, Carl met with the school's head athletic trainer, Dr. Overmyer. They laid out a workout plan for his rehab. Carl would lift weights a couple days a week, especially light weights on his legs. He was adamant about maintaining an upper body workout during the rehab. He liked looking at his six-pack stomach in the mirror and rubbing his hand across it. But after football, his focus shifted 100 percent toward his school work. He knew the only way out of Iowa now was with a degree. He wanted to finish at the top of his graduating class.

Carl loved the college life once his leg got better. He loved hanging out with the guys from the football team, whether it was at the bar, shooting pool, or at a fraternity house watching game film. Carl still watched every game on television. He was beginning to enjoy a social life, something he'd never had before. He was often spotted in the areas in and around campus, his apartment, the library, or the bar. It still hurt him that football was no longer a part of his life, but hanging out with former teammates wasn't bad.

Academics remained important to him, though. He often sat alone and in the back corner of the three-story library just a few blocks from his apartment. It was his personal space. He didn't want any distractions, especially ones coming from the cute girls.

Girls remained very, very low on his priority list, despite a couple hitting on him at the bar. He shrugged them off.

"They just distract me too much," he told a teammate one night. John was a ladies' man. He loved being around women. He constantly flirted with women, a lot of times in front of Carl. He hated that.

"Knock it off. That's disgusting!"

"Ah, what you talking about, Carl? Girls are great. They put all the miseries away with one bat of their eyelashes."

"Yeah. So?"

"You know, that's not so bad once in a while."

"Yes, it is. You lose focus on something, and boom! You can be out the door. Then what?"

"You're thinking too much. You just got to open up, and let a girl please you."

"I will when I'm ready."

Chapter VII

THE SOUNDS OF THE hospital fall silent.

No beeps.

No voices.

He falls into a deep, deep sleep.

Not long after his eyelids get too heavy to keep open, Carl is once again standing in front of his parents' house. This time, it looks like how he remembered it—old, raggedy, and embarrassing. A window frame hangs off the front window. Never once was he proud to call it home. He was embarrassed to have friends over.

Carl is standing at the end of the driveway. A red Chevrolet sits in the driveway, but it's beat up and in bad shape. It looks like it was in an accident. It was. The front of the truck is heavily smashed. A long crack streaks across the windshield. He walks up the driveway toward the house. He passes the car and looks inside it. Nothing. He steps back and looks at it.

He walks away from the car to the front edge of the porch in front of the house. The wood is old and moldy. He walks up the two stairs. The porch creaks with each step. It feels like it could collapse at any second.

He lifts his right arm to knock on the door. His arm goes right through the door.

"Ah!" he screams to himself. He looks at his hand trying to figure out what just happened. He tries to open the door with his right hand, and it goes right through the knob.

"Ah!" he screams to himself again. "What the . . . ?"

He is a ghost.

He walks to his right to look inside the house through the window.

Bill, Steven, and Elizabeth—all grown up—are sitting in the living room, crying. Mom and Dad are nowhere to be found. He isn't either.

He tries to bang on the window for them to let him in, but he falls right through. On the floor, he turns over his left shoulder and looks back at the window. "What was that?" he wonders.

He pushes himself up off the floor and walks up to his siblings.

"Hey, it's Carl. What's wrong?" he asks.

No response.

"Guys!" he says louder.

No response.

"Great. They must not hear me." But Carl continues to watch what's going on, listening.

What in the world is going on here? he wonders.

On the television, the news anchor says, "We're sorry to announce Mary and George Robertson have passed away. Authorities say they were driving in their red, 1959 Chevrolet when apparently George suffered a massive stroke, veered over the center line, and crashed into an oncoming car at an estimated seventy miles per hour. Mary died instantly, police say. Funeral arrangements are pending . . ."

Carl gasps in shock. His eyes are wide. He feels like his heart has stopped.

The news anchor continues with the details of the accident and Carl's parents' background. He stands behind the couch where Elizabeth is crying in the arms of Steven. Bill is sitting in the recliner in stunned silence. His face is buried in his hands; he's fighting with all his might not to show any tears. But one slowly drips out of his right eye and onto the wooden floor.

Carl wonders where he is.

"Try Carl again, Bill," Elizabeth tells her brother.

"Okay," he says.

Bill gets off the chair and walks to the kitchen where his cell phone is in the pocket of his jacket, which is hanging on the back of a kitchen chair. He opens up his cell phone and dials Carl's number.

No answer. It goes to his voice mail.

"He's still not answering his phone!" Bill yells from the kitchen at Steven and Elizabeth. He places his phone on the kitchen counter and returns to the living room. He stands in the doorway between the living room and the kitchen. He leans with his left side up against the wall. He crosses his arms.

"I wish he would pick up his damn phone," Elizabeth tells Steven.

"I know. I do, too," Steven says, holding his sister tight in his arms.

Carl looks at the three of them and suddenly feels enormous guilt.

"So that's why they've been trying to get ahold of me," he tells himself.

He notices through the living room window a black pickup truck pulling up the driveway. It's Chuck.

Carl hasn't seen Chuck in almost ten years, not since he left Carl at the hospital after his knee injury.

"What's he doing here?" Carl asks himself.

Chuck, much heavier than Carl remembers him and with a goatee, opens his truck door, slams it shut, runs up to the house, and knocks on the door.

Bill looks out the window.

"Chuck!" Bill says shocked and excited. He opens the door and lets Chuck in. They firmly shake each other's hands.

"God, I haven't seen you in like ten years! What brings you over here?" Bill asks.

"Your parents. I heard what happened. Are you guys okay?"

"Yeah. We're hanging on," Bill replies. "How'd you know we were here?"

"I called him over here," Steven says.

"Why?"

"I thought it'd be nice to see him and might cheer us up. Besides the fact Carl always treated him like crap, he was still good to the rest of us. Plus Chuck's brother is also a teacher at the high school and is a fellow assistant with me on the football team."

"It's good to see you, Chuck," Bill says. They shake hands again.

"I'm sorry for your loss, guys," Chuck replies. "Where's Carl?"

Carl is standing in the room, but nobody can see or hear him. He's shocked Chuck still remembers him.

"I would've liked to've seen him and told him how sorry I was about Iowa," Chuck says. "I think about that every day. I was stupid and a terrible friend for doing that to him."

"But he treated you like crap," Elizabeth says.

"Yeah, from time to time, he did. But we did have some good times. A lot of great memories."

Wiping tears out of her eyes and off her cheek, Elizabeth tells Chuck, "That's very nice of you. I wish Carl could know that."

"I'm right here!" Carl screams out.

There's no response; he keeps forgetting nobody can see or hear him.

"When was the last time any of you talked to him?" Chuck asks.

Steven, Bill, and Elizabeth look at each other. They can't come up with an answer.

"He's always so busy with work," Elizabeth says. "We can never get ahold of him. We've been calling him all day, and we've gotten no answer."

"What could be so important that he can't return your guys' calls?" Chuck asks.

Elizabeth shrugs her shoulders and shakes her head. "I don't know."

A long pause.

"I don't know . . . But I *do* know," Elizabeth continues. "He's definitely enjoying his life in New York. I think he said he was going to Paris for a business deal. That was, I don't know, a week or so ago. He said he'd call me back, but he hasn't."

"I would, too," Chuck says. "I've heard what he's doing. I'm happy for him. I'm proud of him. I just wish he knew how much people miss him here."

Carl's surprised.

He's thought for all this time that since the day he signed the football scholarship offer to Iowa, nobody wanted to see him again—ever.

He hasn't seen his parents since he graduated from college. But even while in college, he never went home. He loved college so much. He loved to study in the library, multiple hours at a time, and going to class. He had a couple friends he'd hang out with from time to time, mostly in study groups at the library.

There was one guy in particular he'd hang out with often outside of the library: James Patrick.

James was from Des Moines. They were both football players. James decided to pursue academics after high school. He was all-state in football, swimming, and track and field. He won six state championships between the three sports. He dreamed of being a lawyer.

After they met during their freshman year at Iowa in an English class, they realized they'd actually come across each other previously. They'd both attended a football camp, hosted by Iowa. James was a wide receiver. When Carl got to Iowa, they wanted to move him to linebacker, and the coaches were going to until his knee injury.

Carl and James became good friends and remained that way all through college. They did a lot of things together in their spare time. James even showed Carl how to golf. He also introduced some girls to Carl, including one who changed his life—Sydney.

While out at a bar close to campus, Carl saw James, who waved his friend over to a table where he and some other friends were sitting. They sat around a circular table under a dim light. The bar reeked of cigarette smoke, with loud chatter from a nearly full room. Rock music blared on the bar's music system.

"I thought you and I were just hanging out?" Carl asked loudly over the almost deafening music and chatter.

"Yeah. But I ran into John here." James introduced John to Carl.

"Nice to meet you," Carl shouted, shaking John's right hand.

"Likewise."

James then introduced everyone else at the table. First, he introduced Sydney, who was in his economics class. Carl was silent. To him, everything around him quieted down.

"You are so beautiful," Carl said, gently shaking her right hand with his right hand and smiling. "It's a pleasure to meet you."

Sydney smiled. "Thanks. You're sweet and handsome." They hit it off immediately.

Carl and Sydney dated during their sophomore years. She was cute. She was five foot four, 118 pounds with long, blond hair. She was the only girl Carl went out with more than once. He thought Sydney was the one for him. He loved her company. He was always happy around her. Never before in his life had he experienced this feeling, and he loved it.

She felt the same about him.

"Love at first sight," she always told her friends.

This is awesome, he thought one day. *I guess Chuck was right. This really isn't so bad.*

For once, he decided girls might be a good thing. One day, she asked if they could go steady.

"Carl, I really like you. I'd be thrilled if we could start officially dating, like as in boyfriend and girlfriend," she said. "You are so sweet and cute."

Maybe dating and girls isn't a bad thing after all, he wondered.

He told her, "Yes."

Sydney's smile lit up the entire night sky that evening. She was from Kansas City. She wasn't much of a sports fan. She just liked the Kansas City teams—the Royals and the Chiefs. That was okay for him, just as long as it wasn't the Cowboys.

She loved the theater—ballet and opera, especially. He'd never liked that stuff for the longest time. That was until he met Sydney. He just loved being with her and doing stuff with her. He did whatever it took to be with her whenever possible. He just loved being around her so much. He loved every moment of their relationship. He hated being away from her. Even if it was just for an hour, it was still painful.

"Is this what being in love is like?" he asked himself one night before a dinner-movie date. But because he had so few friends, he couldn't ask for insight. James was out with his girlfriend as much as Carl and Sydney were together. He and James didn't see each other much, mostly just in passing around campus. Their conversations were usually short.

"Hey, Carl."

"Hey, James."

"How's Ariel?"

"Good. How's Sydney?"

"Great."

Carl and Sydney spent even more with each other the longer they dated. That was all they did: they would go to class and spend every spare moment with each other. He was falling in love with her. She was already in love with him. His grades began to slip, though.

After two years of dating, the spring semester was drawing to a close. Carl's last final—his biggest one—was to take place the early morning after Sydney's big musical performance, which was her final. She wanted to be an actress in Hollywood. She loved Audrey Hepburn. "She is so pretty," she'd always tell Carl. "I want to be pretty just like her."

"You already are, Syd," he'd say.

"Oh, Carl," she'd reply, blushing.

Carl's marketing tactics final was to take place at 8:00 the following morning. Sydney's play was to begin at 7:30 the night before.

He wanted to study for it. He needed to study for it. He hadn't done much studying all semester because of all the time he spent with Sydney. At the time, it was great. But it was hurting his grades. On his last test for his history class, he'd gotten a D, which was way below his standards. His professor was disappointed with it. His best grade out of his four classes was a C minus. He'd failed his art history class. It was the second straight semester for Carl to have a failing grade in a class. In the fall, he failed what should've been an easy class, marketing. He got one C, three D's, and a failing grade. Carl's advisor noticed his grades were slipping a bit, too.

"Mr. Robertson," the advisor told him one day in a meeting between classes, "if you don't get your grades up, we'll have to put you on academic probation. You could lose your scholarship after that."

"Okay. I'll fix it."

Angry and scared, Carl stormed out of the office to his apartment.

He was still undecided on what to do shortly before the show. He knew he had to study. He had to save his grades and his scholarship. Finally, Sydney told him that it was really important to her that he be there to support her. She smiled at him, just like how she'd done when they first met.

"Okay, Syd. I'll come to the show."

Sydney kissed him on the lips. "Thank you. You don't know how much it means to me to have you there."

The smile worked every time.

He watched with enormous pride throughout the show. "She is so pretty. I'm glad I came."

The show let out at about 10:30 that night. Afterward, the cast decided to have a party at another cast member's house a couple blocks from campus.

"C'mon, Carl. Come with me to the party," Sydney said. She smiled.

He hesitated at first. Sydney gave him her infectious smile and batted her eyelashes as a silent way to beg him. It worked like a charm. It worked every time.

"Okay. Let's go," Carl said.

"Yay!"

That darn smile again.

They hopped into a castmate's car—a blue van—and headed to the party. Inside this two-story brick house with green wood frames around the windows and six bedrooms, the party was already underway. It had started two hours earlier. More than thirty people were already there. Loud music blared at the highest volume from inside. The music was muffled from outside. Sydney and Carl headed for the kitchen where the liquor was set up. Carl grabbed a beer. Sydney went for the Jack Daniels and Coke. Just past the kitchen was a group of six people—three guys and three girls—playing poker. One of the girls playing was from Carl's marketing tactics class, the one which he had a final for in ten hours. He sat behind her in the lecture hall.

Sydney grabbed Carl's hand and took him out back by the swimming pool. They sat on a lounge couch together on the patio. They were alone. It was warm and muggy. Loud chirps came from crickets. It was quiet besides the muffled music from inside the house. They could feel the bass from the stereo underneath their feet on the wooden patio.

Sydney drank her Jack and Coke quickly, put her cup on the nearby table, and hopped on top of Carl on the couch to make out with him. He dropped his beer and wrapped his arms around her. This was the first time they'd made out like that. They kissed each other often. But it was usually a quick peck or two and "I'll see you later."

She took off her shirt, revealing a thin-strapped white tank top.

"Wow," Carl mumbled to himself.

She leaned down and gave him a firm kiss on the lips. The party continued inside.

"I love you so much, Carl," she said.

He hesitated before quickly saying, "I love you, too, Syd."

Sydney paused and looked at him. She wondered why it took him a second to reply. Then she smiled and kissed him on the left side of his neck. Her smile glowed in the dark underneath the nearly full moon hovering high in the sky. It was the first time he'd told her that he loved her. A tear dripped out of her right eye and then her left eye. She stopped, looked at him, and smiled again.

He paused, too, and smiled.

"Wow!" He wondered why he had been such a prick for so long to girls. This was an unbelievable feeling. "Why did I wait this long? Damn it, Chuck."

They continued to kiss passionately. The music still blared from inside the house. A lot of hooting and hollering was going on, too, lots of overlapping chatter and laughter.

James and his date, Ariel, came out and caught them.

"Damn, Carl!" James screamed.

Sydney and Carl stopped kissing.

"That's my man!" James screamed. "We'll go somewhere else." James led his girl down the three wood patio steps to the pool deck. They jumped into the pool, fully clothed.

Embarrassed by what had happened, Sydney put her shirt back on, and Carl buttoned up his shirt. They headed back inside. One girl at the poker table was now without a shirt, only a thin-strapped blue tank top. The girl from his class had no shirt on. A guy had a white tank top on. All three lost articles of clothing lay on top of a pile of poker chips in the center of the circular table.

"Wow, this is some party," Carl leaned over and said to Sydney.

"These parties can be great. I'm glad you're here with me. I usually hate coming to these by myself. It's never any fun."

"Can be great? How can you not have fun at these?"

"Well, in case you haven't noticed, I can be shy sometimes."

"Really? I've never noticed it."

"It's because when I'm with someone I'm comfortable with, I'm not very shy at all. I can be pretty outgoing."

"But you've been that way with me ever since I met you."

"Yes, because . . . I don't know why it is, but I just felt comfortable with you right away. There was just something about you that put me at ease."

"I'm glad you feel that way because I've never been a fan of dating. I didn't have a lot of luck with girls growing up."

"Why not?"

"Well, it's a long story, and I'd actually prefer not to get into it. I don't want to ruin our evening. It's the past, and I'm just so happy to be here with you and have you in my life."

He smiled. She kissed him. They quickly lost track of time, drinking and dancing. Bon Jovi's "Bad Medicine" blared on the stereo in the living room.

Everybody was singing it as loud as they could.

"Your love is like bad medicine!"

"Bad medicine is what I need!"

"Shake it up, just like bad medicine!"

Sydney and Carl were dancing with each other really tight. They were holding each other close while they danced and sang at the top of their voices.

The party was going on 2:00 a.m. Carl still hadn't studied for his 8:00 a.m. final. He looked at the clock on the wall to see it said 2:00 in the morning. He didn't care. He was having the time of his life with Sydney. He didn't want the night to end. He whipped his shirt off and started flailing it around his head. He grabbed a beer out of the nearby cooler and quickly chugged it.

"Woo!" he screamed out.

Sydney rubbed her hands on his well-built chest and stomach.

"You're so hot," Sydney slurred.

"You're not too bad yourself, good-lookin'." He planted one long kiss on Sydney's lips.

The party calmed down at about 5:00 a.m. Some people had left. Others were sleeping on the floor where they had passed out. Carl and Sydney were on the lounge chair outside, holding each other tight.

The sun came up about an hour later.

At 8:00 a.m., Carl opened his eyes and saw Sydney sleeping in his arms. James and Ariel were on the grass by the pool, passed out and still wet from the swim. Carl gave Sydney a peck on the cheek. He took a glimpse inside the house to look for a clock. He rubbed his eyes. He spotted a grandfather clock just inside the window. It was after 8:00. He shot up off the chair.

"What time is it?" he shouted.

Sydney, slow to wake up, said, "Huh? What did you say?"

"I said, 'What time is it?'" Carl looked inside at the clock again and got a better look: 8:05.

"Oh no!"

"What? What's wrong?"

"I'm missing my final!"

He grabbed his shirt and shoes and headed toward the front door. He didn't bother to see if anyone could give him a ride. Everybody was still passed out drunk on the floor throughout the house. His knee still bothered him from the ACL surgery. He couldn't run like he used to. But that was the furthest thing from his mind.

"If I miss that final, I'm in deep trouble!" he said out loud to himself as he left the house.

Sydney stood at the front door after he'd left. "Wait!" He ignored her and headed down the hill toward campus.

He occasionally stopped to catch his breath. He was not in the kind of shape he used to be in. After he couldn't play football anymore, he didn't work out as much—only when he didn't have studying to do, and that wasn't very often. He was heaving all the way back to campus. Cars were passing him along the two-lane suburban road with gravel shoulders leading back to campus.

He started to think, *Please, somebody hit me, so I'll have an excuse to why I missed that test.*

He finally got back to campus after 9:00. He cut through parking lots and courtyards to get to the academic hall where his exam was being conducted. Still limping, more than usual, he cringed in pain. He held on to the railing leading up to the door of the hall. Six concrete steps. He took a deep breath, whipped open the door, and headed down the brightly lit hall. A few students sat on two-seat couches. Each had a textbook and a notebook, reviewing notes. He arrived at room 121 of Williamson Hall, barged into the exam room, and said, "I'm ready for the test."

The problem was it was another class.

"Excuse me, sir," the professor said. "You're interrupting my students. Please leave now or I'll have security escort you out."

"What happened with the marketing tactics class? Did the test get moved?"

"No. That class left a while ago."

He was angry and scared.

He headed to his apartment just off campus to figure out an excuse for why he missed the final. He ran into his professor from that day's final along the way.

"Professor!" Carl screamed.

"Yes? Can I help you?"

"I'm in your marketing tactics class. I missed the final this morning. I had a . . . family emergency that kept me up all night. Can I take the final now?"

The professor smelled the booze all over Carl.

"Where was the family emergency? The bar?"

Carl lifted up the sleeve of his T-shirt and smelled it. He cringed, his forehead folding. It smelled like beer and cigarette smoke. He didn't have an answer or an excuse.

"Please. I'm begging you. They're going to take my scholarship away."

"I'm sorry. It's not my problem. You should be more responsible for your actions. I can't help you. Now excuse me. I have another class to get to." The professor walked away.

"Wait!"

The professor continued to his next class. He looked back at Carl and shrugged his shoulders.

Carl got back to his apartment. He opened his apartment door, slammed it shut, and sprawled on the couch. He was worried. Shortly after 1:00, there was a knock on his front door.

It startled him.

He got up and opened the door. It was his advisor.

"I heard what happened," he said. "I unfortunately don't have a choice." The advisor handed him a letter, walked away and out the building.

Carl closed the door, opened the letter, and read:

Mr. Robertson,

    I regret to inform you that you are being placed on academic probation and your scholarship is being temporarily revoked. You can earn your scholarship back, but you will have to take some allotted summer school classes and pass them with at least a 3.5 GPA. Please see me immediately to discuss your summer plans.

Your advisor

Carl crumpled up the letter and threw it at the door. Another knock on the door followed; it was a softer knock.

He whipped the door open. It was Sydney.

"Is everything okay?" she asked nervously.

"No. I missed my final. I lost my scholarship! And it's all because of your stupid party!"

"Carl, I'm sorry. I really am. Did you have a good time with me at least?"

"How dare you think about yourself! Please leave. I don't want to see you anymore." He pushed her out of his apartment and slammed the door shut. The slam echoed down the hall and throughout his apartment.

He locked the door. Sydney stood at the door and stared at it. She turned to run down the nearby stairwell and out of the apartment, bawling.

"This is why I hate girls!" he screamed out to no one inside his apartment.

*   *   *

Carl is standing inside his parents' living room with Chuck, Steven, Bill, and Elizabeth still grieving over the death of his mom and dad.

The phone rings.

Steven answers it.

"Hello."

Elizabeth and Bill look at each other, hoping it is Carl. It isn't. It is the funeral home confirming the night of the service.

"Yes, that's correct," Steven says.

Silence.

"Okay. We'll be right over."

He hangs up the telephone.

"C'mon. The funeral home wants to go over the arrangements for the service."

"I'll drive," Chuck offers.

"No, thank you," Bill says. "We can take care of it. Thank you."

Bill gets his minivan from out of the garage and helps Elizabeth into the front seat. Steven sits in back. Bill pulls backward away from the house down the dirt driveway. They pass the damaged Red Chevy. Once in the street, Bill shifts into gear and drives off. Carl watches them from the window.

"Wait for me!" he screams and runs out the front door.

When he goes through the door, he is standing outside his condo complex in New York City.

It's a gloomy day. It's cold. He goes through the front door and heads up to his condo. He can't take the elevator, so he goes up the staircase. He gets to his condo. He reaches for the doorknob and falls through.

The place is empty. No couch. No TV. No Yankees banner. Everything is gone.

"Where the hell is all my stuff?"

The door opens. It's the landlord, showing a newly married couple the place.

"I think you guys will really like this place," the landlord says. Carl tries to stop them, but he is unsuccessful.

"It's got a great view of the city."

"Get out!" Carl screams. No one can hear him.

"What happened to the previous tenant?" the man in the couple asks.

"I'm not sure. All I know is he lost his job and couldn't afford the payments. I'm not sure what he's up to now."

"Lost my job?" Carl says, cringing.

The woman of the couple tells the landlord, "We'll take it."

"No!" Carl yells.

The landlord and the couple shake hands and sign the paperwork on the kitchen counter. The same counter Carl slammed his Jim Beam bottle on.

He can't watch as his condo is signed away without him knowing it or being able to do anything about it. He runs out of the complex scared, nervous, worried.

"What's going on?" he hollers. He passes the manager's office on the way back down. He finds a piece of paper on the desk. It's an eviction notice for his apartment. He looks all around him, trying to figure out what's happening. He dashes outside the complex and onto the sidewalk in front of the complex. People walk past him without even acknowledging he's there. To them, he isn't. He heads for the office to see if he can find an answer there. He runs through the streets of New York as fast as he can. He's scared. He doesn't know what's happened to the life he once had. The money. The glamour. The season tickets. Everything. He's losing it all, and he doesn't know why. His life is falling apart.

He gets to his office. The building at least looks the same as he remembers it: fifty stories tall with darkly tinted windows. He goes in and takes the stairs up to his thirty-second-floor office. Peggy sits at the lobby front desk.

"Oh good, Peggy."

He spots Tammy coming down the hall toward Peggy's desk.

"Tammy!" Carl shouts.

No response.

He jumps, screams, and flails his arms trying to get her attention. No luck. Tammy continues a conversation with Peggy about a client. Carl listens in. It's about Runaway.

"Oh no," he mumbles.

He leaves Peggy's desk and heads for his office. He doesn't stay to listen to what happened with Runaway.

Sharon, his secretary, is not at her desk. It's a busty brunette named Caity. Carl stares at Caity. *Who the hell is she?* he wonders.

He spots a plaque outside his office. But it doesn't say his name anymore. To get a better look, he walks up to it: "Mr. Percy Hawkins, Executive Manager."

"No!" he yells out. He's stunned. Speechless.

Percy opens the door. "Hello, Caity. How are you today?"

With her blouse about as tight as one could be, she says, "Good. You, Mr. Hawkins?"

"Doing good. How's the Parker project coming along?"

"Parker project?" Carl wonders aloud.

"It's good. I should wrap it up later this week. Do you want to grab a cup of coffee later?"

"That'd be great," she says.

Carl can't believe his own colleague. His best friend has taken his office, his job. He tries to punch Percy in the face, but he falls right through him. Carl heads back toward the front of the office.

Mr. Berry, the CEO of the company, who rarely makes a visit unless something serious is going on, comes off the elevator. Carl has met Mr. Berry only a few times. He can never remember his first name.

Carl realizes something serious is indeed going on, but he's scared to find out what it may be.

Mr. Berry is at the office to help save the Runaway deal, which Carl and his team finalized and already began work on. Runaway's representatives flew back to New York to discuss the problems with Carl.

"What problems?" Carl asks himself.

"Is all the paperwork finished, Peggy?" Mr. Berry asks.

"Yes, sir."

"Have you had a chance to call Pierre from Runaway?"

"Yes, sir. They'll be here in an hour."

Carl is in the lobby with them, watching and listening. He's fighting back tears. He says to himself, "What could I have done to deserve this? What did I do?"

Pierre and his associates, Alexandre, Henri, Claire, and Camille, step off the elevator and walk toward Mr. Berry, who is still at Peggy's desk. Claire and Camille are still beautiful but look disappointed.

"Ah, Pierre. So nice to see you," Mr. Berry says. "Please follow me into the conference room." Carl follows them.

They all sit down, and Mr. Berry closes the door. Carl stands inside the room thankful no one can see or hear him.

Mr. Berry and Pierre go over what happened with Carl and try to rectify the situation—try to convince Pierre they would be making a terrible mistake to leave Deluxe.

Pierre tells Mr. Berry, "I apologize, Mr. Berry, but we cannot associate with someone who handles themselves the way Mr. Robertson has."

"What way?" Carl asks himself.

"But, Pierre," Mr. Berry says, "I've already fired him."

"We've made our decision. We want to move in a different direction. Good day." Pierre and his associates stand up and leave the office. Camille hands Mr. Berry a check for the contract buyout: $500,000.

"What?" Carl screams out. No one hears him.

Mr. Berry is furious. After the Runaway representatives leave, he walks over to an open area where most of the company's employees are sitting behind their desks. He screams out to them that Carl will never work for another marketing firm anywhere in the world.

"Let that be a lesson to you all," he says.

Carl hears this. He's mortified, stunned, shocked, and scared. Tammy is the only one kept on staff. Everybody else—Tucker, Nick, Caitlin, Steve, and Amber—were all fired. All their desks were empty and unused.

"What's happening?" Carl wonders. "Why is this happening to me? What did I do?"

He heads out of the conference room door and for the window past Caity's desk. Percy is hovering over her, glancing down her shirt.

Carl flies through the glass but doesn't break it. He is falling toward the ground from thirty-two stories up in the air. He's screaming at the top of his lungs.

He reaches the ground, but he's back home in Iowa—not on the pavement of New York City. He's in front of his parents' house again.

*   *   *

It's a week after the untimely deaths of Carl's parents, one day after the funeral. Steven, Bill, and Elizabeth are inside the house cleaning. Chuck comes over to help. He brings over some cleaning supplies. They are cleaning out the house in preparation to sell it.

Carl, standing inside the room with them, notices a newspaper Chuck brought over. It has a story on the front page about Carl's parents' funeral. They were buried at the Oak View Cemetery on the east side of town. There was a big family picture taken when Carl was seven years old with the story. Carl has an angry look on his face in the picture. He always hated that picture. He never liked any picture with him and his parents. There is also a picture of the people attending the funeral.

"Wait," he says to himself. "What happened to the funeral?"

The newspaper story says:

> *Mary and George Robertson were common folks, common friends, common family.*
>
> *Born and raised in Cedar Lake, the Robertsons loved life and the people who made Cedar Lake special. Their deaths were a surprise and a shock to everyone. They leave behind three children and three grandchildren. All were present at Monday's service at Arthur Meadows Funeral Home. More than five hundred people came to pay their respects to two people who bled Cedar Lake.*

"Wait. Three children?" Carl asks himself.

He reads on:

> *Each of the Robertson children is celebrated in Cedar Lake. Bill is a popular man, who has cut just about everybody's grass at some point. Steven is a role model for young children, and his participation in the elementary school reading program is admired by kids and parents alike. And there is Elizabeth. She is an extension of Mary, strong-willed and beautiful.*

"What happened to me?" he asks himself.

The story continues:

There was a fourth child the Robertsons' had: Carl. He's best remembered for bashing the town following his scholarship signing in his senior year. People around town lost respect for the Robertsons that day, and it took years to build the relationship back to the way it was. The less they saw of Carl, the better. As the years passed, the town eventually forgave the Robertsons and everybody—everything—was back to normal.

But they never forgave that young man who was destined for a big future.

"They always had one dying wish," said Elizabeth. "For Carl to return home and apologize for everything he ever did. They believed if he did that, the town would feel better. It's too bad they'll never see it happen.

A teardrop rolls off his face, and he sees it fall straight through the newspaper.

He finishes reading the story:

Steven and Bill apologized for their brother Carl's past behavior.

"I'm sure if he could be here," Steven said during the eulogy at the service, "he'd apologize. My parents loved Cedar Lake, and they loved all of you. They were embarrassed with Carl's actions that day. It bothered them up until the day they died. Their contributions to our community were the only way they knew how to tell you that. I'm sad and devastated they are gone. But they are in a place where they can watch over us and make the world a better place. There's no two better angels for God to have in heaven than my mom and dad. Now they can help my brother.

Mary and George constantly had their house open to feed children and offer playtime. It was like a free nursery. They also had numerous cookouts for anybody who wanted to come.

"I was mad when Carl ripped our town like that," said old friend Barry Kerpinski. "But when Mary and George opened their house to all the kids and strangers, I knew it had

nothing to do with Carl's upbringing. He was just selfish. I'm going to miss Mary and George. God bless them."

No matter what people thought of Carl, Mary and George still had him close to their hearts. His picture hung above their bed in the bedroom of their tiny house outside of town. Pictures of Steven, Bill, and Elizabeth were in the living room. But they wanted Carl in their room with them so they could always watch him and make sure he was okay.

Bill says the reason why their parents' obituary says three children were left behind is because it was a decision Bill, his brother, and his sister all made. He added he wasn't a part of life in Cedar Lake and with their mom and dad, so he shouldn't be recognized for it.

"I just wish he knew how much they loved him," Elizabeth said. "But now he'll never know. I love you, Mom and Dad. I'll miss you."

He is crying harder than he ever has in his life. He drops to his knees.

"Please help me!" he yells out looking up in the middle of the living room with everybody else cleaning up the house. They all disappear. He finds himself in front of a raggedy bum on a city block corner just two blocks from his condo. It's him. He's lost everything. He's nothing. Everything he's ever had, the money, the glamorous lifestyle, the high-paying job—it's all gone.

"No!" he screams. "What do I have to do to change this? Whatever it takes! Name your price. I'm at your mercy."

His hands are buried in his face; he is bawling.

Chapter VIII

*C*ARL LIFTS HIS FACE out of his hands. He's in the middle of an empty field. There's not a speck of life or anything for miles. He's never seen this field before. The sky is gray; the air is a bit chilled.

A sign stands by the road: "Land for Sale." A smaller sign is plastered over it: "Sold."

He notices over his right shoulder his parents. They are young, newlyweds. They hold each other tight with smiles. "Here's where our first home is going to be, Mary," Dad says.

They kiss each other on the lips with excitement. Carl's parents first lived in a small one-bedroom apartment on the corner of Third and Prospect, two blocks from Main Street.

Carl hears a deep voice, "Carl."

He whips around.

"What? Who goes there?" He's searching left and right, up and down. He sees nothing.

"Carl."

"What? Who's there? Where are you?"

"I'm right here."

He spots a man standing behind him. To him, he looks like he's in his thirties or forties. He's walking toward Carl.

"Who are you?" Carl asks.

"I'm you," the man replies.

"Me? You're kidding right?"

"No."

The man is six foot three, two hundred pounds. His physical frame is similar to Carl's. But his facial features aren't. He's got a big red scar down the right side of his face. He's got a spider tattoo under his right eye. He's wearing a long, black coat and blue jeans. His hair is black and pulled back in a ponytail.

"No way you're me," Carl says. "Just look at us. You don't even look like me."

"Want me to prove it to you?"

"You can try. But I'm telling you, you're not me. You just wish you were me."

The man starts, "I've worked at Deluxe Marketing in New York City for five years."

"Everybody knows that."

"My secretary's name is Sharon. She's been married for twenty-seven years. She and her husband, Larry, have two grown sons."

Carl's spooked out a tiny bit but still not convinced. "Lucky guess. I still don't believe you."

"You are wondering why this glorious life you've had all this time is suddenly gone. You're wondering why your parents have died and want to know how to change it."

Silence.

"How'd you know that?" Carl asks.

"It's because I'm your guardian angel, Carl, and I'm here to help you change your past life to make things right. I'm giving you a second chance at life."

"You're my guardian angel? But why?"

"Have you ever given thought to why you treat people the way you do?"

"What's wrong with the way I treat people?"

"That's the problem."

"What do you mean?"

"You have no respect for people. You believe they should bow to you. It doesn't work that way."

"Nobody has ever said anything to me about it."

"Of course not. It's because everybody's scared of you. They'd just rather do what you say and move on, avoiding the possibility of angering you. They avoid you whenever they can. Let me show you what I'm talking about. Follow me."

The man turns around. Carl takes a glance at his parents still relishing the purchase of the land for their first home.

"Come on," the man says.

Carl turns toward the man and follows him, walking away from his parents. They stand side by side, and his guardian angel snaps his fingers.

Carl and the man stand beside each other on a city street in New York. They're in front of Famous Dan's, the establishment the employees at Deluxe typically go to after a successful business deal. It's a few blocks from the office.

"Do you recognize this place?" the man asks.

"Yes, I do. My colleagues come here all the time after a successful business deal. Why?"

"Let's go inside, and I'll show you."

Carl follows the man inside. They walk right through the door. Inside, the man points out a table. "Do you recognize those people?"

It's his assistants, sitting at a table. They are meeting for the first time since they got laid off from Deluxe. They appear to be having a good time, a great time.

He walks up to the table. The man follows.

"Hey, guys. It's me!" Carl says.

Nobody reacts. Carl is a ghost. They trade stories about Carl—bashing Carl.

"He was always so uptight. It was like he was being hung from his underwear," Amber says. The others burst out into a laugh.

Nick says, holding his fiancée Ashlee in his right arm, "He was such a pain." The table agrees.

"I can't believe we all stayed on for as long as we did. He was so mean to us. I'm glad he's gone."

"Gone?" Carl wonders. "What do they mean by gone? Like as in fired?"

"Unfortunately not," the man says. He points at the table to have Carl continue to listen.

"I can't believe we went to his funeral," Caitlin says. "For the way he treated us, I'm glad he's dead."

"Dead? What happened?" Carl asks the man.

"Listen," the man says. Carl turns back around to the table.

"Did you guys hear what happened to him?" Steve asks.

"No, what?" Caitlin asks.

"What happened?" Nick asks.

"Apparently, after he was fired," Steve says, "he lost his condo, too."

"Oh, that was a nice place," Nick says. "Did any of you ever see it?"

"No," they say unison.

"Percy said it was a gorgeous place," Nick says.

Steve continues, "I guess he was banished to the streets. He couldn't find work. Mr. Berry notified all of his business partners and told them if Carl applied for a job at their company to tell him 'no way.' Well, to make a long story short, a couple months later, he snuck up to the top of his condo complex, leaned over, and shot himself in the head. He committed suicide."

Silence.

Carl whips around and over his right shoulder looks at the man. The man slowly nods his head up and down to confirm what Steve said. He points back at the table, and Carl turns back around.

"It serves him right," Tucker says.

"That's awful," Tammy says back to Tucker. "Now granted he was mean to all of us most of the time—"

"Most of the time?" Caitlin, Amber, and Nick say in unison and then laugh.

"Okay," Tammy says. "All the time. He was still our boss, a human being, and you don't want to see people die that way. You should never wish death on anybody."

Carl is happy Tammy is defending him.

"But I have to admit it. He was a pain to work for. Who's ready for round three?"

Everybody raises their hands, and Steven heads to the bar for more drinks. Carl turns around and looks at the man.

"Is that what everybody thinks of me?" he asks.

"Yes."

"Why?"

"Think back to how you treated them. Did you ever give them time off? Did you ever praise them for a job well done?"

Silence. "No. Not really."

"When you treat people the way you do, fewer people want to be around you. Did you ever know why people like John and Kenny didn't want to be around you anymore?"

"They have families?"

"True. But they also didn't like how you would talk to them whenever they wanted to set you up on dates."

"Don't you start on me, too."

"See. That's exactly my point."

"But I love my life. I've got everything I've ever wanted: a great job, a great place to live, money."

"Now look at what's happened to you. Look where it's gotten you. You were too ignorant to even check a phone message from your sister."

Carl is overwhelmed with guilt.

"Why do you hate your parents so much?"

"Because they gave me a horrible life."

"But I thought you said you loved your life."

"Yes. After I got out of there."

"Did you ever stop to think of the things they did for you?"

"Like what?"

"Well, a place to live for starters. They were at all your events growing up. They helped you whenever you needed it. Remember your ACL?"

"Yeah?"

"Who was there at your bedside even after the way you treated them?"

Silence. He starts to realize this man who is claiming to be his guardian angel may be right.

"Okay. Yeah. You're right. It was them," he agrees angrily. "But what does that have to do with it?"

"Everything. Whether you like it or not, they'll always be your parents, and at least yours were there for you. Not everybody can say that. Why didn't you ever want to go home for the holidays?"

"Work kept me from it."

"Did it?"

Silence.

"Most of the time, yes."

"And was it because of you missing your final in college that you didn't want anything to do with women?"

"How'd you know that?"

"I'm your guardian angel. I know everything there is to know about you. Let's go. There's more to see. Follow me."

Carl follows the man through the wooden door with the circular window near the top and out of the bar.

They are back in front of his parents' house. The house is complete. It's brand new. A moving truck sits in the driveway. Mom is six months pregnant with Bill. She sits on a rocking chair on the porch. Dad and the movers get the belongings inside the home.

"Where should the couch go, my love?" Dad asks Mom.

"In the living room, up against the wall," she replies.

It's a hot and muggy August day in the upper Midwest. Dad wipes sweat off his forehead with his shirt sleeve. Mom fans herself with a folder. The house doesn't have air-conditioning. The movers—two burly men—wear plain white T-shirts, blue jeans, and work boots.

"Where would you like us to put the bed frame, Mrs. Robertson?" one man asks.

"In the master bedroom. Thank you," she replies.

"Would you like us to assemble it?"

"If you don't mind, yes."

Carl and his guardian angel stand in the front yard, or what will become the front yard after Dad lays down the grass seed. Right now, it's just dirt.

"Your folks are very nice people," the man says.

Carl looks back and gives no reply.

Two hours later, the movers have moved all of the belongings into the house. Boxes are scattered everywhere, many stacked on top of one another. A couple piles are three boxes high. Only the couch, the bed in the master room, and the kitchen table are set up. The refrigerator will arrive tomorrow. The stove will, too.

Dad drives a red pickup truck to town to pick up a barbeque grill and a few things from the store.

At home, Mom begins unpacking. She pulls out a large picture, their wedding picture. She grabs a hammer out of a small, black toolbox near the front door. She digs for a nail. She walks over to the fireplace and holds the nail just above the mantel. She pounds the nail into the wall with the hammer and sets the hammer down. She grabs the picture, which she'd set on top of a nearby box, and hangs it over the fireplace.

Dad pulls up in the truck, lifts the grill out of the back of the truck, and wheels it to the front porch. He rips open a bag of charcoal and pours it into the grill. He lights a match and starts the grill. Mom continues unpacking inside. Once the fire is going, he whips up a couple cheeseburgers for dinner. The fireflies light up around the grill as the sun dips below the horizon. The crickets chirp at a high rate of speed and at high volume.

"Dinner's done, my love."

Mom and Dad sit on the porch in front of the house and take in their first meal together in their new home—cheeseburgers. Carl and the man still stand in front of the house.

After dinner, Mom and Dad go inside, turn on the fans, and unpack. They listen to up-tempo bluegrass music on the radio. Carl and the man follow them inside.

Carl's mom begins to lay out the plans of the home in her mind.

"Right here is where Bill's crib is going to be," she says, pointing out the area to her husband. It's in the room next to theirs—the smaller of the two bedrooms.

"And right here is where the next baby's bed will go." That's Carl's. "Oh, we're going to have such a wonderful family, don't you agree?"

"Yes, my dear," Dad says.

*   *   *

Three years pass.

Bill has just turned three years old. Mom rushes out of the master bedroom and into the bathroom. She vomits.

"What's wrong, dear?" Dad asks.

"I don't know," she replies. "I feel sick." Carl and the man stand in the hallway, watching.

"Do you want to go to the doctor's office?" Dad asks.

"Yes." Carl and the man follow them out of the house and hop into the back of the Red Chevy with the Robertsons—Mom, Dad, and Bill.

"Won't they see us?" Carl asks.

"Of course not," the man replies.

Twenty minutes later, Mom and Dad sit inside the doctor's office, which is across the street from the grocery store.

"Mr. and Mrs. Robertson," the doctor begins, "you are pregnant. You will have another baby. You're due in July."

Mom is happy. Dad is surprised but also happy. Mom gives him a big hug. Dad smiles. Carl and the man watch inside the doctor's office.

*   *   *

Carl is born July 12. He's seven pounds three ounces and is nineteen inches long. He's a beautiful baby. Carl and his guardian angel are right alongside Mom in the hospital room. Mom holds her newest son tightly in her arm. Dad is sitting on a chair, leaning in close, running his fingers through his wife's hair.

The guardian angel grabs Carl's hand. "Come on. There's much more to see."

Carl follows slowly, looking back at his parents. They fade away.

*   *   *

Carl and the angel are standing inside Carl's bedroom. He's seven years old. He's playing with his miniature cars on the hardwood floor, while the rest of the family is getting ready for a family portrait Mom wants taken on the porch. He doesn't want anything to do with it.

"I hate this, and I hate you!" the little Carl screams out from his bedroom with the door closed. Dad angrily swings the door open and comes into the room. He grabs his son by his right arm and yanks him onto the bed.

"This is something your mother wants!" Dad yells at him.

"But this is so stupid," young Carl says. The elder Carl watches intently. The angel stands back and has his arms folded across his chest.

"I look stupid. This is stupid."

"Gosh, I was an ass," the elder Carl says to himself.

"Yes, you were," the angel replies.

The family lines up outside on the porch. Mom is about three months pregnant with Elizabeth. Bill is nine, and Steven is five. Carl wears a black suit with red and white bow tie, so do Bill and Steven. They aren't fussing. Dad is dressed like the boys, and Mom is in a black-and-white polka-dotted knee-length sundress. A photographer stands on the front yard—with grass.

"Say, 'Cheese,'" the photographer says.

He takes five or six different pictures. The elder Carl watches from inside the house. He keeps a close eye on himself. He watches his actions. Carl doesn't want anything to do with the picture. He also watches how Mom and Dad are behaving. They are doing their best to correct little Carl's behavior.

"Carl," Dad says, "if you don't behave, no TV tonight."

Carl lets out an agitated sigh. "Fine!"

He forces a smile, but it looks awful.

"Okay. I think we're done," the photographer says. "Thank you very much. I should have something for you in a couple weeks."

"Thank you," Dad says.

Two weeks pass, and the pictures arrive in the mail. Mom likes the picture, except for Carl's facial expression. He is in his bedroom playing with his action figures.

"Carl!" Mom screams from the living room. "Get your butt out here!"

"Why?"

"Because I told you to."

He throws his figurines down on the floor, whips the door open, and storms into the living room. His steps creak beneath him.

"Sit your butt down on the couch," Dad says.

He plops down and folds his arms across his chest.

Mom begins with tears, "You ruined the family portrait." She places the photo on the coffee table in front of the couch. Carl picks it up and looks at it.

"It looks fine to me," he replies.

"No, it doesn't. You're not even smiling," she says.

"Yes, I am. Look." Carl points to the one where he is smiling.

"That's not much of a smile," Mom says.

"Do you realize how much this meant to your mom?" Dad asks him.

The elder Carl stands behind the couch, closely observing the scene. The angel asks, "Do you remember this fight?"

"Yes, I do."

"Do you remember how you felt afterward?"

"I remember being really mad."

"Watch what happens next."

The argument continues.

"I hate it here!" Carl yells out.

"Well, when you grow up," Dad says. "You can go wherever you want. Live wherever you want. But as long as you live under my house and my rules, you will abide by what I say and live where we live. Is that clear?"

"Uggh!"

"Go to your room!" Dad yells.

He stands up fiercely and stomps to his bedroom. He slams the door.

Elder Carl and the guardian angel continue to watch from behind the couch. Mom sits down on the couch crying. Dad sits down and gives her a hug. Young Carl slams things in the bedroom. The sounds of toys crashing to the floor echo throughout the house. Bill and Steven are outside playing baseball.

Bill is pretending to be his favorite baseball player: former Phillies pitcher Steve Carlton. Steven is the hitter trying to take Bill yard as Mike Schmidt, the former third baseman for the Phillies. They both liked the Phillies.

Carl hated baseball. He loved football. The New York Giants were his team growing up.

Dad gets up off the couch and heads for Carl's bedroom. Mom reaches for a tissue on the table next to the couch. The bedroom door whips open. Dad doesn't knock. Older Carl follows him into the bedroom; the angel is close behind.

"Son," Dad calmly starts, "do you see how upset your mother is?"

"Yeah. So?"

"So? She's your mother."

"Yeah. So?"

"How dare you talk about your mother like that!" Dad says raising his tone. "We bust our butts for you and your brothers. Why don't you appreciate it like Bill and Steven do?"

"It's because they're stupid. They don't know what kind of shitty life we're living."

Dad slaps Carl across the face with his right hand, knocking him backward into the nearby dresser. The older Carl lifts his right hand and touches his face, remembering that slap.

"Did that hurt?" the man asks Carl.

"Yes, it did. I remember that well." They continue to watch.

"You ought to be grateful for what we do for you boys!" Dad yells. Mom stands at the doorway still crying over the episode in the living room.

"Why can't it be better? We live like homeless people," Carl says.

"At least you have a home," a teary-eyed Mom says.

"Please, honey," Dad says. "Let me handle this." Mom walks back toward the living room and gets another tissue.

"I can't wait to get out of here, and I wish you were dead!"

Dad stops in silence. So does the older Carl.

"What did you just say?" he asks.

"I wish you were dead," Carl says. Mom walks back to the doorway, stops, and stares at Carl and then at Dad. Older Carl notices the expressions on his parents' faces, the silence, and the tears. He never noticed it before. Mom and Dad walk out of the room without saying another word and gently close the door. Older Carl and the man remain inside the room.

"Do you remember that?" the man asks.

"Yes, I do."

"What did that feel like?"

"At the time, it felt good."

"Now?"

"I don't know." A teardrop develops in older Carl's right eye. They hear Mom sobbing in the master bedroom next door.

"I can't believe he'd say something like that," Mom says bawling her eyes out.

"It's okay, sweetheart," Dad says with his arms wrapped around his wife. "He's just ungrateful. That'll change when he gets older."

The elder Carl stands inside his parents' bedroom, watching Dad comfort Mom. He's mortified by what just happened.

"Why did you say that to your parents?" the man asks.

"I don't know. I was mad at them."

"Do you remember your reaction?"

"Yes, I do."

"And?"

"I remember feeling great pride."

"Pride?"

"Yes."

"Why?"

"I don't know. I guess it was because I got them to finally see how much I hated my life and that I couldn't wait to get out of here as quickly as I possibly could."

"Why did you want to get out of here so badly?"

"Just look at this place. We were poorer than poor. It was embarrassing."

"Nobody else seemed to mind it."

"Yeah, but I did. That's all that mattered to me."

"But see what it got you?"

"Kind of."

"Let me take you to another episode where you embarrassed and made a mockery of yourself. Follow me."

Carl is scared but follows the man, looking back at his sobbing mother on her bed. They walk out of the bedroom, down the short hallway, and through the front door. Carl takes a peek at his brothers still playing baseball outside.

They stand outside Carl's high school. It's February. It's Carl's signing day. A teenaged Carl is set to announce his college decision. Only he knows it. He didn't tell anybody, not even his best and only friend, Chuck.

It's lunchtime.

"Let's go," the man looks back and tells Carl.

Carl hesitates.

"What's wrong?" the man asks.

"Oh nothing. It's just I haven't seen my high school in like fifteen years."

"I know that. But let's go. We're going to miss it."

"Miss what?"

"Your Iowa signing."

He and the man come upon a group of people gathered around a table. A couple newspaper reporters sit on chairs in the front row. Mom and Dad sit on chairs on opposite sides of an empty chair behind a table.

"Carl Robertson to the main office," the school secretary announces over the PA system at the school.

Two minutes later, Carl emerges from around the corner from his math class. He carries his three-hundred-plus-page math book, a two-hundred-sheet notebook, and a folder. He wears a tight, plain white T-shirt—his muscles bulging—blue jeans, and white sneakers. He also carries a black gym bag. Inside the bag is a folder.

He sits between his parents behind the table. Cameras click. Flashbulbs go off.

Members of Carl's football team are there, a couple cheerleaders, and a few other students, including his best friend Chuck. Chuck has an enormous smile, like he knows the choice already. He doesn't, though.

Carl pulls out the black bag and folder. The anticipation mounts. He opens the folder; a blank piece of paper is inside. Carl puts the folder back in the bag. The paper remains facedown on the table.

"On this sheet of paper," Carl begins, "is my college decision. I just want to say I considered every offer closely. This was a hard choice for me to make, but I've made my decision."

The elder Carl stands in the doorway of the main office, just enough to see what's happening.

"Do you remember this?" the angel asks.

"Yes. Very much so. This was such a proud moment for me."

"What about your parents? Take a look at them."

He looks at the angel and peeks over the crowd. An enormous cheer erupts. Carl has held up the piece of paper saying, "Iowa."

Cameras and flashes go off.

The group is cheering and applauding the choice. Chuck jumps up and down in the back. "Yes! I knew it!"

The older Carl smiles in remembrance.

One of the newspaper reporters asks him, "Why Iowa?"

"Because it's a great school which could lead me to my lifelong goals."

"What would those be?"

"Live in a big city, making a lot of cash."

"Playing in the NFL?"

The elder Carl braces for what's about to happen next. He cringes.

"That'd be great because this town is a joke. I can't stand it here. Everybody here is a disgrace to humanity. All this lovey-dovey crap is sickening. Have you ever stood on the end of Main Street and just looked down it? This town is a dump, an embarrassment. Everybody here is trash. It's disgraceful. You are all idiots for wanting to live here and calling this a good place to live. You're kidding yourself if you believe that."

He pulls out a picture of New York City and shows it to everybody. They're all standing there in disbelief.

"Now this is a way of life."

His parents are sitting next to him. They are stunned. All of the thirty people in the hallway around the table are stunned.

"Carl! How could you say that?" his mother asks, still stunned. Everybody's mouths are open. Some girls' eyes are tearing up.

"What? I've been saying it since I was six. It's nothing new. I've never been one to hold anything I'm thinking back. The man asked a question, and I answered it."

No words are spoken. It's a quiet scene.

"Any other questions?"

The reporter shakes his head no, still shocked.

"Okay, thanks for coming. Go Hawkeyes!"

The reporter grabs his bag, puts his notepad away, and leaves. He thanks the principal on the way out.

"Please ignore what he said," the principal requests.

Silence.

Everybody storms off back to class. They're angry. The principal, ashamed of what just happened, yanks Carl into the office.

"What in the world was that?" Mrs. Warner asks.

"Look, I've been grateful for what everybody has done. Really. I am. But this town is not the place for me. It never has been and never will be."

"You are a bad representation of this school, the football program, the athletic program, and this town given your actions here today. You're the real disgrace of this town."

Carl slides the chair back rapidly and heads back to class.

The elder Carl plops on the chair he sat on at that age during that lecture.

"Why did you say that?" the man asks Carl.

"It was how I felt at the time."

"And now?"

"Not so good really. Why is that?"

"You're beginning to realize the things you've done were wrong. You feel guilty."

Silence.

"I've got one more thing to show you. Follow me."

"Please don't! I've seen enough!"

He is scared to find out where this last journey through his past is going to take him, but he slowly follows the man out of the school.

They stand in front of a house, a house Carl immediately recognizes.

"This is the house I went to with Sydney in college," he recalls. "This was a party after a theater performance she was in."

"That's right. Here's where your perception of women began to be the way you know it today."

Carl hasn't thought about this place, this party, since he bolted out of there for his final that morning. Everything looks the same as he remembered it: two stories tall and bright-red bricks, green wooden window frames. He hears the loud music inside.

They walk toward the house. Carl peers through the front window. He sees himself kissing Sydney, a girl he hasn't seen since then.

"She was so pretty," he mumbles to himself.

"You remember this party?" the man asks.

"Yes, I do, very well."

They walk away from the window and through the front door. The poker game is going on at the kitchen table. Loud music plays, and people are dancing in the living room. Just like how he remembers it.

"This was fun, though. I have to admit," Carl says.

Suddenly, he spots Sydney leading the younger Carl out of the back of the house onto the patio. Carl and the man follow them.

Carl and Sydney are embracing each other. Carl stands nearby and watches, remembering the moment all too well.

"Do you remember this?" the man asks.

"Of course I do. I thought she was the one for me. All I wanted was to be with her."

"Then why didn't you?"

"Because of the final . . ."

He catches what he says in midsentence.

"See," the man says. "You're blaming your mistake on someone else and not on yourself which is where the blame should be."

Carl, again feeling guilt, slowly turns his head back away from the man and refocuses on himself and Sydney on the chair.

"I was so embarrassed," Carl tells the man.

Sydney and Carl head back inside to rejoin the party, followed closely by Carl and his angel. Carl whips off his shirt and twirls it above his head, singing and dancing with Sydney right by his side. The elder Carl stands off to the side with his angel close by.

"To me, it looks like you were having a good time," the man tells Carl.

"I was. That was the most enjoyable night of my life."

"It's a shame it didn't turn out that way," the man says.

Carl glares at him, acknowledging he is once again right.

*   *   *

It's the next morning. Carl has already missed the final and gotten the notice from his advisor that he's going to be put on academic probation and his scholarship is temporarily being revoked.

There is a soft knock on the door.

Carl storms to the door of his apartment. The elder Carl and the man watch from off to the side. Carl begins to tear up.

"It seems to me you remember this," the man says.

"All too well, I'm afraid," he replies.

Carl whips the door open; it's Sydney. The elder Carl can't bear the sight. He tries to turn away, but the angel grabs him by both shoulders and turns him back around.

"Is everything okay?" she asks nervously.

"No. I missed my final. I lost my scholarship! All because of your stupid party!"

"Carl, I'm sorry. I really am. Did you have a good time with me at least?"

"How dare you think about yourself? Please leave. I don't want to see you anymore." Carl pushes her out of his apartment and slams the door shut. He locks it.

Sydney runs out of the apartment in tears.

"This is why I hate girls!" he screams out to no one inside his apartment; only this time, the elder Carl and the guardian angel are in the room.

"You broke that poor girl's heart, Carl," the man says.

Carl falls to the ground on his knees, crying. He's overwhelmed by guilt, more than he has ever been before. He grabs the angel's hands, looks up at the man, and begs for forgiveness.

"I am an idiot," he sobs, looking into the eyes of his angel. "Please help me change my ways."

The man picks Carl up off the ground. "Follow me."

"No!" Carl says. "No more. You've made your point. Just tell me what I need to do. Your wish is my command. I promise to treat people with respect. I promise I'll change my ways."

Carl continues to sob as the man leads him out of the apartment, passing an upset younger Carl. After going through the apartment door, they are back in front of Carl's childhood home. His parents have already moved in. He's seven years old again. Carl sits on the ground facing his parents' house. The man stands over him.

"Now, here's what I'm going to do," the angel says. "I'm going to send you back, and you will get to relive these episodes and change them. I guarantee you, once you're finished, your life will be better than you could've ever imagined. You have learned a harsh lesson with me. Now you will get the opportunity to change that. I will check back with you when you have successfully completed your tasks. Good luck, Carl."

"Oh, thank you," Carl wipes away his tears with his right arm.

The man disappears.

Chapter IX

CARL STANDS IN THE middle of the living room inside the tight quarters of his childhood home in eastern Iowa. His mother cooks in the kitchen. Pots clang. A knife chops through some vegetables on the counter. Soft country music plays on the radio. Mom is a big country music fan. She loves Willie Nelson. The water in a large pot boils on top of the stove. She is making breaded chicken breast with broccoli and mashed potatoes. Mom is pregnant with Elizabeth.

Dad sits on the couch reading the newspaper. He got home from the grocery store an hour ago. Carl spots Bill and Steven out back playing horseshoes in the yard. Bill is winning.

The elder Carl leaves the living room looking for himself. He turns the corner out of the living room and finds his bedroom door closed with loud Elvis music playing. Growing up, Carl was a big Elvis fan; he loved the music. But he never saw him in concert, which he regrets.

Carl walks through the shut door into the bedroom he shared with Steven.

A bunk bed sits in the far, opposite corner from the door. Two desks sit side by side on the wall with the door. Two dressers stand against the side wall. The walls are bare. The closet, which is next to Steven's desk closest to the window and furthest from the door, is full of sports equipment and toys.

Little Carl lays on his stomach playing with a large collection of Matchbox cars on the floor. With each car, Carl makes a noise—screeching tires, revving engines, crashes.

The elder Carl slowly and quietly walks up behind his younger self—twenty-five years younger.

"Excuse me," Carl says softly.

Younger Carl can't hear him.

A little louder this time, he says, "Carl?"

Younger Carl whips his head over his right shoulder. He's frightened.

"Ah! Who are you?" He screams out, "Mom!"

"No, wait!" the older Carl says. "I'm you twenty-five years from now."

"What?"

Mom comes from the kitchen and bangs on the door.

She hollers through the door, "Yes, Carl? Is everything okay?"

Younger Carl stammers for a moment. "Yes. I was just wondering when dinner's going to be ready."

"Oh. It'll be ready in about ten to fifteen minutes, sweetheart. I'll call you when it's ready."

With heavy steps on the wood floor, which creaks underneath each and every step, Mom walks back to the kitchen to finish supper.

"Who are you?" the younger Carl asks again.

"I'm you twenty-five years from now, and I'm here to change your ways so the both of us can have a better life."

The younger Carl doesn't believe him.

"Yeah right." He goes back to playing with his cars on the floor.

"I'll prove that I'm you," he says.

The elder Carl looks around the room, searching for a clue that would indicate he is the older version of the kid on the floor. He finds a Matchbox car sitting on top of Carl's dresser—a replica of a 1968 silver Camaro.

"See this car?" Carl asks.

"Yeah?"

"You know why it's here?"

"Yeah?"

"It's because this is your favorite car and you don't want it damaged."

Younger Carl is surprised but not convinced.

"Okay . . . Lucky guess."

"Your favorite, our favorite Elvis song, is 'Jailhouse Rock.' You have a traveler's guide for New York City underneath your bed—the bottom bunk. You dream of living in New York City someday."

Younger Carl is startled, frightened, confused, and baffled but also curious.

"Okay," he says dragging on. "So how are you supposed to help me?"

"I'm going to tell you about something coming up, an event that I screwed up at when I was your age, and I'm going to tell you what to do so it benefits the both of us."

"Why?"

"It's these mistakes I made growing up that I'm now paying for as an adult. I will tell you that you will accomplish your dream of living in New York City. But it goes to our heads and we forget all the important things in life, especially friends and family. Because of that, I wind up losing my job and my life. This is my chance, our chance, to make everything right, to live a fulfilling life. It's for the best, for both of us. Trust me on this. You've got to believe me."

Younger Carl stands in shock looking at his older self.

"Can anybody see you?" he asks.

"No. Only you can."

"Are you a ghost?"

"Yes."

"Neat!"

"Not really. It's been quite scary actually."

"Can you like go through walls and doors?"

"Yes. Watch."

Carl walks out and back in through the bedroom door without opening it.

"Say, 'Boo!'"

"Carl!" Mom screams from the kitchen. "Dinner is ready!"

"Okay. I'll be right there."

The Carls look at each other. The older one says to his younger self, "Please. I'm begging you."

Younger Carl walks past his older self, opens the bedroom door, and shuts off the light to go eat supper. He is quiet at the dinner table.

*   *   *

The following morning, the family portrait is to be taken so Mom can send it with the Christmas cards later this year. She has worked on setting this up for weeks. She got a professional photographer to take the picture of the family on the front porch at home to send to their relatives and friends.

She bought a black-and-white polka-dotted knee-length sundress for the occasion. The men wear matching black suits with red and white bow ties. Bill, who is nine, and Steven, five, are already dressed and on the front porch.

Carl is still getting dressed inside. He's taking his time. He doesn't want to go through with it. The photographer Mom hired stands on the front yard, which is covered in grass, waiting and thinking of the different types of pictures he wants to take, the different angles and poses.

Carl agonizes over his outfit, which lies strewn on the lower bunk. Older Carl appears inside the room.

"Ah!"

"Sorry about that."

"What are you doing here? I've got to take this stupid family picture outside."

"That's why I'm here. This is one of those events I told you about last night that I would help you through so we don't do something which will doom both of us. Trust me."

Younger Carl reaches over to the lower bunk and gets dressed, slowly.

"When I had to do this at your age, I had the same attitude. I didn't want to do it. I thought it was stupid. I wanted to go to the library."

Younger Carl stops with his leg in one pant leg, shirt unbuttoned, white tank top underneath and looks up. He wants to go to the library. A new book just came in.

"How'd you know that?"

"I'm you, remember?" The elder Carl continues, "So I made this as hard as I could on my parents to show them how unhappy I was about the idea. Two weeks later, the pictures come back, and we get into a huge argument. It changes our relationship with Mom and Dad forever."

"What did you do?"

"I told them I wished they were dead and that I hated them."

"That's how I feel."

"But that's not how we're supposed to feel. This moment changed my relationship, our relationship, with Mom and Dad. I never wanted to come home for the holidays because I hated them so much."

"They're always in my business."

"You've just got to trust me on this."

Dad pounds on the door. "What are you doing in there?" he hollers through the door. "What's taking you so damn long? Who are you talking to in there?"

"Nobody."

"Hurry up. Everybody's waiting on you."

Dad turns around and heads back outside. The floor creaks loudly underneath his steps.

Carl puts his other leg through his pant leg and buttons up his pants.

"Just trust me," the elder Carl says. The younger Carl buttons up his shirt and clips on his bow tie. He stands at the mirror which hangs off the back of the door. The elder Carl stands and watches as the younger Carl opens the bedroom door and heads to the front porch. Carl turns and looks over his left shoulder just before entering the living room. He sees the elder Carl still standing there inside the bedroom. Everybody's sitting on the swing outside, waiting.

"Sorry I'm late," Carl says. Pause. "I . . . I couldn't find my bow tie."

The photographer starts with his instructions. "Okay," he says. "I'd like you all to move to the top step of the porch."

"Now I'd like Mom and Dad to stand in the back. Dad on the left. Mom on the right. Now I'd like Bill to stand in between Mom and Dad on the next step down below Mom and Dad, and I'd like Carl on his right and Steven on his left."

Bill is the tallest. Carl and Steven are close to the same height, but Carl is slightly taller. The elder Carl watches from inside the house through the living room window.

"Now I'd like Dad to put his left hand on Steven's left shoulder. And Mom, I'd like you to put your right hand on Carl's right shoulder."

She follows the photographer's instructions and places her soft right hand on Carl's right shoulder. He gets a tingling feeling in his body. He shivers. So does the elder Carl inside.

Carl usually hates being touched in a loving way by his parents, but not this time. He smiles and looks up behind him at Mom. She's smiling.

The young Carl peeks at the older Carl standing in the living room window.

"What are you looking at?" Steven asks.

Silence.

Carl looks straight ahead at the photographer. The camera clicks. Carl turns back and looks up over his shoulder and at his Mom. She's smiling. She looks down at him.

"You look pretty, Mom," he says.

"Awww, Carl. That's so sweet of you." She leans down and gives him a quick, soft kiss on the top of his head, rubbing his right shoulder with her right hand.

Dad watches with pride after overhearing what his second-oldest son just said, by far the nicest thing he's ever said.

Inside, Carl feels a shiver in his body.

"Whoa. That was weird," he says to himself.

"Okay. Everybody look at me," the photographer says. "Big smiles now. One, two, three."

Click.

"Another one. One, two, three."

Click.

The photographer continues taking the pictures. Carl still watches from the living room window. He smiles.

This isn't so bad, the young Carl thinks to himself. The older Carl carefully watches his own expression—smiling—and his parents' expressions; they're also smiling.

"All right, last one," the photographer says.

Click.

"Wait!" Mom says. "How about a funny picture?"

"Okay!" Carl screams out. Bill and Steven are surprised. They know he's usually not into this type of stuff.

"Let's lift up our pant legs," Carl tells his brothers.

They each lift up on their right pant leg, showing off the black socks pulled up to mid-calf underneath. Mom whistles. The boys all smile.

"That's cute!"

Click.

*　　*　　*

Two weeks pass. The mailman comes up to the door. He normally leaves the mail inside the box, which sits next the road. But he's got a large, light-brown envelope, which reads in bright-red, bold letters: "Do Not Bend."

Mom and Dad are sitting on the couch watching television when they spot the mailman coming up to the door.

"Oh! The pictures are here!" she says, bouncing up off the couch and to the door. The elder Carl watches from the back of the room. The boys—Bill, Carl, and Steven—are outside playing football.

Dad gets up off the couch after Mom and heads to the back door through the kitchen.

"Boys!" Dad yells. "Come inside. The pictures are here."

The younger Carl wants to keep playing, but then he spots his older self watching from behind the bushes and follows his brothers inside. Carl playfully tosses the football at Bill's back and hits him.

"Gotcha!"

"Nice throw!" Steven says.

"Shut up," Bill angrily replies.

Mom and Dad sit on the couch while Bill, Carl, and Steven sit on the floor behind the coffee table, in front of their parents. Mom rips open the envelope. Older Carl watches from the outside through a window from the backyard. The younger Carl notices him and turns away quickly.

"Aww! They're so cute!" Mom exclaims, gawking at the pictures. She turns them around to show to Bill and Steven. They all smile. Then Carl. He gives a wide smile without regret or hesitation. He laughs softly underneath his breath.

"What a great picture!" Mom says. She flips through the picture printouts and then lets out an enormous laugh.

"That's so funny!" she says, looking at the picture where Carl and his two brothers rolled up their pant legs in the goofy picture. Mom is laughing hysterically in the picture and at the picture. "These turned out great! I'm so proud of you boys."

Outside, Carl feels a tingle in his body.

They all point and laugh at each of the pictures. In one, Carl is making a funny face—unintentionally.

"What are you doing there, Carl?" Bill asks.

"I don't know," Carl replies with a soft chuckle and a smile. "I think I was holding back a sneeze."

"You look like you have to fart," Steven says.

Everybody, including Carl, laughs.

"Honey," Mom says, looking at Dad, "go get that picture frame from the kitchen."

Dad gets up and picks up a large brown picture frame off the table, which Mom had bought at the store yesterday, and brings it into the living room.

"Frame this one," Mom says, handing the picture to her husband, hiding it from the boys. Dad takes the picture back into the kitchen and frames it.

He returns to the living room with a nail and hammer in his left hand. The picture sits underneath his arm with the back of the frame facing out. The boys still don't know which picture Mom has selected to be added to the wall next to the baby pictures of each kid. They're scared. Dad pounds the nail into the wall with the hammer.

Dad sets the hammer down on the coffee table, pulls the picture from underneath his arm, and hangs it on the wall. All the boys moan.

Mom laughs. Dad is smiling with his hands on his hips as he admires the picture.

It's the picture of them holding up their pant legs with Mom and Dad laughing hysterically behind them.

"Mom!" Bill says. "Why that picture?"

"It's funny," she replies.

Carl, who does not normally make a fool of himself or enjoying doing so, is not upset. He's happy. He looks at the picture basking with pride and joy. He is proud of something, and he is not upset with his parents.

"It's a great choice, Mom," he says.

The elder Carl shivers.

"Let's go out for ice cream," Mom says.

"Yay!" the boys say in unison. Everybody gets up and heads for the front door. Dad grabs the car keys and slams the door behind them. Just before they get in the red Chevy, they all chatter over each other about the pictures, especially the funny picture.

The doors on the car slam. The engine starts. Dad puts the car into reverse, backs down the driveway, and heads to town for ice cream. Older Carl stands next to the garage, watching his family leave. He makes eye contact with his younger self. They smile at each other.

* * *

"Good for you, Carl," a male voice says.

Carl whips around. It's his guardian angel.

"Way to steer the kid in the right direction," he says. "Did you see how happy your mom was?"

"Yes, I did."

"And how do you feel?"

"Good actually. Let me ask you something."

"Sure."

"Sometimes I get this tingling feeling in my body. What does that mean?"

"It means you are feeling goodness, and a change is being made in your adult life—a good change. Every time something changes positively for your adult life, you will get that sensation. That's how you'll know you have succeeded in turning your life around. So far, you're one for one."

"Did you happen to see how my mom and I looked at each other on the porch?"

"Yes, I did. Why?"

"Even though that wasn't physically me, I felt good about it. I never looked at my mom that way. I wasn't ashamed of her."

"It was physically you."

"What?"

"That was physically you. Right now, you are just a ghost, a figment of your imagination for your younger self. What you feel here is what you feel in real life then and now. You are learning some of the important aspects of life with a chance to fix up your past. Keep up the good work, and you will be a better you in no time."

"Can I ask you something else?"

"Sure."

"Why was this opportunity given to me again?"

The man smiles and claps his hands twice. He disappears. Carl stands in the middle of Main Street in downtown Cedar Lake. He turns to his left and spots the family inside the ice cream shop, eating their ice cream. He walks up to the window.

They each got two-scoop cones. Everybody but Mom got vanilla. Mom got chocolate. They are all smiles and laughing, still about the goofy picture. This is one of the first times they've had quality time together. It's not the last. Carl's always been the sour one. But his interaction with his older self is suddenly changing him. His younger self has this weird feeling. He doesn't know where it came from or why. He's got a different feeling about family than he has ever had. He likes it. He's proud to be out in public with his family, especially his parents.

The elder Carl watches. A tingle runs through his body yet again.

"Wow," he says to himself.

The younger Carl spots his older self standing on the sidewalk looking into the shop. They smile at each other.

"What are you looking at, sweetie?" Mom asks.

"Nothing, Mom." He takes a big lick of his ice cream cone.

A week later, the younger Carl suggests the family go camping in Minnesota for a weekend. Carl used to hate camping. But he suddenly has the urge to do things with his family.

The last time the family went camping, Carl faked the stomach flu just so he could go home.

"My tummy hurts really bad," he said to his mom and dad. He pretended to throw up.

Another time they tried to do something as a family was just weeks earlier when they had gone to Wisconsin for a canoeing trip. Carl tagged along, but he hated every minute of the trip. He hated being spotted in public with his parents, even if it was in front of complete strangers.

They weren't bad-looking people. Their clothing style wasn't terrible, either.

Dad had an athletic build from his days as a football player and a wrestler, while Mom was quite slender. She had an hourglass figure. Carl was still embarrassed. He always thought they looked hideous.

The younger Carl stops with half a scoop left on his vanilla cone and shakes his head. He gets a chill running down his spine.

"What's wrong, Carl?" Mom asks.

"Nothing. I'm just having fun." He smiles.

Mom smiles.

Dad, Bill, and Steven look at each other—surprised.

The family returns from its ice cream trip.

They're singing in the car with the radio. Johnny Cash's "Folsom Prison Blues" is on. The elder Carl is sitting on the front porch steps as the red Chevy pulls into the driveway. He stays there while the family walks past him, ignoring him—like he's not even there. Only Carl, who's the last one inside, spots him.

They smile at each other.

*   *   *

"A family isn't all that bad, hey, Carl?" a male voice says. It's Carl's guardian angel reappearing.

"You again?"

"Yes. I told you I'd check in on you to see your progress. By the looks of it, all is well."

"I have to admit I do have a refreshed feeling. I've always felt bitter about things. I never really understood why. But now I don't. I feel happiness. Why?"

"It's because you are learning there is good that can come out of life outside of dollars and success. This is why you were granted this opportunity. So you could learn that and the importance of it."

"Does everybody get this chance?"

"No."

"Then why me?"

Two claps of the man's hands, and they stand in front of his high school.

Chapter X

THE SCHOOL LOOKS AS it did when he was a senior there—newly-built, red bricks, and large windows in the lobby. The grass is green and neatly trimmed. A couple small snow banks are scattered throughout the parking lot. It hasn't snowed in two weeks. The temperatures have been near forty degrees for almost two weeks straight. It is forty-two degrees today, unseasonably warm for this time of the year. The sun is bright on a clear day with a steady but weak breeze. A sign stands in front of the building welcoming you to Cedar Lake High School. On the sign is a message: "Robertson Signing Day Today."

Carl remembers the sign.

The hustle and bustle of the start of the school day takes place while he's standing on the lawn. Three yellow school buses sit in front of the school. A fourth one pulls in. A black minivan drops off two kids next to the buses. A pack of four senior girls, dressed in winter coats and tight jeans, giggle as they walk past Carl. They don't see him.

He recognizes each of them.

"Wow," he says to himself. "Katie Johnson."

She is a busty brunette every guy in the school wants to date. She's captain of the cheerleading squad and is on the tennis team.

On her right is Amber Connelly. She's also a busty brunette. She has the prettiest blue eyes in Cedar Lake everybody says. Amber doesn't play sports. She studies. She and Carl are common table partners in the library. But nothing ever grew from there. She wants him to ask her to prom. He's not interested.

To Katie's left are Nicole and Mary Jennings—blond twins. They're considered the bombshells of the school.

Amber dated Chuck for a brief period until he caught her cheating on him with one of the receivers on the football team. Carl and the receiver, Jon, don't get along because of it. Their relationship is strictly football. That's it. That's why Carl isn't interested. He often holds a grudge.

A loud, long ring sounds from the school. It's the 7:25 bell. Class starts in five minutes.

Carl is walking toward the front door when he spots his seventeen-year-old self running down the street toward him. The teenaged Carl runs up the driveway to the school parking lot and dashes around a couple parked cars and toward the front door of the school. He spots the elder Carl walking toward the school.

He stops. He tries to remember him. He hasn't seen his older self in ten years.

It's 7:27.

"Today is a big day, as you know!" the elder Carl shouts to his younger self.

He stops.

"Yeah, I know. What's your point?"

"Remember what I told you when you were seven?"

"No. Not really."

"This is another major moment that I screwed up when I was your age, and I'm here to make sure you do it right this time for the sake of both of us."

It's 7:28.

"Hurry up. I'm going to be late."

"When you sign your letter of intent, be excited and do not be an idiot. I basically said the town was garbage and I couldn't wait to leave. I lose many ties to our hometown. At that time, it was great. Now, I'm telling you it's not so great."

"But I do want to get out of here."

7:29.

"Just trust me. It's for a better future for both of us."

"Okay. Whatever. I gotta go."

The teenaged Carl whips the school's front door open just as the 7:30 bell sounds.

Teenage Carl runs down the hallway to his first-hour classroom —social studies. He stops running short of the classroom. He takes a deep breath, exhales, and walks in. It's 7:31.

"Oh hi, Carl," Mr. Davis says as Carl walks in.

"Hello, Mr. Davis. I'm sorry I'm late."

"It's okay. Today is your big day. Just make sure you give props to your favorite teacher and we'll be okay."

Carl smiles. "All right, Mr. Davis."

Carl takes his seat in the third row, fifth seat back from the front of the classroom. The elder Carl enters the school.

"Wow," he says to himself.

Old memories run rampant through his mind. He sees the principal, Mrs. Warner, leaving the office and walking down the hall in a long black dress with small polka dots. She carries a walkie-talkie in her right hand. Her high-heeled shoes click with each step on the tile floor.

Bright white lights illuminate the vacant hallway. The morning announcements begin over the PA system.

"Good morning, students," it begins. "Drama Club will meet after school in the cafeteria today. Anybody interested in participating in this spring's play must attend."

"Yuck! Drama Club," the teenaged Carl whispers to himself in the classroom.

"Debate has practice also after school today in the auditorium," the announcements continue.

"Football players . . ."

Both Carls are listening.

"You are to meet with Coach Chapman at lunch today for Carl Robertson's special announcement. Students who wish to watch should meet outside the main office during the first lunch period. Congratulations, Carl. We're all very proud of you."

The students in his class applaud. One classmate, Jeff, leans over from behind Carl, says, "Congratulations!" into Carl's right ear, and gives him a couple soft pats on his right shoulder.

The elder Carl continues walking through the halls, remembering what it was like to be seventeen. He passes the gym where a class is taking place. They're playing floor hockey. Gym was Carl's second-hour class. His third-hour class was math. Then it was lunch period.

He loved gym class, especially when they played games like floor hockey or soccer. He was one of the best athletes in the school, so it was easy for him to dominate those games. He always took them seriously, maybe too seriously. But he is extremely competitive.

He suddenly comes across the football team photo hanging on a wall opposite the gymnasium entrance. It is from his senior year. He looks for himself in the photo. He searches left and right, going one row at a time, top to bottom.

He is not in the picture. He's not in any of the football pictures, which rest on a white concrete wall.

"They took me out," he says to himself, feeling guilty.

First hour is over. The doors in the hallway fly open. Students pile out of the classrooms and jam into the narrow but well-lit hallways. Hundreds of conversations overlap each other. Carl stands in the middle of the hallway with kids coming at him from every direction.

Teenaged Carl then walks past. He spots his older self.

"Remember what I told you," the elder says.

The younger nods his head up and down slightly to acknowledge him. He doesn't want to be caught talking to nobody. People will think he's crazy. He doesn't want that. He wants people to envy him.

"Gosh, I remember all too well," Carl says, watching his younger self just smile and nod as people walk by him giving him a pat on the back or a high five or congratulating him. The elder Carl feels what it's like to be appreciated. The anticipation mounts throughout the school for Carl's big announcement. He is the center of attention today. He loves it. He's basking in the glory and the attention.

The teenaged Carl turns to his left into the boys' locker room so he can change for gym class. Today, the class is to do a weight-lifting session in the weight room, which is next to the gym.

He finds his locker. Number 331. It's in the first row, fifth locker back along the right once inside the locker room. It's a full-length locker about as tall as he is. He winds the combination lock: 18-30-22.

The elder Carl stands inside the locker room, just around the corner from his younger self's locker. The locker room is dimly lit with blue, green, and white floor tiles and kind of muggy next to the door leading out to the gym. The younger Carl spots him out of the corner of his right eye. He ignores him. He doesn't want to be caught talking to nobody.

In comes Chuck and walks to his locker, across from Carl's. He just came from his Advanced Placement history class.

"How was social studies, man?" Chuck asks.

"Okay. How was history?"

Chuck shrugs his shoulders. "Eh."

Carl takes off his shirt, revealing his tightly toned body. Chuck takes his shirt off and is not as defined.

"Man, you're going to be a big man on campus next year," Chuck says. "There's no doubt in my mind about that."

"Thanks."

"Hey," Chuck starts, "I heard Katie Johnson wants to go out with you."

"Yeah, I heard that, too."

"So? What are you going to do? Aren't you going to ask her out?"

"I don't know. Maybe."

"You should, man."

"Why?"

"I think she's coming to your signing today at lunch."

"Okay."

"Just okay? Dude. She wants you."

"Okay."

"Man, Carl, you need to lighten up."

"I don't care. I've got other things to worry about."

"You're crazy."

"Chuck," Carl looks at Chuck sternly, "I'm tired of having this conversation with you. I've told it to you a thousand times. So just shut the hell up about it and drop it. Got it?"

Carl stands in the corner watching this whole conversation with Chuck. He remembers it well. He remembers being irritated, just like how he always is when people try setting him up on dates. Nothing changes fifteen years later.

Nicole Jennings is in Carl and Chuck's gym glass. She's wearing short gym shorts, a white T-shirt, white tennis shoes, and white socks.

"Hi, Carl," she says, ignoring Chuck.

He gives half a smile in return.

They walk into the weight room, and it's quiet. It smells like the rubber that makes up the floor and the iron the weights are made of.

Carl and Chuck take a seat on a bench press bench while Nicole sits on another bench press bench behind them.

"Hey, Carl," she whispers. He turns over his right shoulder.

"Good luck today. I can't wait for your announcement."

He halfheartedly smiles.

The bell rings to start class. The elder Carl stands in the doorway inside the weight room. He remembers these smells all too well. He spent a lot of time in here when he was in high school—a couple hours a day, almost six days a week.

Coach Chapman is the teacher for the class.

"Hey, Carl," he says. "You ready?"

"Yes, sir."

"All right. Get on this bench and show everybody why you're going to a Division I college! Chuck, spot for him."

Chuck stands up and comes around the back to be his spotter. Carl waves his arms in a circle, loosening up. He holds his right arm across his chest for ten seconds. He does the same with his left. He circles his arms again. Coach blasts Metallica's "One" on the stereo.

Carl heaves out three deep breaths and lies down on his back. He puts his hands on the bar, adjusting his grip. He lets out two more deep breaths.

"Are you ready, man?" Chuck screams.

Carl nods and lifts the bar.

Three hundred pounds is on the bar. Carl slowly drops the bar down to his chest and pushes it up fiercely.

"One!" Coach screams. Nicole watches in amazement.

"Two!"

"Three!"

"Four!"

"Five!"

Carl is cruising. He's barely sweating. He's barely straining. The class begins cheering loudly for him. They clap and yell with each rep. Principal Warner walks past, hears the commotion inside the room, and opens the door. The elder Carl stands in the back with pride.

"Yeah," he says to himself, remembering that moment.

"Six!"

"Seven!"

The principal watches in amazement.

"Eight!"

Carl begins to struggle.

"Nine!"

"C'mon, Carl, give me one more!" Coach shouts. His classmates cheer him on. Nicole stands in awe a few feet away.

Carl digs for an extra boost of energy to finish this last rep. He slowly lifts the bar up, his face turning red, his body shaking. He grinds his teeth together. He screams to motivate himself.

"Ten!"

Chuck helps Carl put the bar back on the resting spot, and Carl sits up to a loud cheer, high-fives, and applause from his classmates, including Nicole. Carl notices her behind everybody. They make eye contact.

The elder Carl notices this. He remembers feeling a chill down his spine. The younger Carl shivers.

"What's wrong, Carl?" Chuck asks.

"Nothing," he replies. "That felt great!"

The principal comes over and gives him a pat on the back.

"We're very proud of you," she says.

Carl smiles.

"You're the man, Robertson!" Coach shouts.

*   *   *

The bell sounds, ending third hour and beginning the lunch period. A table is set up outside the main office. Carl's mom and dad are standing there next to a couple coaches from the football coaching staff. They're talking, reminiscing.

"You must be very proud of Carl," one coach says.

"You have no idea," Dad replies. Mom smiles brightly.

Students begin to assemble in a large group around the table, waiting for their star athlete to arrive and announce his college decision.

Chuck is there right in front.

Nicole, Katie, Mary, and Amber are also there. Chuck checks out Katie and her somewhat revealing wardrobe.

"Hmmm," he says to himself. "Carl better ask her out today."

Thirty of Carl's friends, classmates, teachers, and administrators stand around the table still waiting for Carl.

"Carl Robertson to the main office," the school secretary announces over the PA system at the school.

He comes around the corner. Everybody cheers. They applaud him. Dad comes over and gives him a firm handshake. Mom follows with a big hug. Coach Chapman extends his right arm and firmly shakes Carl's hand.

The elder Carl is standing beyond the group, leaning against the wall. They make eye contact. The elder Carl smiles and nods, while the younger continues to the table where three chairs sit.

A couple newspaper reporters sit on chairs in the front row. Two newspaper photographers also sit in the front row. Mom and Dad sit on chairs on opposite sides of an empty chair behind a table.

Carl sits between his parents behind the table. Cameras click. Flashbulbs go off. The principal stands off to the side holding a small disposable camera. She takes a picture and winds it back up for another picture.

Members of Carl's football team are there, a couple cheerleaders, and a few other students, and, of course, his best friend, Chuck. Chuck has an enormous smile, like he knows the choice already. He doesn't, though. Nobody does, except Carl.

The elder Carl continues to watch, remembering this day all too well. It's a day he hadn't thought much about since it happened.

The young Carl pulls a folder out of a black gym bag. He opens the folder and takes out a blank piece of paper. He puts the folder back in the bag and puts the paper facedown on the table.

"On this sheet of paper," Carl begins, "is my college decision. I just want to say I considered every offer closely. For those who didn't know, I had offers from Iowa, Iowa State, Wisconsin, Michigan, Nebraska, and Minnesota. I narrowed it down to Iowa, Iowa State, and Michigan. I can't stand Minnesota."

Everybody cheers. He smiles.

"Thank you, everybody, for your support. This was a hard choice for me to make, but I've made my decision."

An enormous cheer erupts. Carl holds up the piece of paper saying, "Iowa."

Cameras and flashes go off.

The group is cheering and applauding the choice. Chuck jumps up out of his front-row seat and goes behind all the people screaming, "Yes! I knew it!"

The cheers go on for a few minutes before one of the newspaper reporters shouts over the crowd and asks him, "Why Iowa?"

"Because it's a great school which could lead me to my lifelong goals."

"What would those be?"

"Live in a big city, making a lot of cash."

The students cheer and laugh. Carl smiles.

"Playing in the NFL?"

Young Carl spots his older self from the corner of his eye and takes a long look over at him. The older Carl smiles and nods. The young Carl turns his head back toward the reporter and says, "That'd be great. But . . ."

He hesitates.

The elder Carl watches from the side nervously, biting his lower lip with his top teeth. The area is silent.

"I'll just be happy with whatever happens. I just want to have a great-paying job wherever that is. I have no preference. I just want to be able to someday come back to Cedar Lake and be able to show this great town they have someone to be proud of. I want to give Coach Hall a run for his money someday as the greatest to ever come out of here."

A thunderous cheer erupts from everyone in attendance. The elder Carl sighs. "Phew!" Then he feels a strong chill throughout his body. He shakes.

His younger self smiles and looks back at his older self. He shivers, too.

"You okay, man?" Chuck hollers out, worried.

"Yeah. Just a chill. I'm okay."

Katie smiles from her chair which was in the second row to Carl's left. She holds a piece of paper, grabs a pen out of her purse, and writes her phone number on it. "Call me."

The questions from reporters continue. The elder Carl raises his right hand and gives a thumb-up and points it at his younger self, who smiles. The elder Carl walks away from the commotion. They fade in the distance. So do the cheers and chants of "Car-l! Car-l! Car-l!"

He turns the corner just past the main office and is a couple steps shy of the school's front doors when he spots the guardian angel waiting for him.

"Nervous were you?" he says.

"Yes, I was."

"Would you like to know if you and Katie Johnson ever went out?"

"Sure."

"You did. She gave you that piece of paper afterward, and you called her after school."

"I did?"

"Yes. In your previous life, you didn't because she didn't want to be around you, much like a lot of people did after you bashed the hometown everybody loves so much, including her. Remember that?"

Sighs.

"Yes, I do."

"She didn't want to have anything to do with you. Nor did a lot of people. After you said that, she and her friends, who were all there, left. She crumpled up that piece of paper and threw it away. Who went with you to prom?"

"Nobody. Chuck and I hung out." He stops.

"Let me guess, Katie and I go to prom together."

"You do. She's prom queen, and you're prom king. You're more popular than you ever were before. People liked and respected you because you were no longer viewed as an idiot and an asshole. After that, you saw how many lives you touched and how many people genuinely cared about you; they were proud of you. This gave you a new outlook on having positive relationships with people. That's why you felt the big shiver you did. You have now learned here the importance of family and friend relationships. You went on plenty of dates after that. Now you've got one more event to fix."

"How long did Katie and I go out?"

"About three months before she went off to college at Florida."

"What happened to her?"

"She's still in Florida, but now working at Disney as a tour guide. She's married with two little girls. Now c'mon. There's one more thing you have to do."

"One more question."

"What is that?"

Silence.

"Never mind."

Chapter XI

*C*ARL STANDS IN FRONT of a familiar building. It's three stories tall, all red brick and faces a small pond. He spent many hours in this building as an undergraduate at the University of Iowa. If he wasn't here, he was not far away at the school library.

It's the fall semester of his sophomore year at Iowa. The sky is bright blue without a cloud in sight. A brisk wind whips across campus. The leaves are turning from their spring and summer green to fall orange and red. A few leaves lie on the steps in front of the building. It's in the low fifties. It's a glorious fall day in Iowa City. He spots a clock on a lamppost a few feet away: 11:29 a.m.

It's Wednesday.

"Do you recognize this?" a male voice asks.

Carl whips around and sees his guardian angel again.

"Yes, I do," he replies, pointing at the building. "I had classes in that building. This is Campbell Hall."

"That's right. But do you know why we're at this particular building?"

Carl pauses to think.

"If I remember correctly, it was my marketing tactics class."

"Yes, it was."

The front wooden doors of the building swing open. The man points at the door.

"Just watch."

Carl turns around and watches.

The twenty-year-old Carl is the fifth person to emerge from the building. He wears a University of Iowa football solid black sweater with yellow letters, blue jeans, and white tennis shoes. His book bag is draped over his right shoulder. He doesn't notice his older self watching him from across the sidewalk. He reaches into his right front pants pocket and pulls out his cell phone.

There is a voice mail from James Patrick.

Carl lifts up the phone to his right ear and listens to the message: "Hey, dude. It's James. Meet me in the food court in the union when you get out, okay? Later!"

He puts the phone back in his pocket, looks at his watch—11:32—and heads for the union. He walks with long strides, turning his shoulders to the side to fit through a group of people with whom he just walked out of the building. The elder Carl follows him. He looks back, and the man is gone.

Five minutes later, Carl opens a glass door to the union and heads up two flights of stairs to the food court. He walks past a Subway and a Taco Bell before he comes upon James sitting at a table by himself. They wave at each other. Carl sits across from him and shakes his hand.

"Hey, dude," Carl says. "What's up?"

"Not much. I still have another hour until my economics class. We have a quiz today."

"That sucks."

"Well, not really. I'm having someone meeting me here from class so we can do a quick study session."

"Then what do you want me here for?"

Before James can answer, a high-pitched female voice says, "Hi, James," behind Carl. He turns around to see who it is. They lock eye contact and smile.

"Carl, you remember Sydney, right?"

Carl quickly stands up and extends his right hand.

"How could I forget?" he stammers with a continuous smile. "How are you?"

"I'm good," she replies, grabbing his hand softly. Carl melts with the soft touch of Sydney's hand. "It's nice to see you again."

Carl offers her his seat. "Here, you can have my seat."

"Thank you." She takes his seat, and he pulls up a chair from a nearby table and sits next to her. James sits there with a grin. The elder Carl leans against the wall not far away and out of younger Carl's sight. He smiles, remembering the moment.

For the next few minutes, no quiz preparation takes place, at least for Sydney. Carl and Sydney talk and stare at each other. James eats his lunch—a fish sandwich—and occasionally glances at his notebook and a textbook from his economics class.

"What's your major?" Carl asks.

"Theater. What's yours?" she replies.

"Marketing."

"Where are you from?" she asks.

"Cedar Lake. You?"

"Kansas City."

"Hey, would you like to go out to a dinner and movie sometime?"

"Yes. I'd love to. Let me give you my number."

"Great."

She reaches into her purse, which hangs off her right shoulder, for a piece of paper. Carl loans her his pen. She writes down her number.

"Call me," she says.

"I will. I better let you two get to your quiz. I'll see you later, Sydney."

"I can't wait," she replies with an infectious grin.

Carl stands up, fist-pumps James, and says, "I'll catch up with you later. I'll be at my apartment for the rest of the day. I don't have any more classes. Come by later."

"Okay. I should be there after two or so."

"See you then. Bye, Sydney."

Carl slowly walks away from James and Sydney at the table. He stares back at her as he walks away. He bumps into another student, who almost drops her tray with a soft drink and sandwich on it.

"Hey watch out!" she says.

"Sorry," Carl replies, stumbling over his words. He's lost in another world. The elder Carl continues to lean against the wall and remembers the whole interaction well. He stares at his younger self as he goes down the hall.

* * *

Thirty minutes later, Carl gets back to his apartment just off campus. On his entire way back, he did nothing but think of Sydney.

"Wow," he constantly mutters to himself. "She's hot! She's beautiful!"

Once back, he opens up the front door to his complex and heads up the stairwell to his apartment. He reaches for his keys. They jingle in his pocket and in his hand as he pulls them out. He is shaking more than usual. He's a bit frazzled. He unlocks his apartment, walks in, and closes the door behind him softly.

He shakes his head.

"Wow," he says to himself.

"I know. She's something else," a male voice says.

"What? Who's there?" Carl asks.

"It's just me," his older self replies.

"How'd you get in here?"

"Remember, I'm a ghost. Only you can see or hear me, and I can walk through things and change places in the blink of an eye. I'm here to make sure things go right with you and Sydney—I mean us and Sydney."

The younger Carl takes a deep breath. He tosses his book bag on the couch and goes to get something to eat from the kitchen.

"You know why I'm here, right?" the older Carl asks.

"What happens with me and Sydney?"

"Well, I'll be happy to tell you a lot of good things at first."

"At first?"

"Yes. At first. Eventually, you'll be invited to a party by her . . . We'll be invited to the party. It gets kind of crazy."

"How so?"

"You two are going to go there and have a great time. So good of a time that you will lose track of time and miss an important exam. You lose your scholarship, and we lose respect for women because of it. This is when I find myself believing that women are obstacles for our life dreams. I . . . we no longer have a desire to date because of this one event, and it changes the way we approach all sorts of relationships. That's why I'm here."

"But I still kind of feel that way. I still would rather study than go out. But this girl gave me a new feeling today."

"I remember."

"So what are you saying? Should I not go out with her?"

"No. I'm not saying that."

"Then what are you saying?"

"Hold on. Let me finish. After you lose your scholarship, she comes by to console you—see if you're okay—but you go nuts at her. You get really angry at her. You break up with her and break her heart. You two never see each other again, and women are a minor detail in your life from that point on. Very minor."

"You're joking, right?"

"No, I'm not. Remember the signing?"

"Yeah, why?"

"Well after that, women weren't a high priority in our lives. But when Sydney came along, we were willing to give it another shot, until it ended in disaster. Again, my sole purpose is to change the biggest mistakes in my life with you so we both can have great lives—the family picture when you were seven, the Iowa signing, the party with Sydney. All of these events are connected, and if they're not fixed, our adult life will be a disaster. All hell will break loose. Believe me. I've seen it."

A loud and male voice shouts through the apartment door. Then a couple of hard knocks follow.

"Hey, Carl! You in there? Let me in. It's James."

The younger Carl pauses and looks at his older self. Then he turns around and shouts back at the door. "I'll be right there."

He turns his attention back to his older self.

"So when is this 'test' going to happen?"

The elder Carl has disappeared. The younger Carl walks to the door and opens it.

"Hey," James says, standing in the open doorway to his friend's apartment. "What the hell took you so long?"

"Nothing. I was just . . . changing shirts."

"No, you weren't. You still have the same one on."

Silence.

"I changed my mind. So anyways, tell me more about that Sydney chick."

"She's hot, isn't she?"

The elder Carl stands outside the apartment, just down the bright hallway, listening to James and Carl's conversation. James walks in, and Carl leans out into the hallway and looks down at his older self.

They briefly stare at each other. Carl leans back into his apartment and softly shuts the door.

*   *   *

James leaves Carl's apartment at about 7:00 that evening. They played video games almost the entire time he was there and talked about Sydney. Carl asked question after question about her. He wanted to know everything about her.

"All right, James. I'll see you at the gym tomorrow."

Carl opens the door to his apartment to let James out. He turns around and looks at Carl.

"Good. Sydney's going to be there."

"Really? Why?"

"She likes to work out, too."

"Awesome."

"I'm telling you, man. She's got a nice body, too."

Carl grins.

*   *   *

The next day, Carl doesn't have a class until after 2:00. Neither does James or Sydney.

Carl and James arrive at the gym at 10:30 in the morning. They put their gym shorts and cutoff shirts on and head for the weight room.

Carl grabs two forty-five-pound dumbbells and lies down on a nearby bench to do a chest exercise. Rock music plays softly on the stereo inside the weight room. About ten guys are scattered around the room. There are just two girls. The room has a black rubber mat throughout. It's well lit. A large fan softly whirs from a nearby corner. There is light chatter. Some weights clang together. A tall, muscular man lies on a bench next to Carl and is doing the bench press. He has three hundred pounds on the bar. His male friend stands behind, giving him a spot. The muscular man grunts loudly, trying to lift one more repetition. Carl watches closely and ponders challenging him.

"Hi, Carl," a female voice says behind him. He stops, gently puts the weights down on the floor, and looks back.

"Oh, hi, Sydney. It's very nice to see you again. I didn't know you worked out here."

She is wearing black mesh shorts, which go to mid-thigh, with a tight white tank top. Her long blond hair is pulled back in a ponytail. She holds a small water bottle in her right hand.

"How long have you been here?" she asks.

"About ten minutes or so. You?"

"Same. I come in here every Tuesday and Thursday to work out because I don't have a class until two fifteen. I usually like to run on the treadmill."

"Oh. I'm usually in here on Mondays and Wednesdays. That's why I never see you here." He pauses. "You look really pretty today."

"Thanks. I was on the swim team in high school."

"Oh. So are you a sports fan?"

"Sort of."

"What sports do you like?" Carl asks.

"Swimming for sure. I've been doing it since I was like five. But I mostly just like the teams from home—the Chiefs, the Royals."

"Okay. I can accept that."

"Why?"

"I hate the Cowboys. I love the Giants. I don't have to hate you from the start now."

They share a laugh. James, meanwhile, is running a brisk pace on the treadmill. He runs three to four miles every day on the treadmill. He also played soccer in high school.

"You look good, too, Carl," Sydney says.

"Thanks. I used to play football."

"Used to? What happened?"

"I tore my ACL before fall football practice last year. I can't play anymore."

"That sucks."

"Yeah, but I'm getting over it. Listen, you still want to go to the movies tomorrow night?"

"Sure."

"Great. Where can I pick you up?"

"I live in the dorms. Wells Hall. Fifth floor. Room 505."

"Pick you up at six?"

"That'd be great. I can't wait."

"Likewise."

"I'll see you later."

*　　*　　*

Carl is rushing around at 5:00 on Friday evening to get ready for his first date with Sydney. He wants to look good for her. She already does it for him. It's the least he can do, he thinks to himself. Never has he felt so nervous about how he looks for a girl. He wants to look his best. This girl is different to him.

In his closet, he finds a pair of light-brown khaki pants, brown shoes, and a light-blue, button-down, long-sleeve shirt. He stands at the mirror. "Yeah. This will work."

He grabs his wallet and keys off the dining room table. He grabs his jacket off the couch and heads out the door. He locks up his apartment. His elderly neighbor, Ruth, is walking down the hall with a bag of groceries in her right hand.

"Oh hi, Carl," she says to him. "You look awfully handsome this evening."

He normally doesn't interact with her. But because he's in such high spirits, he thanks her and offers to carry her things to her apartment.

"Thank you," she says. "Do you have a date or something tonight?"

"Yes, I do, with a very pretty girl named Sydney."

"I'm sure you two will have a good time."

"Thanks."

He heads downstairs and walks to Sydney's dorm on the opposite side of campus from his apartment. He slightly limps along the way. His knee is flaring up on him a little bit. He looks at his watch: 5:45. He's twenty minutes from the dorm.

He extends his strides to a power-walk pace. "I can't be late."

Along the way, he passes the football stadium. He stops and looks at it. Since his ACL injury, he's tried to avoid the football stadium to keep his mind off football—a sport he once cherished.

In the weeks after the injury, he couldn't bear the sight of the football stadium. He would cry. He just stares hard at it.

"I do miss playing football," he says to himself. "But I guess everything happens for a reason."

He feels a chill go down his spine. He wonders what it was. He continues on without thinking any more about it.

He looks at his watch: 5:51. Still ten minutes until Sydney's dorm. "I've gotta hurry up."

Carl starts a slow jog, trying to pick up time. His knee is still bothering him. Sydney sits in the lobby of her dorm hall. She couldn't wait any longer. She is excited for this date. She came down at 5:30.

Carl whips past tree after tree, student after student still going to class. Never has he been in this big of a hurry to meet a girl. There is something special about her. He wants to find out what it is.

At 5:59, he turns the corner to get to the front of Sydney's dorm complex.

At 6:00, he pulls the door open swiftly and heads into the lobby. There she is. She's looking prettier than he ever could've imagined.

He stops to collect himself and catch his breath from running and gently bends and extends his leg, trying to work out some of the lingering pain. He also has to catch his breath from the sight of the gorgeous Sydney.

"Wow!" he says. "You look absolutely amazing." He continues to breathe heavily.

"Thanks," she says. "You look really cute."

He's still heaving breaths. She asks, "Why are you so winded?"

"I ran all the way here. I got caught up. I helped a neighbor with her groceries."

"Aww. That's so sweet of you."

"Plus my knee was beginning to flare up."

"Are you okay?"

"It should be fine."

Sydney is wearing a sleeveless, knee-length black dress with a pleated skirt. The top of the dress angles down enough to reveal a little cleavage. She paid a hundred dollars for it yesterday just for this occasion. She bought it after class. She also carries a small matching black purse. It hangs around her right forearm.

"You are stunning," he says.

She grins with an infectious smile.

"Are you ready?" he asks.

"Yes, I am."

The two are turning toward the lobby front door when her roommate walks in from her business class. She whistles.

"Wow, Syd," the roommate says, "you look hot!"

She blushes. Carl smiles with pride.

"You must be Carl," she says, extending her right hand to shake Carl's. "I'm Cindy. She's told me a lot about you."

"Really?" he replies. "Hopefully they were good things," he adds with a smile and a chuckle.

"Yes, they were," she replies.

"Okay, Cindy. Leave us alone," Sydney says, still blushing. Her cheeks are noticeably red.

"Have a good time, you two." Cindy wishes them well.

Carl opens the door for Sydney to go outside, and they walk to the movie theater, which is just a few blocks from campus. Cindy watches them leave.

It's a cool evening—low 40s. It's supposed to get into the 30s that night. Sydney shivers. Carl offers her his jacket. "Here you go." He puts it around her shoulders.

"Oh, thank you." She clutches it tightly. "It's warm."

Carl wraps his right arm around her shoulders. They walk almost in stride all the way to the movie theater, which is only a couple blocks from Sydney's dorm on campus. They talk about their days. The knee is feeling better.

"I had a quiz in my marketing class today," Carl starts.

"How'd you do?"

"I did pretty good. We'll get our scores Monday. I think I nailed it, though."

"That's good."

"How was your day?"

"Tough."

"How come?"

"I didn't have any classes today. So I was in my dorm bored all day."

"Was somebody a little anxious?" Carl asks with his voice rising at the end.

"You could say that," she replies grinning.

*   *   *

The movie ends shortly after 8:00 in the evening. It's much colder outside than it was earlier. The two are shivering. They look for a campus taxi. Carl flags one down—a gray van. They get inside.

"Where to?" the cabdriver asks.

Carl and Sydney look at each other. She whispers, "Where do you live?"

"I have an apartment to myself a couple blocks from the football stadium. Why?"

"Let's go there. I don't want to be with my roommate. She'll just pry into our business."

"Hampton Square, please," Carl tells the driver.

"Okay," the driver replies.

Sydney inches closer to Carl's side on the seat inside the van. They're the only passengers. The radio is off, but the heat softly blows from the front of the van. She rests her head on his shoulder, as they make their way to Carl's place. He wraps his right arm around her, and she reaches for his left hand to hold it.

She reaches up and gives Carl a light kiss on his right cheek. He looks at her amazed. She is staring at him. She's smitten. He is, too.

They get to his place. He gets out the right side and holds out his hand out for Sydney to hold on to.

"Thank you," Carl tells the driver.

"Good night," he replies. He pulls away.

Carl and Sydney hold each other tight as Carl looks for his keys in his jacket pocket, which sits around her shoulders. They walk up the steps to the complex's front door. He spots his older self standing on the corner of the block, leaning against a light post. The younger Carl glances at him and looks back at Sydney.

"Ah! Here they are," Carl says, pulling out his keys.

He unlocks the door, and they head upstairs. Ruth is coming down the hallway and going to the laundry room on the first floor.

"Oh hi, Carl. Is this your lovely date? She's gorgeous. You were right."

Carl's now blushing.

"Thank you, miss," Sydney replies.

"Good night," Ruth says.

"Good night," Carl and Sydney reply in unison.

Carl finds his apartment key and opens the door. They go inside, and he locks the door behind them. Sydney hands Carl his coat back and thanks him.

"Can I get you anything?" he offers.

"Yes . . . You!"

She wraps her arms around him and gives him a long kiss on the lips. He is caught off-guard briefly but then places his hands on her hips. He accidentally pokes Sydney's right hip with the keys.

"Ouch!" she says.

"Oops. I'm sorry."

He tosses the keys onto the couch and puts his hands back on her hips. She wraps her arms around his neck and kisses him again.

"Wow. You're not only hot, but a great kisser," she says.

"Thanks. You're pretty good yourself," he replies.

They continue kissing. The apartment is dimly lit. Just a lamp in the living room window is on. It's slightly cold. He likes it that way.

They kick off each other's shoes to the side. She unbuttons his shirt, slides it off, and lifts the white undershirt he has on underneath over his head. Bare-chested, he keeps his hands on her hips.

"Let's go to your bedroom," she says.

He doesn't reply. He just leads her back. He takes her hand, and they walk back to the bedroom of his apartment. The floor creaks underneath each of their steps. He flips the light on and closes the blinds to his room.

She sits on the edge of the bed, and he sits down right next to her. They turn to face each other and kiss once more before a handful of loud knocks echo throughout the apartment.

"What is that?" she asks.

"Who could that be?" he asks. "Let me check."

"No. Stay here. They'll go away."

"I'll be right back."

He gets off the bed and goes to the front door. He picks up the white T-shirt Sydney took off of him off the floor near the couch, puts it on, and opens the door.

"Yes. Can I help you?" Carl asks an elderly man standing in the doorway.

"Yes. I'm Jerry. I'm your next-door neighbor. Ruth's husband. You helped her with the groceries earlier."

"Oh yes. What's the problem?"

"I just wanted to say thank you. It's rare to find good guys such as yourself around these days."

Carl, slightly agitated because he's missing out on Sydney, replies, "It's no problem. I'm glad to have helped. Good night."

Carl begins to close the door before Jerry puts his left hand on the door to stop it.

"Is there something else?" Carl asks.

"Yes. I'm sorry. I'm putting up a new shelf. I'm trying to at least. Could you spare a minute and help me out? I'm not as strong as I used to be."

Silence.

Sydney leans out of the bedroom doorway and watches the conversation intently.

"Sure. Just give me a second," Carl says.

He gently closes the front door, and Jerry walks back to his place. Carl goes to Sydney in the bedroom. She sits on the edge of the bed.

"Who is it?" she asks.

"My neighbor. He needs help with a shelf. Can you hang tight?"

"Well," she replies slowly, "I should probably get back to my dorm. I have practice in the morning."

"Rehearsal? For what?" Carl asks.

"I'm in the theater group. We've got a play at the end of this semester."

"Oh yeah. I'm sorry."

"But I had a wonderful time tonight. Let's do this again."

"I'd love to." He's bummed she has to leave.

"Here's your jacket," she says.

"No. Hold on to it. It's cold out. I can get it from you later."

"Will you be without a jacket?"

"Nah. I've got another in the closet there." Carl points at the closet in his room.

"Thank you." She stands up and gives him another strong kiss on the lips.

"You're welcome. I had fun tonight."

"I did, too. I can't wait to see you again. When will I see you again?"

"How about tomorrow? We can meet at the union?"

"Sure. I'll come after my first class, which ends at about eleven."

"Great. See you then."

He has a psychology class at 11:10.

"Actually," she starts again. "Carl, I really like you. I'm usually pretty shy. But there's just something different about you. I'd be thrilled if we can start officially dating, like as in boyfriend and girlfriend. You are so sweet and cute."

He pauses and then replies, "Yes. I'd be thrilled to."

They embrace each other excitedly. They emerge out of the bedroom and walk across the apartment. Carl opens the door for his new girlfriend. Jerry is standing in the doorway to his apartment.

"Oh," he says, "I didn't realize you had company. I'm sorry."

"That's okay," Carl says.

"I was leaving anyways," Sydney says. "Good night, Carl. See you tomorrow."

"Can't wait."

* * *

Three months pass.

Carl and Sydney are smitten with each other. The relationship has taken off. They spend every waking moment with each other. Whenever they have spare time, they are with each other.

It's the end of the semester. He is getting ready to attend Sydney's show. The elder Carl is at Carl's place with him.

"Isn't she something special?" the elder asks.

"Oh yeah. What are you doing here?"

"Tonight is the night I warned you about."

"Warned me about?"

"Yes. This is the night where I screwed it up with Sydney. I'm here to make sure you don't do it for our sake."

"I don't know how you could've screwed this up. She's an amazing girl. I've never felt this way about anyone."

"You're right."

"So how did you screw this up?"

"Well, she's going to ask you after the show tonight to go to a party."

"But I can't. I have that marketing tactics final in the morning that I've barely studied for."

"Exactly."

"So what did you do?"

"I went to the party, had a great time, lost track of time, missed the final, got put on academic probation, and lost the scholarship. It only got worse from there."

Silence.

"So you're saying not to go to the party?"

"I say go to the party. But don't lose track of time. Explain to her why, and I guarantee she'll understand."

The younger Carl, wearing a black suit with thin white pinstripes, white dress shirt, and black tie, puts on his watch and heads out the door to the show. The elder remains in the apartment.

On the way to the theater hall, the younger Carl carefully thinks about what his older self just told him. He tries rehearsing what he's going to say to Sydney when he sees her and when she asks him to go to the party afterward. It's an unseasonably warm evening in December, forty-three degrees. There are numerous puddles on sidewalks and roadways on his way to the hall. It's been unseasonably warm for the past couple of days. Nine inches of snow fell three days ago. It's a quiet night. He looks up and sees a full moon high in the sky. He passes the football stadium and smiles.

He arrives at the Performing Arts Center where Sydney's performance is set to take place. He stands outside looking at the large building with tall windows. A tall Christmas tree stands inside. It's lit with plenty of white lights draped from the branches from top to bottom. He sees people gathering inside and outside the building.

A group of four students, friends of other performers, walks past him. They share a laugh.

"Well. Here goes nothing," Carl softly says to himself. He walks toward the front door.

Inside, the chatter echoes throughout the lobby. Carl walks toward the Christmas tree until he feels a set of arms wrap around him from behind.

"Hey, Carl," Sydney says excitedly.

"Hey, Syd." He turns around, and she gives him a peck on the lips.

"I'm glad you came."

"I am, too."

She smiles at him. "You better go take your seat."

"Okay. Where should I sit?"

"Wherever you want. There are no assigned seats."

"Okay."

"See you after the show."

He smiles back at her as she turns around, walks down a connecting hallway, and turns the corner to head backstage.

He finds a seat somewhat close to the stage. He sits stage right seven rows back. There are forty rows in three sections. The capacity is 450 people. He sits in an aisle seat. He extends his right leg into the aisle and rubs his knee.

The loud chatter that filled the lobby echoes into the auditorium. A few people sit spread out in the auditorium. Nobody is seated in front of him. A group of six students, each holding a spiral notebook and a pen, sits three rows behind Carl. Each auditorium light is on. The stage is dark.

A woman shouts an announcement in the lobby. "Ladies and Gentlemen, please take your seats. The show is about to start."

The chatter continues, and more people file their way inside the auditorium. The chatter is now inside. One stage light comes up. A man in his forties walks from the side of the stage to a microphone placed underneath the light at center stage.

"Ladies and Gentleman," he says, "can I have your attention?"

The chatter quickly softens. Others whisper, "Shh."

The room is now silent. Faint chatter is heard backstage.

"Thank you," the man says. "Welcome to the show."

The room of about three hundred people applauds. Carl gently follows suit, looking around him to see if he knows anybody. He doesn't see anybody. While the man, one of the professors in the theater department, describes the evening's plans, Carl begins to think and reminds himself not to forget about his final. He goes over some notes he remembers from his notebook, which sits on the kitchen table at his apartment.

"Enjoy the show," the man says. The elder Carl leans against the back wall as the lights dim. The auditorium is almost pitch-black with only the dim aisle lights on.

A stage light comes up. First onto the stage is Sydney. Once again, Carl is flattered by her stunning beauty. She wears a long white gown, holds a book, and is seated on a chair facing the audience underneath a light on stage left. Her right leg is crossed over her left. A small wooden table sits to her right. A box of tissue sits atop the table. She recites her opening line.

"I don't how she does it," she says, with her voice echoing throughout the auditorium, as she pretends to be fighting back tears. She reaches to her right to grab a tissue.

A male actor's voice screams from off-stage.

"Gloria!"

Carl watches with enormous pride throughout the show. *She is so pretty. She's so talented.*

The show lets out at 10:30. The audience rises to their feet for a standing ovation. Carl follows suit. The cast walks out hand in hand to take a couple of bows. The stage lights dim, and the auditorium lights shine brightly. The audience begins to file out of the auditorium and into the lobby. Carl walks past a couple of groups of people standing in the aisle, talking about the show.

Sydney is standing next to the Christmas tree, waiting for Carl.

"You were magnificent, sweetheart," he says. He spots a small table near the door he walked through from the auditorium. A woman is selling roses.

Sydney smiles. "Thank you."

"Can you hang on a second?" Carl asks.

"Sure," she replies curiously.

"Close your eyes, though."

"Okay," she replies nervously, but obliges.

He walks up to the woman's table and asks for two roses.

"Absolutely. Here you go."

"How much?"

"Seven dollars."

He reaches into his pocket, grabs a ten-dollar bill, and hands it to her.

"Keep the change. I'd like to donate it to the department."

"That's very kind of you, sir. Here's an extra rose for your generosity."

He gently squeezes the three roses and walks over to Sydney, who has her back to him. He taps her on the shoulder.

"Here you go, my love."

She opens her eyes, turns around, and has a big, infectious smile.

"They're beautiful." She kisses him softly on the lips.

A fellow female cast member comes up to Sydney.

"You were great, darling," Lisa says.

"Thanks."

"Listen, we're having a party not far from here. You should come."

Sydney looks at Carl.

"C'mon, Carl. Come with me to the party."

Out of the corner of his eye, the younger Carl spots his older self standing at the end of the hallway outside the theater. They make eye contact. The elder's arms are folded across his chest. The younger holds Sydney's hands. She looks at him with a grin. It is her silent way of begging. He melts every time she does it. It works every time.

"Okay. Let's go," Carl says.

"Yay!" She leads him outside of the theater hall, holding his right hand with hers. They hop into a castmate's car—a blue van—and head to the party.

Inside this two-story brick house with green wood frames around the windows and six bedrooms, the party is already underway. It started two hours earlier. Carl and Sydney arrive at 11:00. Thirty or more people are already there. Loud music blares from inside the house. Sydney and Carl head for the kitchen where the liquor is set up. Carl grabs a beer. Sydney goes for the Jack Daniels and Coke. Just past the kitchen is a group of six people—three guys and three girls—playing poker. The guys are winning for the most part. One of the girls playing is from Carl's marketing tactics class. He sits behind her in the lecture hall.

"I should probably only stay for a bit, Sydney," Carl says.

"How come?"

"I've got an eight o'clock final that I've barely studied for." The elder Carl watches from behind the kitchen counter.

"How come you haven't studied for it?" Sydney asks.

"Someone's distracted me," he replies with a smile.

Sydney is slightly offended. "What? Are you saying I'm distracting you? Keeping you from your studies?"

"Yes. But that's a good thing. I love being with you. But I really have to do well on this final."

"Well," she replies perturbed, "how long were you going to stay?"

"About one. Is that okay?"

She begrudgingly sighs. "Fine."

"It means a lot to me. Do you want to dance?"

"Okay."

Carl grabs her left arm with his. The drinks are in their right hands. He pulls Sydney in tight by grabbing her butt with his left hand.

"You've got a nice butt," he tells her.

She laughs. "Thanks."

They grind against each other, having a great time. The elder Carl stands in the doorway between the kitchen and the living room, which is the dance floor. The elder spots James taking his date by the hand outside from the kitchen.

They dance throughout the night. Sydney finds a straw cowboy hat sitting on top of the bookshelf. She puts it on. Carl makes repeated runs to the liquor spot in the kitchen. Sydney's all about the Jack and Cokes tonight. Carl is more conservative, drinking one beer for every two of Sydney's drinks.

Carl lifts up his left arm, shakes it out, and looks at his watch: 12:33. Sydney grinds her backside up against Carl. She's wearing a tight shirt that accentuates her tight body and tight, low-rise blue jeans. He whips her around, grabs her butt again, and plants one long kiss on her lips.

"Let's go upstairs," Sydney says to him a little slurred.

He looks at his watch: 12:41.

"We probably shouldn't," he tells her.

"Why not?" she asks angrily.

"Because it's almost one, and I need to study for that final."

"It'll only be for a few minutes. I promise."

"I really think I should get going." The elder Carl observes from his same spot by the kitchen doorway.

Sydney's angry.

"I'll make it up to you," he says. "I promise."

"You better," she slurs. She turns away from him and heads into the kitchen. Her drink glass is empty. Time for another round.

"I'll call you later," he says to her as she walks away. She ignores him.

Carl leaves the party and takes a cab back to his apartment. The elder Carl follows him out and watches his younger self head home.

*   *   *

Carl gets back to his apartment at 1:15. He's got less than seven hours to sleep and study.

The elder Carl appears twenty minutes later with younger Carl studying hard.

"Hey, Carl," the elder says.

"Thanks a lot. Sydney's mad at me." Carl has his marketing textbook open on the dining room table. A folder lays strewn with papers scattered everywhere. A dim lamp hangs over the table. The rest of the unit is dark. Outside of their conversation, there is not a sound in the room or the building. Everybody but Carl is asleep.

"It'll be fine. Just trust me on this. She'll realize it in the morning."

"Realize what?"

"How mean she was to you. You are doing the right thing here. Trust me."

He studies until 4:00 a.m.

*   *   *

Carl wakes up at 6:00. He rolls over to his left and slams his hand on the buzzing alarm clock.

"Five more minutes," he says. He hits the snooze button and falls back asleep. There is a soft knock on his front door.

He throws on his robe and goes to the door. He peeks out the peephole and unlocks the door. His course work still sits on top of the dining room table.

"Yes, Sydney?" Carl says leaning on the side of the door. He lets out a big yawn and covers his mouth with his right hand.

"Look . . ." she starts with a clearer voice than she had a couple hours ago. "I'm sorry for last night. I was really mean to you."

"It's okay." The elder Carl watches from inside the apartment, just past the couch. "It's no big deal."

"Yes, it is," she replies. "I should respect what you need to do. Homework and studying is more important. I dragged you to that party anyways."

"No, you didn't," Carl replies quickly. "I wanted to go with you to the party. I'm glad I went because I was there with you. I had fun."

"Really?" she asks.

"Yes. Really." Sydney smiles at him.

"I'm glad you're not mad at me."

"I'm not. And I promise to make it up to you. After finals, we'll go somewhere very private for you-and-me time."

"I think I'll like that. I'm actually glad you did what you did now that I think about it."

"Why?"

"Well, you know I'm a virgin, right?"

"No, I didn't."

"Well, I've always wanted to save myself for marriage. Last night, I was ready to give that up. But you didn't take advantage of me, which I probably would've regretted later. I should be thanking you."

"It's okay. I really like you. I don't want you to feel uncomfortable. Well, I've got to get ready and head to the library. I'll call you later. Okay?"

The elder Carl quivers behind him.

"Good," she replies.

Carl begins to close the door.

"Wait! One more thing," she says.

"What's that?"

Sydney slowly lifts up her shirt, revealing a tight, firm stomach with a belly-button ring. "Here's a little motivation for you. If you ace that final, I'll show you more."

She grins.

Carl smiles, leans out into the hallway, and gives her a kiss on the lips. "Thanks. That should help." His smile grows bigger.

"Good luck, baby!"

Carl gently closes the door. Sydney heads down the stairs and outside to go back to her dorm.

"Told you," the elder says, and then he quivers as another moment once gone wrong is corrected.

"Now go nail that final!" the elder says, walking out the door.

Once in the dimly lit hallway, the guardian angel is standing there—waiting.

"Good work," he says.

Silence.

"You should be grateful. You've gotten the chance to correct the biggest mistakes in your life so you can have an even more fulfilling life from here on out."

"So what happens next?" Carl asks.

"You got an A."

"Awesome."

"You don't lose your scholarship, and you don't have to take any summer courses. Instead, you spend the summer with Sydney in Kansas City."

"What happens to us?"

"Well, the two of you date for the rest of your college years."

"Then what?"

"Well, she moves to Los Angeles to become an actress. You begin work on your internship."

"Why don't we move out there to LA together? Or to Atlanta?"

"You both realize you've got amazing opportunities that you can't pass up. But don't worry. You promise each other to write and call as often as possible and stay in close touch."

"How close?"

Chapter XII

CARL AND HIS GUARDIAN angel stand on a vacant two-lane dirt road in front of Carl's childhood home. A steady breeze passes by them, with lots of clouds moving swiftly. The sun occasionally peeks through a break in the cloud cover. It is fifty-two degrees. They stand looking at the house together, which is in average shape. The lawn hasn't been cut in weeks. There are boards on the windows. A "For Sale" sign sits on the front lawn. No red Chevy in the driveway.

Carl turns to the man.

"What's wrong with the house now?"

"Nothing. Your parents moved out."

"What? When?"

"After you got your promotion at work, you bought them a brand-new house on the edge of town."

"Why?"

"Well, because of the changes you just made with your life, your relationship with your parents changed for the good. You talk to them more. You see them more."

"Do I visit them for Christmas?"

"Yes."

"Is the house nice?"

The man smiles.

"There's one thing I don't understand, though," Carl says.

"What's that?"

"Football. Why couldn't I go back and change the football injury I had?"

"That was because that was an inevitable event. No matter what, that was going to happen."

"Why?"

The man begins to open his mouth to reply, but his voice echoes the sounds of a sporadic and high-pitched heart-rate monitor. He disappears in front of him. Everything around him turns a bright white. He shields his eyes.

"What's going on?"

The beeping continues.

He slowly opens his eyes and stares at a light beaming down on him. He awakes from his dream. He looks to his left and sees a pretty nurse with brown hair in a ponytail.

"Hello?" he groggily mutters.

"Mr. Robertson," a nurse says. "Good to see you're awake. Everything's going to be just fine."

"Where am I?" he asks still groggy.

"You're at the hospital."

"Why?"

"Well, your friends brought you in here because you suddenly got really sick."

"My friends?"

"Yes. I believe Percy is the one who brought you in. He and some others are waiting for you in the waiting room. We'll let you see them in a second."

There are two soft knocks on the door, which is half open.

"Hello?" Dr. Joe Young asks, carefully walking into the room. "How are you feeling, Mr. Robertson?"

Silence.

"Confused."

"Well, you've been out for a while. Can you sit up for me just a little bit? I'd like to take your temperature. Just relax. We should have you out of here in no time. Okay?"

"Okay," Carl replies still confused.

He spots a clock on the wall. It's just after 5:00 a.m. in the morning.

"What happened to me?"

"Well, Mr. Robertson . . ." Dr. Young begins. He hears a couple soft knocks on the door.

"Carl?" a male voice asks.

"Yeah?"

Percy comes into Carl's room.

"Carl! Are you okay, man?"

"Yeah. I think so. What am I doing here?"

"You got really sick, man. We thought you were going to die."

"We?"

"Yeah. Kenny, John, Tammy, Tucker, Nick, Caitlin, Steve, Amber, and Sharon. They're all in the waiting room."

"Really? Why?"

"It's because we care about you, man. Where else would we be?"

"I don't know. Sleeping at home?"

"Nah. We care about you too much. We want to make sure you're okay."

Carl is even more confused than he was before.

I thought I was nobody's friend, he thinks to himself.

He rubs his eyes with his fists. An IV hangs off his right arm. He has a pulse monitor on his right index finger. He wears a long white hospital gown. He has a pair of white thermal socks on his feet. The room is a bit cool.

"It's cold in here," he says. "Can you turn up the temperature?"

"Sure," Dr. Young replies.

He walks over to the nearby thermostat to turn up the heat a couple degrees. Then everybody walks into the room—Kenny, John, Tammy, Tucker, Nick, Caitlin, Steve, Amber, and Sharon. The nurse follows them in.

"What happened?" Carl asks Percy.

"Well, I think you had too much to drink with no food in you. But whatever it was, you got real sick real fast, and we had to get you to the hospital."

"Why?"

Percy's confused.

"Well, you were in pretty bad shape, man."

"I'm sorry about that," Carl starts. "Look, I'm sorry for being an ass for all these years. I never meant to hurt any of you like the way I have. From now on, I'm going to treat you all with the respect you deserve."

Percy pauses and is confused. Everybody looks at each other also confused.

"What are you talking about?" Nick asks.

"I'm always a pain in the butt, especially to my team."

"No, you're not. We think the world of you, Mr. Robertson. You're a great role model for us."

"What are you talking about?"

"Carl," Percy starts. "What the hell's gotten into you?"

"I don't know. I'm just a little confused."

"Why?"

"I don't know. I guess I must've really passed out."

"Yeah. Everybody's been waiting for you to wake up."

"Why?"

"We wanted to make sure you were okay. Like I said, you were in bad shape."

Dr. Young looks at Carl's group of friends and colleagues and asks them to head back to the waiting room. He wants Carl to get some more rest.

"Mr. Robertson, I need you to relax so your memory can clear up."

Sharon looks at her boss and says, "Carl, we'll be in the waiting room when you're ready to see us again."

The nurse leads the group out of the room and back to the waiting room down the hall from his room. The doctor follows closely behind and gently closes the door.

Carl is left alone with his thoughts. He rubs each of his eyes with both fists and yawns.

"Confused, are we?" a male voice asks.

His guardian angel peeks out from behind the curtain to the left of Carl's bed.

"What are you doing here?" Carl asks.

"I'm just here to tell you that because of the changes you made to your past, everything is now the present from that past. That life you once knew never happened."

"Huh?"

"That life you had where you treated everybody like garbage never happened. You're now living the life you made for yourself. That's why everybody was confused by you."

Carl is speechless. The heart-rate monitor continues its high-pitched and sporadic beeping.

*   *   *

Two days later, Carl is released from the hospital.

"Thankfully it wasn't alcohol poisoning, Mr. Robertson," Dr. Young tells him as he signs the release papers. Carl is standing in the corner near a storage closet in which there is a set of clothes—blue jeans, a black T-shirt, white socks, and a pair of black tennis shoes.

The room is warm. The sun beams through the window. No lights are on.

Percy steps off the elevator and walks down the hall and into Carl's room.

"Hey, Carl. You ready to go?"

"I am. Doc?"

"Sure. Just sign here."

He extends a clipboard toward Carl and hands him a pen. He quickly etches his name on the sheet of paper.

"All right, Mr. Robertson. You're ready to go."

"Thanks."

Percy leads Carl out of the room, down the hall, and to the elevator. He's on the fifth floor. The elevator is on the sixth floor.

The elevator doors slide open. It's vacant. Percy and Carl step on, and the doors softly close. Carl is quiet.

"What's wrong? You okay?" Percy asks.

"Yeah, I'm just a little tired."

The doors slide open, and a group of people are waiting for him. It's Sharon, Nick, Tucker, and Caitlin.

"Mr. Robertson," they say in unison. "How are you?"

"I'm doing okay," he softly replies.

Caitlin and Sharon walk up to him and give him a soft hug. Nick and Tucker extend their right hands and shake their boss's right hand.

"Glad you're okay," Tucker says.

Carl, followed by Percy, Caitlin, Sharon, Nick, and Tucker, steps out of the hospital and into the bright New York City sunlight. It's a clear and warm afternoon, close to sixty-five degrees. Horns sound softly around them.

Suddenly, a cab pulls up. At first, Carl doesn't pay any attention to it. The right rear passenger window buzzes down.

"Carl!" a female voice shouts. Carl recognizes it. He squints his eyes, trying to get a better look. The door swings open.

"Liz! What are you doing here?"

"Sharon called me to tell me you were here."

"Look. I'm sorry I didn't get back to you."

"Don't worry about it. You're better now. That's all that's important."

"Thanks, Liz. Is everything okay?"

"Yeah, why?"

Carl pauses. "Nothing." He smiles. He leans over and gives his sister a big hug and tells her, "I'm sorry."

"Sorry for what?"

"For not being a better brother."

"What are you talking about? You're a great brother."

"I am?"

"Yes. Why do you think you're not?"

"I don't know."

Liz leans in and hugs him.

"Now hurry up. We've got a surprise for you back at home."

"Where?"

"Your condo."

Carl smiles and whispers softly to himself, "Good. I didn't lose it."

"What was that?" Liz asks.

"Oh nothing," he replies.

Percy leads Carl into the cab Liz rode in to the hospital. He opens the right rear passenger door for him, and Carl slides in. Liz hops in through the left door. Percy says, "See you later, Carl."

"Aren't you coming with?"

"I'll meet you there."

"Okay." He waves at his friend and smiles.

"Luxury Living, please," Liz tells the driver.

"Sure thing," he says, softly steps on the gas, and pulls away from the curb.

Carl quickly notices the nameplate on the back of the front seat. It's the same guy who'd talked like his dad a couple days earlier. The driver says, "Hello, sir. How are you today?"

Carl is silent and nervous.

"Carl?" Liz asks. "Are you okay?"

Silence.

Carl shakes his head back and forth quickly. "Oh. Sorry about that. I'm doing good, I guess. Thanks."

"Good. I'm glad to hear that."

Carl looks nervously out his window. For some reason, to him, everything just looks bright. People are smiling on the sidewalks as they walk. Liz is on her cell phone. She's trying to be discreet, not revealing too much. Carl isn't paying much attention to her. He has a close eye on the city passing by him.

"Yeah. We'll be there shortly. See you in a few," she says.

She closes her cell phone and puts it in her purse, which sits on the backseat between them.

"Who was that?" Carl asks.

"Nobody," she says, trying not to smile.

Five minutes later, its 11:37 a.m., and Carl spots the bank on the corner with the clock one block away from his condo. The driver stops at the curb in front of the Luxury Living complex. The bellman reaches out and opens Carl's door.

"Hello, Mr. Robertson. I'm glad to see you're doing much better. The staff was worried about you."

"Thank you. I suppose," Carl replies.

He gets out of the car, and Liz darts around to the other side and grabs him by the right hand. The bellman opens the front door to Carl's complex and wishes them a good day.

"What are we doing here?" Carl asks.

"This is where you live," Liz replies.

"I do?"

"Yeah. Why not?"

Silence.

"Nothing," Carl says.

Liz and Carl get onto the elevator and go up to his floor. He's still trying to piece things together from his dream to what they mean now in his real life.

The elevator doors open on the twelfth floor. He and Liz walk to his place. She holds her brother's right hand, hurrying him down the hallway. She reaches into her purse where she has Carl's keys and unlocks the door. Before opening the door, she says, "Close your eyes."

"Why?" he asks.

"Just do it."

He closes his eyes. Liz gently grabs Carl's right hand and leads him inside his place.

"*Surprise!*" a loud group yells at the top of their voices.

Carl opens his eyes. He is stunned and flattered but also confused. Everybody from the office is standing inside his place. So are Kenny, John, and their families. Almost fifty people are gathered inside. A banner hangs from the ceiling.

"Welcome Home, Carl," it reads.

He quickly looks around to see if everything is in place from where he remembered it—the Yankees banner, the couch, the refrigerator. Suddenly, he tears up.

"This is incredible. You didn't have to do this."

"Yes, we did," Amber says. "We were really worried about you. We're glad to see you're okay."

Carl walks up to Amber and gives her a big hug. He then hugs people all around the room.

"This is amazing. Thank you, guys. I don't know what else to say."

"You don't have to say anything," Sharon says. "Now let's go cut that cake."

It's a chocolate cake, Carl's favorite, sitting on the kitchen counter. He walks into his kitchen, quickly scanning the area with his eyes. He peeks into the garbage can. It is empty.

The cake has "Welcome Home" etched in cursive and blue frosting.

Sharon leads him to do the honorary cut. Carl looks around the room and notices everybody who's there. He thinks to himself, *This is incredible. This really isn't so bad after all.*

"Who cleaned up my apartment?" Carl asks anybody who's listening.

"Percy and I did," Liz says.

Carl reaches over to his sister who is standing nearby with his right arm and gives her a big one-armed hug.

He looks around the room. He rubs his hands softly up and down his chest and smiles. He looks up to the ceiling and hollers, "Thank you!"

Tammy looks at him, confused. "What was that?"

"Nothing. It's nothing. Now cut that cake before I fire you!"

Everybody laughs. Carl grins.

Then, out of the corner of his right eye, he notices two familiar faces standing just beyond the kitchen counter—Mom and Dad.

He blinks a couple of times, making sure he's not dreaming. They're not a figment of his imagination. They're not an illusion.

"Mom? Dad? Is that you?"

"Yes, Son," Dad says. "Of course it's us. Who else would it be?"

Carl's overwhelmed. He tears up. He smiles. He briskly walks around the counter and up to Mom and Dad and gives them each a hug, the biggest hug he's ever given them.

Dad embraces him tightly. Mom cries.

"We're glad to see you're okay," Mom says, wiping away tears.

"Me too," Dad adds.

"I'm so glad to see you here, alive," Carl says.

"Alive?" Dad asks.

Carl pauses.

"Nothing. Nothing."

"What is it?" Dad asks curiously.

"Nothing. It's nothing. Let's have some cake."

"No, sweetie," Mom says quietly. "What kind of dream did you have?"

"Well," Carl starts. "I had a dream when I was at the hospital that you two died in a car accident, and that Liz and everybody kept trying to get ahold of me to tell me that, but I kept on ignoring it. I was too wrapped up in work."

"Well," Liz says, "I was trying to get ahold of you. Yes. That's true. But you were slammed at work. I understand that. It happens to me at work all the time. But I was just trying to make sure you knew what was going on and that Bill and Steven were on top of it."

"Where are they?" Carl asks.

"Who?" Liz says.

"Bill and Steven."

"Oh. They couldn't make it. Cedar Lake had its rivalry football game with Felton this weekend, and Bill couldn't get the time off of work."

"Did they win?"

"I'm not sure," Liz says. "He's supposed to call you later today after the game."

"But I do remember something about Mom and Dad and you being upset," Carl continues.

"Yes, I was."

"Why?"

"I was rushed to the hospital," Dad interrupts. "It turns out I had a minor heart attack."

"Really? Are you okay?"

"Yes. I'm much better now. It was a wake-up call."

"We were all scared," Mom adds. "At first, we weren't sure he was going to make it."

Liz interrupts. "And that's why I was trying to get ahold of you, to let you know that it happened, and try to provide you updates on his condition."

"When did you get released?" Carl asks Dad.

"About a day or two ago."

"How long were you there?"

"Oh, I'd say a couple days or so," he replies looking at Mom. She nods her head in agreement.

"Listen. I'm really sorry about that and everything else that's gone on."

"It's okay. Everything worked itself out. Everybody is back to normal. Now let's have some of that cake."

Some members of the party close in on the conversation. Caitlin, Nick, and Tammy inch closer.

"Carl," Caitlin says curiously, "tell us more about this dream you had."

"Well, I was just so arrogant," Carl says. "I just didn't want anything to do with my parents in this dream. I hated them even."

"Arrogant?" Mom says.

"Hated us?" Dad says.

"Yes," Carl replies.

"Why would you hate us?" Dad asks.

"It's because I had this embarrassing life growing up," Carl continues. "And I wanted to get out of Cedar Lake so bad, and when I finally do, I shut it off and erase it from my memory. I didn't want to have anything to do with it anymore. I treated everybody so horribly."

"When did you have this dream?" Liz asks, confused.

"At the hospital," Carl replies.

"When?"

"I don't know."

"Carl," Liz says. "You've never been like that. You've always been so sweet."

Carl's colleagues all nod together.

"Sounds like it was some kind of dream," Mom says. "Glad it was only a dream."

"Yes. That's why it's a dream, I guess," Carl says, smiling.

He cuts the cake.

*   *   *

Everybody enjoys a piece of the chocolate cake. Carl's working on his third piece. A couple loud knocks echo over the overlapping conversations inside his condo.

Everybody stops.

"Who's that?" Carl asks.

Liz goes to the door and opens it. It's Percy.

"Hey, Carl. What's going on? How's the party?"

"Did you put this together?"

Percy smiles.

Carl walks over from the kitchen and firmly hugs Percy.

"Thanks, man. Thanks for cleaning up my place, too."

"No problem at all. Anything for a friend."

Percy's cell phone goes off.

"Hello?" he says.

A pause.

"Oh hey! How are you?"

Silence.

"I'm good. What can I do for you?"

Silence.

"Sure. He's right here."

Percy hands his cell over to Carl. He's confused. "Who is it?" he asks. Percy just smiles.

"Hello?" Carl asks nervously.

"Hi, Carl," a female voice replies.

"Who is this?"

"It's Claire. Claire from Runaway."

"Claire! How are you?"

"I'm good. You?"

"I'm doing better."

"Yeah, I heard you were hospitalized for a little bit," she replies with her French accent.

"Yeah, it was pretty scary. But I'm doing better now."

"That's good."

"Yeah, so what's up?"

"Well, I wanted to know if you wanted to come up to Boston this weekend. I've got tickets to the Yankees-Red Sox game. Third row behind the Yankees dugout."

"What! Get out of here! I'd love to!"

"Great. And what would you say to dinner afterward?"

He pauses.

"I'd be happy to."

"Great. I'll fax the flight itinerary to your office."

"I can pick it up for you, Carl," Percy jumps in.

"Wait. Did you set this up to?"

Percy smiles. Carl smiles back. He shakes Percy's hand. "Thanks."

"I'll pick you up at the airport."

"Great. See you soon!"

Percy hangs up the phone.

"Don't tell me you got me tickets to see the Yanks in Boston and bought me a plane ticket there?"

Percy just smiles.

"You set me up on date?"

Percy just smiles.

"Thank you."

*　　*　　*

Carl stands in the airport terminal at Boston Logan International airport on a chilly late afternoon in late September.

It's overcast with high winds. He stands next to his tall, red suitcase waiting for Claire to pick him up.

Two soft blows from the horn of a blue four-door BMW sound as it pulls up to the curb in front of Carl. Claire buzzes down the passenger-side window.

"Hey, Carl. How are you? How was the flight?"

Carl smiles. "It was good."

Claire gets out, with her car running and the four-way flashers blinking on and off. She wraps her arms around him and gives him a soft rub on his back with her right hand.

"I'm glad you're okay."

"Thanks."

He is mesmerized by her beauty. *That at least didn't change,* he thinks to himself. He puts his suitcase in the trunk and gets in Claire's car.

"Where are you staying?" Claire asks.

"I believe the Hilton."

"Ah. Nice hotel."

"Thanks for asking me up here. I've never been to Boston."

"Really? Let me show you around then."

"Okay."

Claire drives Carl around Boston for the next two hours. They drive past the harbor. Then later, they pass Fenway Park—home of the Boston Red Sox. In his mind, they're the hated Red Sox. In everybody else's mind in Boston, they're the beloved Red Sox.

Carl's Yankees T-shirt and hat are in his suitcase. He knows it's a sin to wear any Yankees stuff in Boston, just as it is a sin to wear Red Sox apparel in New York City. He can't wait for tomorrow afternoon's game. It's a 1:00 p.m. start. The weather forecast calls for sunshine and slightly warmer temperatures, maybe in the fifties.

"Where do you want to go next?" Claire asks.

Carl stops to think as he snaps a picture of Fenway. "Where's your apartment from here?"

"Oh. It's just up the street actually."

Claire's roommate, Camille, is out of town this weekend. She's in Chicago, promoting the Runaway business.

"Really?" Carl asks. "Can we check it out?"

"Sure."

Claire pulls up to her complex. "Here we are," she says.

Carl looks up at it. "Wow."

It's a tall building, brand-new and thirty-six stories tall. Claire and Camille live on the fourth floor. "Would you like to check the place out?" Claire asks.

"Sure. Why not?"

She pulls her car around the corner and into the parking garage. They get out of her car in the dark garage.

"C'mon," she says, reaching for his right hand with hers.

She leads Carl to the nearby stairwell. He notices she's wearing tight blue jeans. He thinks to himself how nice her butt looks. Claire pushes the door open and leads Carl down a single flight of stairs outside, around the corner, and to the front of her complex.

She opens the door, which is unlocked from 10:00 a.m. to 7:00 p.m. They walk past an empty desk and to the elevator. The doors slide open. They step inside, and the doors close. It's silent as the elevator moves up to the fourth floor. She inches closer to Carl. He looks at his watch: 5:53 p.m.

The doors slide open on the fourth floor, and they head down to Claire and Camille's apartment at the end of the hall: Number 426.

Claire pulls the keys out of her purse and unlocks the door. The door swings open. It's a large, two-bedroom unit. A light-blue carpet lies throughout the unit. It's a spacious apartment. She gently closes the door behind them. The dining room is to the left with a ceiling fan hanging above the table. Just beyond the table is the kitchen, with white tile floor and light-brown cupboards and countertops. To the right of the table is the living room, which has a beige sectional couch facing the unit's window. It looks out onto the street in front of the complex. A forty-seven-inch flat-screen TV sits in the corner on top of a black entertainment center. Down the hall are the one-and-a-half bathrooms and two bedrooms. Claire's is first.

The light-blue carpet on the floor complements the light-purple walls. A king-size bed rests against the far wall. Two dressers and a walk-in closet are to the right.

Claire points out Camille's room across the hall. The full bathroom is at the end of the hall.

"This is a very nice place you girls have here," Carl says, smiling and nodding.

"Thank you," Claire replies.

They suddenly lock eyes and are speechless. A muffled sound of a garbage truck passes outside.

"Want to get a drink?" Claire asks.

"Sure."

*   *   *

Claire and Carl arrive at a tavern just a few blocks from the apartment. She orders an Appletini—one and a half ounces of vodka with one ounce Sour Apple Pucker. He orders a Miller Lite on tap. They find a corner table and sit down.

"When I heard you were in the hospital," Claire starts, sipping on her drink, "I was really worried about you."

He puts his drink on the table after taking a short swig. He clears his voice. "You were?"

"Yeah."

"Why?"

Silence.

"I don't know."

Carl looks at her. She's speechless.

"What? What is it?" he asks.

"I think you're cute, Carl. Really, really cute!" she blurts out.

He smiles.

"Really?"

"Yes. I was immediately attracted to you at our first meeting a couple weeks ago. I haven't stopped thinking about you."

"Really?"

"Yes."

"I had no idea you felt that way about me."

"That's why I begged Percy to get those tickets. It's because I knew that'd be one way to get you up here to see me. It's the only thing I could think of to make it easy for me to ask you out and you not be upset by it."

"Why would I be upset?" Carl asks.

"Remember? You basically told me at dinner once that you didn't want to mix business with pleasure."

"I did?"

"Yeah."

"I'm sorry, Claire." He searches for an excuse. "I was just tired."

"Tired?"

"Yeah. Tired."

She pauses and sips on her drink.

"Okay. So why now?" he asks. "Why do you want to see me now?"

"Because I want to get to know you better."

He pauses and quickly thinks about what he should say to her.

"Well, Claire . . ." he starts. She looks with wide eyes and curiosity. "I'm attracted to you, too."

She stares back at him across the table and flashes a big smile. A dim lamp hangs above their table. Loud conversations overlap around them. Rock tunes play on the jukebox.

"Seriously?" she asks.

"Yeah. Seriously."

"Well, good," she replies. She finishes off her drink. "We're going to have fun."

"I think so, too."

*   *   *

The next morning, the sun shines down on Boston. It's forty degrees at 10:00 a.m. Carl rolls out of his king-size bed in his hotel room. He walks over to the curtains and slides them back, looking out from his fifth-story room.

He stretches. He opens the door to his room and sees a newspaper lying on the floor. There is a huge preview story of the game on the front page. He sits on his bed and begins reading the article.

The phone in his room rings softly. He reaches over with his right hand and picks it up.

"Hello?"

"Sir, this is the front desk. You have a telephone call. Do you accept?"

"Who is it?"

"Claire."

"Yes. I'll accept.

"Okay. I'll transfer the call."

"Okay."

A brief silence follows on the other end of the line.

"Hello?" Carl asks.

"Carl! It's me. Claire."

"Oh. Good morning."

"Good morning to you, too. Listen, I'm going to have to meet you at the game. A customer called me this morning, and he is in town and wants to grab a cup of coffee. I'll meet you at the front gate."

"Okay. What time?"

"Twelve."

"Twelve it is. See you then."

* * *

Carl asks the concierge to call him a cab at 11:20 a.m. He wears his navy-blue Yankees T-shirt and white hat with the Yankees logo on it.

The valet cringes at him but with a smile. "How can you wear that here?"

"I'm here for the game today. Can I get a cab?"

"Sure. Right away."

A yellow cab pulls up fifteen minutes later. "Where to? Oh wait. I'm guessing the game?"

"Yep."

"Lucky," the driver replies.

Just as Carl is about to get in, he notices a gorgeous woman across the street coming out of an apartment complex. It's Claire. A man sees her to the door. Carl stops.

"Sir? Can you get in?"

"Just a second," Carl replies. He squints trying to get a better look. He watches Claire closely from across the street. He's about to raise his right arm and shout across the street to get her attention.

Then she places one long kiss on the man's lips. He grabs her butt with both hands.

Carl's angry. Heartbroken.

Claire walks away and then spots Carl watching her. Carl steps away from the cab and walks back up the stairs into the hotel. Claire darts across the street after him.

"Carl!" she screams. He ignores her.

He gets to the elevators, and Claire comes in through the front door. "Carl!" she screams out, her voice echoing throughout the lobby.

"Get away from me!" he yells back at her.

The elevator is all the way up on the top floor. She closes in on him.

"Get away from me!" he yells again.

A security guard comes around the corner and notices what's going on.

"Sir, is this woman bothering you?"

"Yes! Please get her away from me."

The elevator bell sounds noting its arrival at the lobby floor. Two couples walk off the elevator and between Carl and Claire.

Carl turns toward the elevator and rushes onto it. The guard asks him, "Sir, what would you like me to do with her?" Claire stands next to the guard.

"Please kick her out," he quickly replies just as the doors close. He notices a tear roll down her right cheek.

He's heartbroken. He cries.

*   *   *

The next morning, Carl wakes up at 4:00 a.m. and calls the concierge to help him with his suitcase and to call for a cab to take him to the airport. His flight leaves just after 8:00. He's up practically all night, heartbroken.

He checks down the hall after the bellman arrives to see if Claire is anywhere nearby. No sign of her. He sighs.

The phone in his room softly sounds.

"Hello?"

"Sir, it's the front desk. Phone call for you."

"Who is it?"

"Claire."

"Don't want it."

"Okay, sir."

There is a knock on the door to his hotel room. He peeks through the peephole and sees a bellman. He opens the door, hands him the rolling suitcase, and closes the door behind him. He follows the bellman down to the lobby to check out and go to the airport. On the way to the airport, he thinks about what his life was like before his dream and what it's been like since.

He thinks about women, dating, and love.

"I guess I'm supposed to still hate women," he mumbles softly to himself.

Chapter XIII

A MONTH PASSES SINCE CARL'S scare at the hospital and his heartbreak in Boston.

The Runaway deal is in full swing. It's already prospering well for Deluxe Marketing. It's a partly cloudy day in New York City. He walks leisurely to work today. It's his first day back in the office. The sun shines occasionally on the city. A small breeze whips through the streets. He wears a light-gray suit coat and pants with shiny black dress shoes and a white-collared, button-down shirt—no tie.

He carries a black briefcase in his right hand. No cell phone. That is still at his office. He reaches into his pocket to get his phone to check the time. He forgot his watch. No cell phone.

"Now where the hell did it go?" he mutters to himself. Then he tries to recall where it might be. "At the office?"

He's sad. He arrives at his office building. It's tall with dark-tinted windows, just like he remembers it. He stops in front of it from across the street.

The night guard, Bill, is leaving for the day after finishing his night shift. "Hello, Mr. Robertson. Welcome back."

"Thanks, Bill. It's good to be back."

Bill's wife pulls up in her car. "Hi, Carl. Nice to see you," she hollers out from inside the car.

Carl looks back and waves. "Thanks. Good to see you, too."

He rides the elevator up to his office. Up-tempo orchestral music plays on the speaker. He is alone.

The elevator doors slowly slide open. A banner hangs across the hallway inside the office: "Welcome Back, Carl."

He walks past Peggy's desk after stepping off the elevator. "Hello, Mr. Robertson! So good to see you back. Alive and well."

"Thanks."

He turns the corner toward his office. Sharon is sitting at her desk, talking into her headset. She stops once she spots her boss coming at her.

"Hello, sir. It's great to see you this morning." She gets up out of her chair, comes around the desk, and gives Carl a hug and a peck on the right cheek. He places his right hand on his right cheek.

"Why did you do that, Sharon?"

"I'm just so happy you're here and that you're okay."

"Thank you." He hugs Sharon firmly.

Percy comes down the hall, too.

"Hey, man!" he shouts at the top of his voice with a wide smile. "Welcome back!"

"Thanks. It's good to be back."

For the month Carl was out, Percy managed all of his accounts, including Runaway, and his team.

Carl embraces Percy with a big hug.

"Thank you for saving my life."

"You don't have to thank me. I'm just doing what any good friend should do in that situation."

"And thanks for taking care of my work while I was gone. I owe you big-time."

"Don't worry about it."

Percy and Carl exchange fist bumps, and Percy turns back toward his office down the hall.

The door to Carl's office is closed. He walks slowly up to the door and looks at the nameplate to make sure it says his name on it. It does.

"Whew," he says softly but loud enough for Sharon to hear it and see it.

"What? What's wrong?" she asks.

"Oh nothing. Just glad to be back."

"Gotcha."

He reaches out with his right hand for the door handle.

"Oh!" Sharon quickly stops him. "I almost forgot. You have a message from Claire. She's called numerous times."

"Toss it."

"Why?"

"Just do it."

"Okay."

He again reaches for the door handle on his office door before Sharon quickly says, "There's someone here to see you."

He opens the door slowly and looks in. "Who?" He's scared.

A woman stands up with her back to him out of a leather pull-up chair in front of his desk. She turns around.

"Hi, Carl," Sydney says, looking prettier than he remembered and standing in his office. She wears tight blue jeans with brown zip-up boots up to mid-calf. The jeans are tucked inside the boots. The boots are leather. She wears a plain black button-down blouse with a white spaghetti-strap tank top on underneath. Her blond hair is long and curly. A small black duffle bag sits on the floor to the right of her chair.

He is blown away, amazed, and stunned.

"Sydney!"

He gently closes the door. Sharon leans out of her chair to watch.

"Wow," he says. "You look amazing. What are you doing here?"

"Thanks, Carl. You look great, too. I'm here auditioning for a part in a play. You invited me to stop in a couple months ago. Remember?"

"Really?"

"Yeah. Didn't you check your cell phone messages?"

"No, sorry. It's been hectic. Don't know if you heard—"

"Yes, I did. But that was a while ago."

"I'm sorry, Syd. I haven't been in the office in a while, and I can't find my phone."

He thinks to check his desk. He walks past Sydney with a big smile on his face. He puts his keys on the desktop and pulls out a drawer. His phone rests on top of a stack of papers.

"Here it is."

The phone battery is dead.

"Look, Syd," he says. "I'm really sorry."

She's silent.

"It's okay."

"Did you have your audition yet?"

"Yeah, I had it early this morning."

He walks around his desk and reaches with both his arms to hug his college sweetheart. They embrace each other tightly. They lean back, look each other in the eyes, and embrace each other tightly again.

"Wow," Sydney says. "I never realized how much I missed your hugs."

He smiles and blushes. So does Sydney.

"I see you've done pretty well for yourself," Sydney says. "Mr. Big Shot."

"You seem to be doing well yourself, too. How long has it been since we've seen each other? I don't even—"

"Almost three years," Sydney quickly interrupts.

"Oh. That long? It doesn't seem like it. It's certainly great to see you again. I've missed you."

"But we haven't talked in a couple months. Don't tell me you forgot about me."

"No, I didn't. Just a little scatterbrained."

Sharon stands just outside Carl's office. She leans close to the door trying to hear the conversation going on inside. Amber and Tammy notice her.

"What are you doing, Sharon?" they ask in unison.

"Shhh!" Sharon whispers. "Carl's got an old college friend in his office, and she's beautiful!"

"He sure draws the attention of a lot of women," Tammy says.

"I don't blame them," Amber replies. "He's pretty cute."

Tammy and Amber leave Sharon's desk. Sharon still has an open ear to the door.

"So where are you staying?" Carl asks his longtime college girlfriend.

"The Marriott."

"Nice hotel, I hear."

"Yes, it is."

"Where do you live now?"

"What do you mean?"

"Huh?"

"I'm in LA. Remember?"

"Sorry."

"What's wrong with you, Carl?"

"I'm just a little overwhelmed by your beauty."

She smiles and blushes.

"Do you like it there?" he asks.

"Oh, I love it! You should come out there sometime."

"That'd be awesome."

Their conversation stops.

"Hey," Carl says, stuttering, quivering. "Is there a restaurant at your hotel?"

"Yes, there is. Why?"

"Well, would it be okay for us to have dinner there tonight?"

"I'd love to. I'm in room 1241. Meet me there at seven thirty, and we can go down there together. Sound good?"

"Sounds perfect. I'll see you then, Syd."

"I can't wait."

Sydney smiles, leans over, and hugs Carl. She puts her right hand on his butt and squeezes it gently.

Still feels as good as it did in college, she thinks to herself.

He grins, feeling Sydney's hand on his butt. She reaches down and picks up her bag, which has her audition clothes inside it. "I'll see you tonight."

"See you tonight," he replies. He reaches out with his right hand and opens the door for her. Sharon hears them coming toward the door and quickly leaves to get back behind her desk. Carl walks Sydney out of his office and to the elevator.

Sydney steps inside. "Bye, Carl."

"Later."

The doors slide closed. He whips around with an enormous grin on his face. Peggy notices it at the front desk. She smiles. He happily walks back to his office. Sharon is behind her desk, grinning from ear to ear.

"Sounds like you have a hot date tonight, yes?" she asks.

"Of course. She's beautiful, isn't she?"

"Yes!"

"What are you guys going to do tonight?"

"She's staying at the Marriott. We're going to have dinner at their restaurant."

"Sounds lovely."

"She's just an incredible girl. I just can't believe it's been so long since I've seen her. She's just amazing."

* * *

Carl packs up his things at his office at 3:30. He got little work done today. He thought about Sydney all day long. His phone rings loudly.

"Hello?" Carl asks. "Hey, Pierre, how are you?" It's 3:13 p.m.

"Good. I heard you had a scare. You went to the hospital. Yes?"

"Yeah, I did. It was quite scary. But it's changed my life."

"That's good to hear. I'm glad everything's okay. We were worried about you."

"Thank you. That's kind of you."

"I just called to let you know we're having great success so far."

"Well, I'm glad to hear that. We're happy with it, too. In fact, we couldn't be more pleased on our end."

Silence.

"That's great."

"Sorry to cut you a little short, Pierre. But I gotta let you go. I've got a couple errands I need to do. You have a good day."

"Likewise."

Carl hangs up the phone. He collects his things, whips his suit jacket from the back of his chair, and heads for the door. He stops.

"Oh wait!" he says to himself. He walks back around his desk, opens the top drawer, and retrieves his cell phone. He puts the phone into his right pants pocket and heads out the door, gently closing it behind him.

"Good day, Sharon," he says excitedly.

* * *

Carl glances at the clock on the wall of his condo: 6:57.

He grabs the keys off the counter and his coat off the back of the couch. His cell phone is charging in the kitchen. He shuts out the lights, leaving just the kitchen light on, and closes the door softly.

He briskly walks down the hall toward the elevator. He presses the down button. The elevator doors slide open. He reaches out with his right hand and pushes "1" on the floor panel, and the doors close. He's alone.

He bounces on his toes anxiously; he's nervous and excited. He wonders, *How is she going to look tonight?* It's quiet.

The elevator doors slide open. He's on the first floor. He quickly walks out, past the front security desk, and out the doors. He whistles for a cab and checks his watch: 7:05.

"Still plenty of time," he mutters.

He whistles again, throwing up his left arm.

A yellow Chevy Lumina pulls up to the curb. The driver buzzes down the window and says, "Hello, sir. Where you headed?"

"The Marriott, please."

"Right away." The driver gently presses on the accelerator and pulls away from the curb.

Carl sweats in anticipation. He bounces his legs up and down in the backseat. The driver looks in his rearview mirror. "Big night tonight?"

"Yes. I'm going on a date with a girl I haven't seen in three years."

"Is she hot?"

Carl smiles at him. "She makes a Victoria's Secret model look like child's play."

"Impressive," the driver says.

Carl checks his watch: 7:19.

"How much further?" Carl asks.

"A few more minutes."

It's 7:23. The cab pulls up to the front of the Marriott. A bellman reaches out with his white cotton-gloved right hand and opens the door for Carl. "Welcome to the Marriott, sir. Can I get your bags from the trunk?"

"No. That won't be necessary. I'm here visiting an old friend. She's staying here."

"Oh. That's outstanding, sir. The lobby's right through that door."

Carl turns to the driver and hands him a fifty-dollar bill out of his pants pocket. "Keep the change." The tab was $19.35.

The driver's eyes open wide, and he smiles. "Thank you." He gets back in his cab, and another man gets in the backseat and closes the door.

Carl stops in front of the main door to the lobby and looks up. He sighs. "Here we go." He pushes his way through the gold revolving door. A six-foot tall chandelier hangs twenty feet above the center of the lobby. It's fully lit, illuminating the room. Soft conversations overlap one another. A man plays a soft, but quick, medley on the piano to Carl's right.

"Carl!" a female voice shouts.

He searches for its source and finds Sydney coming off the elevator to the right of the lobby desk in front of him. She's stunning.

She wears a full-length and slightly low-cut blue dress, which glistens underneath the fully lit chandelier. Her back is bare. Her long blond hair is straight. A light-blue sash drapes over her shoulders. She carries a small white purse. Her heels click with every step. She wears light-pink lipstick and a touch of pink blush on her cheeks. Her teeth are pearly white.

"Wow, Sydney," he stammers and shakes. "You look incredible. I've never seen you like this."

"Thanks, Carl. You look pretty handsome yourself."

He wears a black suit and a button-down dress shirt with thin white pinstripes. He wears a white tie and freshly shined black shoes. He spots the clock behind the front desk: 7:25.

"I thought I was coming up to your room?" Carl asks.

"I couldn't wait to see you."

"I couldn't wait to see you, either."

He smiles at her, gazing deep into her blue eyes. She stares right back.

"Are you ready?" Carl asks.

"Definitely. Let's go."

He forms a loop with his right arm. She slides her left arm through. They walk in stride to the restaurant just past the elevator Sydney got off of.

A host dressed in a black and white tuxedo asks, "Two of you this evening?"

"Yes," Carl replies.

"Would you like a private table?" he asks.

"Yes," Carl replies.

"Certainly. Right this way."

The host leads Carl and Sydney to a secluded room in the back corner of the restaurant. It has a red curtain that slides in front, and there are three wooden walls enclosing a table with two chairs. A small red couch sits in the corner. A dimly lit lamp hangs above the table.

Carl pulls out Sydney's seat and scoots her chair in after she sits down. The host hands each of them a long black menu and opens it for both of them. He reads off the evening's specials. The soup of the night is chicken and broccoli.

Carl ignores him. He stares at Sydney, while she listens to the host.

"And for you, sir?" the hosts asks.

"Oh. I'm sorry. I got lost for a moment. I'll have a water and a bottle of your finest champagne."

Sydney smiles.

"Right away, sir."

Carl and Sydney sit in their secluded room—alone.

"My goodness, it is so good to see you again, Sydney," Carl starts. "After you came to my office today, I didn't realize until then how much I'd missed you."

"Really?"

"Yeah. I thought about you all day."

"Really? Why?" She smiles.

*　　*　　*

Ten loud clock chimes sound from the center of the restaurant.

"Oh. It must be ten o'clock," Carl says. Their table is empty. Sydney had a fresh garden salad. Carl had a nine-ounce sirloin steak. He pours the remainder of the bottle of champagne. It is their fourth bottle.

They spend the entire evening catching up, just like it was old times all over again.

"I remember that," Carl says, laughing hysterically.

Sydney laughs along with him.

"We were so drenched that night," Carl continues recalling a time in college when they had been walking home from a movie one night and it began to rain unmercifully. Neither of them had brought an umbrella.

She laughs, sips her champagne from her glass, and gently places it back on the table, laughing again. The waiter gently draws the curtain back.

"Is there anything else I can get you two this evening?" the waiter asks.

Carl and Sydney look each other and smile.

"Hey," Carl starts, "can we take a bottle of champagne to our room?"

Sydney opens her eyes widely in approval and smiles.

"Yes, sir. You can just add it to your bill."

"Oh. Can I just pay for it now?"

"Sure. What would you like?"

"The same bottle please."

"Yes, sir. Right away."

He reaches across the table with both of his hands and grabs Sydney's. He holds them firmly. She blushes. They stare at each other.

The waiter returns with the bottle and the tab for the evening. Carl gives him two hundred-dollar bills to pay for the bottle and the tab. Sydney's looking at her small makeup mirror. The tab is $119.37.

"Keep the change," Carl says.

"Thank you, sir. You two have a wonderful evening."

They get up and push aside the curtain. The only other patrons are an elderly couple sitting at a table nearby. They're sharing a piece of strawberry cheesecake. The restaurant closes at ten.

Carl holds Sydney's left hand softly and leads her to the elevator. "Is it okay if I come up to your room?"

She kisses him on the lips.

"What do you think?"

"No?"

She gently slaps him on the shoulder.

"Okay. Yes."

They smile at each other. They stand in front of the gold double elevator doors leading up to the guestrooms.

The elevator doors slide open.

"What floor are you on?"

"Twelve."

"That's the same floor I live on at my condo."

The doors slide closed. They're alone. A soft orchestral song plays on the elevator's speakers. He leans against the back of the elevator. Sydney leans into him, wrapping her arms around his neck and looking into his eyes. His hands are on her hips. They kiss.

The doors slide open. They turn to the right down the hall to room 1241. Sydney gets the key out of her purse and slides the card in, and the door opens. She leads him inside and gently closes the door behind him.

*　　*　　*

The first major snowfall of the year hits New York City—six inches.

Three months have passed since Sydney and Carl got reacquainted. Every weekend they exchange flights. One week he flies to Los Angeles to Sydney's place, and the next week, she flies to New York. They do this for three months.

He loves her place.

It's a beachfront condo, three-stories, white with black window shutters and frames, and has a wooden patio walkway leading right to the beach of the Pacific Ocean. She watches the sun set almost every night.

"It's so beautiful, isn't it?" she asks Carl during his first weekend trip to LA.

"Yes, it is. Even more beautiful with you here."

She blushes and kisses him. They lay on a lounge chair on the balcony of her condo, watching the sun set.

*　　*　　*

It is one week before Christmas.

Carl calls Sydney on the phone.

"Hey, baby. How are you?"

"I'm great now. You?"

"Likewise. I miss you!"

"I miss you, too!"

"Listen, I've got a great idea for Christmas. Why don't we go to my parents' house? They're dying to meet you. I've told them a lot about you."

"All good things, I hope?"

"Of course."

"Sure. That'd be fantastic. My parents are actually going to Sweden to visit my cousin for Christmas, and my sister is in Rome on a study abroad trip."

"Okay. I'm flying in tomorrow. I'll get you a plane ticket for Thursday, Christmas Eve."

"How will you be able to get a plane ticket on such short notice at this time of the year?"

"Don't you worry about that."

"Okay. I'll see you then, hot stuff! I love you!"

"I love you, too, Syd!"

They hang up the phone.

He picks up the phone in his office and calls the airport. A woman answers.

"May I help you?" she asks.

"I'd like to hire a private flight out of LA for Thursday. Who can I talk to about that?"

"Umm. Let me transfer you to someone who could help you. Can you hold please?"

"Sure."

A soft jazz tune plays through the phone.

*   *   *

Sydney is playing Christmas music inside her condo and singing along. It is seventy degrees outside her place. It's sunny.

She goes through her closet, sliding one outfit across to the next. She grabs her University of Iowa sweater, yanks it off the hanger, and tosses it onto the bed behind her. She grabs a pair of skin-tight blue jeans, which hung next to the sweater. She zips up her large rolling suitcase and takes it to the front door. She grabs a light jacket from the closet next to the front door. She opens the door, shuts off the living room light, and gently closes the door.

A limo sits at the end of the walkway leading to her condo. A man wearing a long black tuxedo jacket, black slacks, black shoes and socks, and a black hat opens the right rear passenger door.

"Hello," he says. "May I take your suitcase?"

She hands it to him and gets inside the limo. He places her heavy suitcase in the trunk, gently closes it, and gets into the car.

They drive past Los Angeles International Airport.

"Sir?" she asks curiously.

"Yes, ma'am?"

"Where are we going?"

"It's a secret, requested by Mr. Robertson."

She smiles. "What is he up to?" she asks herself.

The driver pulls into a lot near the airport. A long, white private jet awaits her.

"No, he didn't," she says to herself.

"Here you go, ma'am."

"Thank you. What do I owe you?"

"Nothing. It's prepaid for."

She shakes her head back and forth. He leads her to the airplane while holding her suitcase. A female flight attendant welcomes her aboard.

"Sit anywhere you like."

Sydney is smiling and embarrassed.

*   *   *

Carl arrives in Des Moines just after 2:00 in the afternoon on December 23. It is fifty degrees, and there's no snow on the ground anywhere. Steven picks him up at the airport.

"Carl!"

"Steven!"

They wave at each other. They hug and pat each other on the back.

"It's so good to see you," Steven says.

"Likewise. It's good to finally be home again. It's been too long."

Steven pauses.

"Again? You came home for Christmas last year. Remember?"

"I did?"

"Yeah. You made supper."

"Oh yeah. Duh!"

Carl doesn't recall. He just plays along with it.

"What else did that dream do?" Carl wonders softly.

"So Mom told me you've got a guest coming."

"Yes, I do. Her name is Sydney."

"Sydney, huh? How do you know her?"

"We dated in college."

"Oh that Sydney! I've heard a lot about her from you and Mom."

"She's amazing. She was in New York a while back auditioning for a part in a play. She stopped by my office, and well . . . you know."

"Thatta boy," says Steven, extending his right hand toward his brother for a fist bump.

More than an hour later, Steven pulls up to Mom and Dad's house. It's a cool afternoon under cloudy skies. Carl's speechless.

"Wow," he says.

"Wow?"

Both pause and look at each other.

"Carl, are you feeling okay?"

"Yeah, I'm fine. Why?"

"You're acting weird."

"It's just . . . It's just I haven't seen this house . . . in a while. I forgot what it looked like."

"Okay," Steven says, confused.

Steven grabs Carl's suitcase out of the trunk and helps his brother with it inside.

"Carl!" Mom yells from the top of the patio.

The house is two stories tall with white siding and blue window frames. It has a large living room window. A cobblestone path leads up to the patio, which is white with blue posts. A black BMW sits in the driveway.

The house has wood floors throughout, but the floor doesn't creak with every step. They have a glowing shine to them. It almost looks like a freshly polished dance floor. A tall staircase leads up to the second floor from the greeting area. To the left, inside the front door, is a den for Dad. To the right is the living room. Straight ahead is the staircase, and to the right of the stairs is a long hallway leading to the kitchen and dining room.

"Wow," Carl whispers. Steven doesn't hear him. Carl's never seen this place, at least that he can remember.

This must be the house I bought them, he thinks to himself.

*   *   *

On Christmas Eve, Carl and Steven get into the black BMW and drive to Des Moines to pick up Sydney from the airport.

"I can't wait to meet her, man," Steven says to his nervous brother.

"I think everybody will love her."

Carl's cell phone goes off. He looks at the caller ID: Unknown.
"Hello?"

"Carl, please listen to me," a female voice says loudly. It's Claire.
"Leave me alone."

He quickly hangs up the phone. His phone rings again. It's Claire again.

"Who's that?" Steven asks.

"Just some girl who cheated on me."

"That sucks. Who is she?"

"I prefer to not get into it, okay?"

His phone rings once again. He lets it ring again. Once it stops ringing, he turns it off.

They get to the airport and drive to a small area just past the terminal. A long private jet rolls in and stops. Moments later, a beautiful girl emerges from the airplane.

"Is that her?" Steven asks.

"Yes, it is."

"Wow."

Sydney stands next to her tall, purple suitcase. She's wearing a dark-blue scarf, blue jeans, white tennis shoes, and a long winter coat. Her breath steams with every exhalation. Carl gets out of the car on the passenger side and walks up to her.

"Hey, baby," she says.

"Hey, gorgeous."

Steven gets out of the car, too.

"You're too much, Carl," she says. "That was incredible."

"Thanks. Glad you liked it."

Carl, gently holding Sydney's right hand with his, turns toward his brother.

"Sydney, I'd like you to meet my brother, Steven."

Steven and Sydney exchange handshakes.

"Wow. Everybody was right. You're gorgeous." He turns to Carl. "Nice work, bro!"

Sydney blushes. "That's kind of you."

Carl looks like he wants to bash his brother's face in for embarrassing him. Instead, he opens the front door for Sydney. Steven hops into the backseat and closes the door. Carl struggles to lift Sydney's suitcase.

"Geez, what's in here? Bricks?"

"Nope. Clothes."

Carl drops her suitcase in the trunk. He goes to the driver's side and gets in the car. Steven reaches over the seat and hands his brother the keys.

Driving back from the airport, Carl sweats.

"Carl, what's wrong, honey?" Sydney asks.

"What? Oh nothing. Just a little warm."

He's nervous.

They pull up to the house. Sydney is in awe. Carl is still in awe.

"What a beautiful house," she says, gasping for breath. "You bought this for your parents?"

"I guess you could say that."

"Carl. It's magnificent."

Mom and Dad stand on the porch. It is thirty degrees. A slight breeze sweeps across the property from right to left. The sun is out, with minimal cloud cover. Mom and Dad wave hello.

Sydney steps out of the car and waves back. "Hello." She smiles.

Carl and Steven get Sydney's things inside the house.

"Mom, Dad, I'd like you to meet Sydney," Carl says.

Sydney extends her right hand for a handshake. Mom grabs her arm and pulls her in tight for a hug. Dad embraces her in his arms, too.

"It's so nice to finally meet you," Mom tells her.

"Agreed," Dad follows. "Carl's told us so much about you."

"Good things, I hope," Sydney replies.

"Absolutely," Mom and Dad say together, smiling.

Mom wraps her right arm around Sydney and leads her into the house.

Dad turns back to Carl. "She's beautiful, Son."

"Thanks, Dad."

*   *   *

"Time for presents!" Mom yells from the kitchen after finishing up cleaning the dishes from a nice ham dinner she made.

Everybody finds a piece of furniture to sit on in the living room where a large fire burns in the fireplace. A Christmas melody plays on the stereo in the corner of the large room. Carl and Sydney sit next to each other on a love seat next to the couch facing the fireplace. She places her right hand gently on Carl's left leg.

The Christmas tree, which is ten feet tall, is to the right of the fireplace, fully lit with a bright white angel perched atop it. More than seventy wrapped boxes sit on the floor underneath and around the tree.

Elizabeth, who flew in last night, sits on the floor in front of the tree, ready to pass out the presents. Carl's hands moisten. He wipes them off on his blue jeans.

"Is everything okay?" Sydney asks.

"Yes."

Carl puts his left arm around her shoulders, and they lean back into the couch. All ten people in the room have their first present from under the tree. Mom and Dad never were big spenders. That at least he could remember from before his dream.

"There's a lot of presents, Mom," Carl says.

"There's always this many," Mom replies.

"Okay. Now!" Elizabeth shouts.

Paper rips and flies from all the family members. Carl gets a new briefcase from Bill. Sydney gets a fleece sweater from Mom and Dad. She holds it up for everybody to see.

"It's so soft," Sydney says. "Thank you."

Elizabeth reaches over and grabs more presents to pass out.

An hour passes. The presents are all accounted for and opened. Carl also gets three new movies, a Yankees jersey, a Giants jersey, a six-pack of silk ties, dress socks, and a new iPod stereo.

All the gifts have been opened, except for one.

"Hold on a minute," Carl says, pushing himself off the couch and into the guest bedroom just past the left side of the fireplace. He reaches into his suitcase for a small velvet box. He also grabs a small wrapped box from the bedroom. Nothing's in it. Just bath towels to make it feel like something's in it. He places the small box in his pocket. He walks out of the room and directly to Sydney.

"Here you go, S-S-Sydney," Carl says, stammering slightly.

Nobody knows what's coming, except Carl.

She carefully reaches out across the small table in front of her and takes the present from Carl. He asks her to come around and sit on the coffee table. She hesitantly agrees. He sits on the table with her on his left. He wipes his hands against his pant legs again. Sydney rips at the paper and opens the box.

"Towels?" she says confused.

"Keep looking. There's something else inside it."

"Okay."

Sydney continues to look for something else. "I'm not finding anything."

She looks up, and Carl's on his right knee, holding out the open black velvet box. Inside is a beautiful, two-carat diamond ring.

"Will you marry me?" Carl asks.

"*Yes!*" she screams. Sydney pulls Carl up off his knees and plants one long kiss on his lips. Everybody in the room cheers, applauds, and whistles. Mom cries from her chair next to the couch.

Carl and Sydney hug each other tightly. Tears roll down Sydney's cheeks. Carl takes the ring out of the box and slides it onto her left ring finger. She shows it off to everybody in the room.

She's bawling and smiling.

While staring at his fiancée, Carl suddenly catches a glimpse of something outside. It's an illusion of the three stages of his life he helped fix in his dream. They stand outside smiling. Carl stands there and stares back at them.

"Whatcha lookin' at, bro?" Bill asks.

"Nothing. It's just an illusion."

Carl returns his attention to his new bride-to-be. He takes another quick peek outside.

The illusions disappear.

Chapter XIV

*O*CTOBER 25. IT'S THE wedding day for the future Mr. and Mrs. Robertson. Carl and Sydney are ready to tie the knot after ten months of being engaged.

It's a gorgeous mid-autumn day. The birds chirp from a nearby bush in front of the church. The sun beams down heavily. Not a cloud is in sight. It is fifty-three degrees. A soft breeze coasts through the parking lot, ruffling the remaining leaves on the trees in front. The organ plays soft medleys for the guests coming in.

Carl is nervous and excited. So is Sydney. Both are wide-eyed and smiling. His groomsmen try to calm him down in a small classroom in the school connected to the church. Her bridesmaids do the same in a much larger room, a couple rooms down the hallway.

Percy is Carl's best man. Bill and Steven are the groomsmen. Elizabeth is the maid of honor. Sydney's sister and her cousin from Sweden are the bridesmaids.

The men, all dressed up, file into a small classroom just beyond the entrance into the church, and they wait.

Sydney is making the final preparations. Elizabeth hands her a bouquet of flowers to carry down the aisle. She gives her soon-to-be sister-in-law a big, firm hug.

The anticipation mounts.

Guests arrive one by one.

Carl's entire team from Deluxe shows up. Many of Sydney's classmates from college arrive. James Patrick arrives with his wife, Ariel. Sydney's parents arrive and then Carl's parents.

The church is large, big enough for five hundred people. A large pipe organ sits upstairs. A twenty-three-year-old woman plays welcoming tunes.

Carl and Sydney are getting married at Trinity Lutheran Church in Kansas City, Sydney's hometown. They will spend a week in

Hawaii for their honeymoon. Carl's parents paid for it as a wedding present.

Carl frequently checks the clock on the wall of the room. It feels like time is going slowly. The pastor gently knocks on the door, leans in, and asks, "Are we ready?"

"Yes," Percy says.

Carl stands up, throws his coat over his shoulders, and looks into a mirror. A tear rolls down his right cheek.

"I never thought this day would come," he says with tears increasing.

Percy walks up to him and puts his left arm around him. "You don't have to wait anymore. This is your day."

Carl turns around and hugs Percy tightly. Carl turns to his brothers and hugs both of them.

"Thank you for being here, guys," he says.

"We wouldn't miss this for the world," Bill says.

"No way," Steven agrees.

Another soft knock on the door follows.

"Hello, Celeste. How are you?" Carl asks his very soon-to-be mother-in-law.

"I'm great. You look so incredibly handsome."

"Thanks . . . Mom."

She smiles. Carl smiles.

"I've got something for you," she says.

She hands Carl a white envelope with a card inside it. On the front, it says, "Carl." He turns it over and opens the envelope. He places the envelope on the table, looks at the front of the card, and reads it.

"My heart belongs to you."

Carl's eyes fill with tears again. He opens the card.

"I never thought that love could be this endless, deep, and true, until the day I gave my heart and all my love to you." Carl's eyes continue to moisten.

It's from Sydney, and she signs it, *"I'm so thrilled, happy, and honored to become your wife today. I love you!"*

Carl loses it. He bawls. His mother walks past and sees him crying. She comes inside the room and starts crying herself, hugging him tightly.

"I'm so proud of you," she says, struggling with her words through tears.

Bill rushes to the desk on the far wall and grabs a tissue box. Elizabeth sees her brother with his eyes beet red from crying. She hugs him.

"I'm so happy for you and Sydney," she tells him.

"Thanks, Sis."

The pastor says, "It's time."

"Let's go do this, man," Percy says. "Let's get you married."

Carl smiles, sniffling.

The wedding bells sound. Carl follows the pastor down the aisle, followed by his two brothers and Percy. Soon after, Carl passes his guardian angel, resting against a wall to his right.

He smiles and winks at Carl. He smiles right back and mouths, "Thank you." The angel disappears.

The sound of a bell, a ring, finally sounds good to Carl Robertson. He listens to the charming sound intently. He smiles. He cries.

Standing at the front of the church, Carl turns to look up the aisle. A curtain at the end of the aisle is pulled back. Sydney slowly walks toward him in a long white gown. Her dad walks in stride alongside his daughter. She has tears in her eyes.

Carl peeks to his left and sees his guardian angel once again.

About the Author

Nicholas Dettmann is a veteran journalist from Milwaukee, Wisconsin. He has worked at daily newspapers in Idaho Falls, Idaho; Michigan City, Indiana; and West Bend, Wisconsin. He has also appeared in numerous newspapers around the country, including the *Houston Chronicle*, the *Milwaukee Journal Sentinel*, and the *Baltimore Sun*.

He has won writing awards at the local, regional, and national levels. Nicholas graduated from the University of Wisconsin-Milwaukee with a degree in journalism and mass communications. In 2010, Nicholas wrote a story about a high school swimmer who suffered from dwarfism. His dream was to become a Paralympian. The Wisconsin Newspaper Association wrote, "Good story and nice storytelling getting the reader into the story."

Nicholas was first published in 2001 at only nineteen years old when he wrote a poem, "Remembering," honoring the memory of a classmate. It received an Editor's Choice award from Poetry.com.

His writing idols include Rick Reilly, Mitch Albom, John Grisham, and Tom Hallman Jr. In his spare time, Nicholas enjoys reading, exercising, swimming, and spending time with family and friends. He is also a member of the Society of Professional Journalists, where he serves on the Awards and Honors committee.

His specialties in writing include personality profiles.

Nicholas is married to Elizabeth, and they have two cats, Daisy and Dory.

CPSIA information can be obtained at www.ICGtesting.com
Printed in the USA
LVOW111158290212

270957LV00003B/7/P